BATTLETECH:
GREY WATCH PROTOCOL
BOOK ONE OF THE HIGHLANDER COVENANT

BY MICHAEL J. CIARAVELLA

BATTLETECH: GREY WATCH PROTOCOL
By Michael J. Ciaravella
Cover art by Florian Mellies
Design by Matt Heerdt & David Kerber

Published by Catalyst Game Labs,
an imprint of InMediaRes Productions, LLC
7108 S. Pheasant Ridge Drive • Spokane, WA 99224

*For my grandparents: Rose Moreno,
and Stephen and Josephine Ciaravella:*

*When you taught me to read, you taught me to fly.
I miss you.*

CHAPTER 1

"We have received confirmation that New Home, Bryant, and Keid have been attacked by the Capellan Confederation. Requests for further information from the Prefect's office have received no response, forcing this reporter to wonder: What is happening to the Republic?"

—Armin Sanswell, *Northwind Today,*
30 September 3150

CELESTIAL PALACE SITUATION ROOM
ZI-JIN (FORBIDDEN) CITY, SIAN
CAPELLAN CONFEDERATION
30 SEPTEMBER 3150

For most citizens, Sian represented the ideal to which other planets aspired. The capital of the Capellan Confederation was one of the best defended planets in the Inner Sphere, a place of grand deeds that most Capellans spoke of with a quiet reverence and respect.

For *Sang-shao* Lindsey Baxter, it would always be a place of dread.

Thanks to the nomadic nature of being raised in a military unit given near-autonomous control, she'd spent her formative at a variety of different stations, but one of the few areas of consistency centered around the rare moments when her father, Stephen, would take his family to Sian when he was summoned.

As she thought back, her memories slid into her own scattered visits during her time at the Sarna Military Academy, usually when she had been called forth for advanced training programs she couldn't have taken advantage of elsewhere.

She caught herself frowning, and quickly schooled her features as she remembered the skeptical looks she had received from many of her contemporaries at deciding to attend what was considered the least prestigious of the Capellan military academies. Still, she had always known that her future lay in the family business, and she intended to uphold the tradition of service her family had maintained for five generations. Her only true regret was that her father had not lived to see her ascend to a command in the regiment he had so loyally served.

Unfortunately, all of those pleasant memories were overshadowed by the memory of her last visit, when she had been ordered to report to the capital in the wake of the Battle of New Canton.

The day everything changed.

She vividly remembered being summoned before the Strategios, the strategic planning committee of the Confederation, and futilely attempting to explain how one of the most respected units in the Capellan Confederation Armed Forces had been bested by units of the Republic of the Sphere. She had been lucky to return from that foray merely tarnished, having not been in command at the time of the defeat. The Strategios told her that her refusal to abandon the body of her commanding officer, Faith McCarron, had been one of the few admirable moments in that dark chapter of her unit's history.

Her immediate superior, Donald Hopkins, had not been so lucky. She remembered her shock as a pair of Death Commandos dragged him from the chamber, his eyes wild as the Strategios decreed that he had not done enough to stem the tide of the Republic incursion, the he had failed the Chancellor and, by extension, the Confederation itself.

For a brief moment she had feared they would strike the Fourth McCarron's Armored Cavalry from the rolls of the CCAF due to their perceived failure, but luckily House McCarron had long ago earned enough good karma to overshadow the stain on the regiment's battle record.

Thinking of her former commander caused her to glance at her current CO, Cyrus McCarron. The eldest son of Xavier McCarron, the overall commander of McCarron's Armored Cavalry, was said to be the spitting image of his illustrious forebear at that age. To be honest, she couldn't see it, but she knew she was not as prone to fanciful jumps in logic as some of her fellow warriors. Yes, their eyes were the same color, and he had worked hard to hide that his hair was beginning to thin on top by keeping his hair cut short in military fashion, but his chin was not as sharply defined, nor were his cheekbones as gaunt, giving him less of a hawkish appearance. In fact, from the right angle, one might mistake him for a prosperous construction foreman rather than the heir-apparent to one of the most storied units in the Capellan Confederation.

Still, she counted herself lucky that she had never been on the receiving end of one of his famous dressing-downs: she was told that when he was truly disappointed in a member of the unit, the McCarron fire was visible in full measure.

Together they stepped up to yet another internal security post, proffering her identification for review. It was a sign of the immense respect the CCAF had for the McCarrons that they had come this far into the Celestial Palace unescorted, especially with the Chancellor rumored to have been pulling back from public appearances in the wake of security concerns.

Despite clearly recognizing them, the guard carefully checked both sets of identification: the verigraph on the card, visual confirmation of their pictures, and the biometric scans. At his side, a second security officer watched closely, his weapon at the ready to respond instantly to any threat. Beyond the obvious security in place at the main door, and the multiple checkpoints they had gone through to get this deeply into one of the most secure buildings in the Confederation, she had absolutely no doubt that unseen Maskirovka agents were confirming everything about them while they waited, with additional security forces prepared to use deadly force if they proved to be a threat.

When the security team was finally convinced they were not assassins, the guard nodded respectfully to McCarron, and stepped back to allow them inside. The door opened soundlessly, and as they passed, she could see its steel-reinforced interior, complete with heavy bolts that could lock it down in case of emergency. The room probably could withstand nuclear horrors, like those the Word of Blake had rained down on other worlds during their Jihad.

As they stepped into the secured meeting chamber, Lindsey was surprised to see how cavernous it seemed with only two other occupants. One, a young *sao-wei*, waited at the room's control console, but her focus was immediately drawn to the room's other occupant as she instinctively snapped to attention.

Seated at the far end of the large conference table that dominated the center of the room, a woman in a full CCAF dress uniform sat with her gaze focused on one of the many large ceiling-mounted screens, giving her normally severe face a sickly pallor.

Standing rigidly at attention, her eyes locked forward, Lindsey fought the urge to straighten her uniform. To her horror, her commanding officer merely gave an insouciant nod to the other woman. "*Sang-jiang-jun.*"

From her seat, *Sang-jiang-jun* Isabelle Fisk, Strategic Coordinator for the entire CCAF, gave McCarron a hard look before allowing her gaze to slide over to Lindsey. The elder warrior had more silver in her hair than when she had spoken at Lindsey's academy graduation, but neither the power of her gaze nor the sharpness of her uniform betrayed any signs of advancing age.

"As you were, *Sang-shao*," she responded with a curt nod before glancing at McCarron. "At least your subordinates have the proper respect for their seniors."

Cyrus gave an infuriatingly thin smile and bowed properly, the fleeting expression the only thing marring his proper form. "Apologies, *Sang-jiang-jun*. It has been too long since I have seen you, and I seem to have forgotten myself."

No doubt the *sang-jiang-jun* registered the gentle chiding of how long it had been since Cyrus had been personally deployed against the Republic, but Fisk refused to rise to the bait. Gesturing to the table, she waited until her two guests had settled before taking them both once again under her gaze.

"Thank you for coming so quickly. With the tactical situation being what it is, I thought it important to brief you personally." Her gaze flicked back to McCarron. "Cyrus, you recently returned from an inspection of your units on the front lines. What is your opinion of the current status of Operation Tiamat?"

Cyrus raised his chin thoughtfully, but if he was surprised by the question, he did not show it. "From what I have seen, everything seems to be going exceptionally well. We have been pushing back the Republic on nearly every front, and despite some costly battles, we have been extremely successful. While I expect nothing less from my own people, I have been especially pleased to see the gains made by CCAF regulars on New Home and Bryant. I have heard that the cleanup efforts on Keid and Epsilon Indi are also progressing well."

Although the Strategic Director had narrowed her eyes at his careful separation of "his people" from the CCAF regulars, she also clearly heard what he had not said. "And your thoughts on our new allies?"

Lindsey looked at her commander, curious as to his response. The recent Unity Pact between the Capellan Confederation and the Draconis Combine was still a very recent measure, and while it had proven successful so far, she knew many still looked on it with suspicion. The ties between the Confederation and the Combine hearkened back to the Kapteyn Accords of the early 3020s, but like so many other things, that alliance had shifted in the wake of the Clan Invasion.

"While I doubt I have more current intelligence than you do, the strikes on Asta, Altair, and Fomalhaut seem to have done a good job of holding the Republic's attention. Coupled with their help in disrupting the Federated Suns border, it seems as if the Pact is working as designed."

Lindsey turned back to the *sang-jiang-jun,* but couldn't help but to wonder if there was more that McCarron had not said. Like many mercenaries, the McCarron family had a historic distrust of the Combine since the days of Takashi Kurita's "Death to Mercenaries" order, and such memories remained powerful. Still, if Fisk had any reservations, she did not voice them as she continued, "I specifically wished to discuss Keid. The Fifth Sian Dragoons have crushed the militia forces on planet, but they have found no sign of the Republic Standing Guard. We are declaring the battle for the planet a complete victory.

"Due to the results on Keid and several other planets where the Republic forces did not receive reinforcements, the Maskirovka believes the Republic is suffering a severe shortage of reserves, and is in the process of pulling back to a new defensive position on all fronts."

Lindsey nodded, understanding where the Mask was coming from. Ever since Gray Monday, each major power had attempted to take a bite out of the Republic of the Sphere, avariciously seeking the young nation's technological wealth and the strategically vital planets for themselves. Over the last several months, most of the various attempts had been repelled or had become embroiled in other conflicts, but three major forces still besieged the Republic. Aside from House Liao, both Clan Wolf and Clan Jade Falcon had been making exceptional progress in snatching the various worlds that had been sacrificed when the walls of Fortress Republic had gone up, and all three nations were still doing everything in their power to capture the prize that they all coveted: Terra, the birthworld of humanity. *Could this be the turning point?* She smiled slightly at the thought. *Are we finally within a stone's throw of ending the threat of the Republic of the Sphere?*

Fisk switched her gaze between the two officers. "Full reports should already be en route to your personal servers, but I can tell you that Strategios has decided this recent intelligence indicates a vital weakness in the Republic's defenses, one we must take advantage of immediately."

McCarron leaned forward, clearly hearing the hesitation in Fisk's voice. "That sounds like a very rational decision, but I am very curious as to what *you* think, *Sang-jiang-jun.*"

To Baxter's surprise, Fisk smiled thinly. "While I am loath to agree with my colleagues on principle, their information does seem to be based on solid evidence. I must admit to a certain level of concern, however: Were I Devlin Stone, I would attempt to show weakness in the face of our continued advance in an attempt to lure us into overextending our resources and provide him with an opportunity to exploit. As the defender, he has both shorter supply lines to exploit and the ability to move more quickly between fronts. If we advance too quickly, a Republic counterattack could shatter any force we could afford to send in."

"Or show us to be a tempting target to one of our neighbors," McCarron replied. "Even if the Clans don't want to divert themselves from their invasion, I would not put it past one of the Free Worlds League fragments or a Border March to attempt to take advantage of the situation."

Fisk nodded. "I happen to agree. Unfortunately, I also cannot deny that militarily, we are at the strongest point we have been since the fall of the Star League. House Davion, our greatest natural threat, is currently neutered from the loss of New Avalon and Julian Davion's focus on attempting to gain some small fragment of his nation back. If the data can be trusted, there is no better time to strike."

McCarron nodded sagely, but still kept his own counsel. While the CCAF's training and advanced technology had been improving steadily, this was the first opportunity since the last war with the Republic to face a true challenge to their equipment or their tactical doctrine. Too many lives had been lost on both sides when the Capellans had refused to bow down to Stone's fledgling Republic, and she knew of too many who had lost loved ones. Much like Fisk herself, McCarron had fought Stone's Republic for too long to underestimate the tactical and strategic skills of the Republic forces, and he knew they had to move forward with caution. When he spoke, however, his voice was gilded with the conviction of a true warrior. "As always, McCarron's Armored Cavalry is ready to serve the Confederation. How may we do so?"

Fisk glanced at her aide, and the young officer quickly pulled up several map views on the hanging screens, highlighting the Confederation border with the Republic. "In the wake of our deliberations, the Strategios have devised Operation Clarity—a plan to strike at the very heart of the Republic." Fisk looked down to lock eyes with Baxter. "The Chancellor himself has personally requested that the Fourth take part in this effort."

Although she refused to let anything show in her expression, Lindsey felt a warm rush of pleasure at the compliment. Since she had taken command of the re-formed regiment, she had been working tirelessly to bring it up to the high standards set by her predecessor, and relished the validation of the hard work her team had put forth.

Cyrus gave her a small smile of approval, as if psychically aware of what she was thinking, and then turned back to the *sang-jiang-jun*. "It is our honor to have the faith of the Celestial Wisdom, ma'am."

Fisk nodded before continuing. "The Fourth will be part of an elite task force tasked with striking at the heart of the Republic—a world that holds not only a high intrinsic strategic value, but a place where a victory would be of immense historical importance to the Confederation."

Lindsey said the name aloud even before the planet lit up red on the display:

"Northwind."

The *sang-jiang-jun* favored her with a small smile. "Northwind. Aside from the historical consideration that makes it such a tempting target, it happens to be the closest of the four worlds within easy reach that still has a working hyperpulse generator. If captured, its interstellar-communications capability would be vital in coordinating any potential strike on Terra itself, giving us an advantage over both the Wolves and the Falcons."

Lindsey gave another thin smile, as if in agreement, but she was fully aware of the topic Fisk was so carefully trying to avoid: during the Fourth Succession War, First Prince Hanse Davion of the Federated Suns had offered the Northwind Highlanders their historic homeworld in return for abandoning the Confederation in one of its greatest hours of need, a betrayal that had brought the Capellans to the brink of destruction. While the Confederation had since regained nearly all of what it had previously lost, the memory still smoldered in the hearts of many loyal Capellans.

"What forces are we expected to encounter?" McCarron asked, pulling up a close-up of the planet's information on the smaller screen in front of him. "Considering our successes along that front, the Republic has to realize Northwind is a tempting target."

Fisk tapped the table in agreement. "According to Maskirovka intel, the only forces currently on planet are the Twelfth Hastati Sentinels. While they are an elite regiment largely drawn from the ranks of the Northwind Military Academy and the Highlanders regiments, they still only constitute a single regiment. The Highlanders themselves are still posted on Terra as one of its primary defensive forces, and post-Tiamat data indicates that the Twelfth will not be receiving any sort of reinforcement anytime soon."

The *sang-jiang-jun* gestured for another screen to be brought up, this one showing the breakdown of forces for the proposed operation. "The Fourth MAC will be part of a task force including Warrior House Imarra, Laurel's Legion, and the First Canopian Lancers."

To an armchair tactician, such a massing of forces might seem like overkill for a single planet, especially in the wake of an era where a single BattleMech might be expected to lead the defense of an entire planet, but no less of a tactician than Hanse Davion himself had proven the necessity of three-to-one odds during the Fourth Succession War. While the CCAF had suffered greatly from the lesson, it was only fitting that they would use that same strategy against their own enemies. "We will retain our independent command?" McCarron asked, and Fisk nodded carefully. The Big MAC had always held a special place in the command structure of the CCAF, and traditionally took precedence over both CCAF regulars and mercenary units, but a Warrior House was a very different animal altogether.

To Lindsey's surprise, Fisk focused on her as she responded, almost as if apologizing for something. "While the mission will be technically under the command of *Gao-shiao-zhang* Jiang Hui of House Imarra, the Fourth will retain its autonomy to achieve its mission objectives without undue interference." As if sensing Lindsey's concern, Fisk smiled slightly, a fleeting expression that almost made Lindsey reply in kind, but she was careful to maintain her neutral expression. "The House Master is a bit unconventional, but like you, the Celestial Wisdom has personally requested his participation. You should have no problems working with him."

Lindsey bowed her head respectfully, while Cyrus Gave a more neutral nod. While not the answer he was hoping for, it certainly could have been worse. McCarron's Armored Cavalry was not the most orthodox fighting unit in the CCAF's roster, but when given an objective, they knew how to get the job done.

Despite the Strategic Director's assurances, however, McCarron still did not seem fully convinced of the plan. "That may be all well and good, *Sang-jiang-jun,* but that assumes that the Republic's unwillingness to send reinforcements to besieged planets also means they are unable. Northwind is likely to be a very different proposition."

For a moment, the *sang-jiang-jun* considered how to respond, and then looked at McCarron squarely. "I will be honest with you, *Sang-shao*: I happen to agree. However, while we have factored that into our strategic planning, we also cannot let the possibility paralyze us from doing what must be done. The greatest risk is the Highlanders themselves: with the majority of them defending Terra in the wake of the last attack by the Steel Wolves, they are within striking distance of Northwind, and they are likely to immediately return to their homeworld if they hear it is being attacked." Fisk smiled thinly at the two officers. "The Maskirovka has devoted significant resources to monitoring for any sign of weakness in the Republic's Wall, and the director assures me that we should have ample warning if they abandon Terra. Of course, and that any such departure would signify a critical shift in their relationship with the Republic."

"Not to mention leaving Terra with one less defender," McCarron responded, clearly seeing the benefit. "If they should counterattack Northwind, we can always bunker down and hold them off for as long as necessary, giving you the opportunity to devote additional forces to the strike at Terra itself."

"Exactly," she responded, a flash of her old fire evident in her eyes. "It's a calculated risk, but it also happens to be our best opportunity to seriously damage the Republic's command-and-control abilities and negate their interior advantage."

McCarron gave a small nod, apparently convinced. It was a gamble, but he would not have stayed in the military life if he did not like playing the odds. "We serve the will of the Chancellor, *Sang-jiang-jun.*"

"Indeed," came another voice from the rear of the chamber, and this time the four occupants of the room shot to their feet as one. As they rose, a hidden panel slid open in the wall, and Daoshen Liao, the divine Chancellor of the Capellan Confederation, stepped into the room, flanked by two of his black-suited Death Commandos.

He glided among the shadows, the light from the monitors reflecting the red and gold silk of his robes, while his eyes seemed an even darker black than the shadows themselves. Lindsey took what little comfort she could in the rigors of her military training as she stared straight ahead, locked at attention. The Chancellor had been rumored to be with the rest of the Strategios on Liao, keeping a personal eye on the military operations from the front lines, but seeing him here only underscored the vital nature of her upcoming mission. She couldn't help but feel a small thrill of trepidation at the enormity of what she was being asked to do, but she kept her breath slow and even to avoid betraying her thoughts.

Approaching the table, the Chancellor nodded once, allowing them to relax, although none dared to resume their seats. "It is clear that you understand the vital nature of the mission, *Sang-shao*. Several of the other Great Houses have hesitated to give us the respect we have earned while still seeking to take advantage of our gains. It is imperative that we take Terra before any other nation, providing the entire Inner Sphere the unquestionable confirmation of our legitimacy to lead humanity to its rightful destiny."

"Of course, Celestial Wisdom." McCarron bowed his head deeply, none of his former insouciance with the *sang-jiang-jun* apparent when faced with the Chancellor.

Once again, Lindsey kept her eyes locked on the Chancellor as he spoke, despite her urge to glance over at her senior officers. While she feared no risk in the service to the Confederation, she was well aware that Task Force Chong Che's attempt to breach the Wall in 3146 had utterly destroyed the Third Liao Guards and the Seventh Capellan Defense Force.

"You are right to be concerned about the nature of the mission. However, it is imperative that we do everything in our power to take and hold Northwind. It is of vital strategic importance to our nation to enhance our own war efforts, and the loss of the HPG to another nation would put us at a grave disadvantage along our own border." His dark eyes roamed the room, taking them all under his gaze. "Devlin Stone is a wily foe, and I would put nothing past him. It is our duty to ensure that the threat he poses to the Confederation is neutralized once and for all."

To Lindsey's horror, his gaze slid over to hers, and she locked eyes for an agonizing moment with her sworn lord, feeling like she was drowning in the restless ebony waters she saw there. "This will also go to great lengths toward forgiving previous shortcomings, solidifying the place of highest esteem that McCarron's Armored Cavalry has always held in the Confederation."

McCarron gave a deep, respectful bow, which Lindsey instantly matched, but her mind was completely awash with what the Chancellor had said.

The gauntlet had been thrown. Regardless of who was truly in charge of the mission to Northwind or whom she would have to fight, she was determined to secure the planet for the Chancellor and the Confederation. She owed it to Faith McCarron and the memories of all of those who had been lost to the Republic.

The honor of the unit would allow for nothing less.

CHAPTER 2

"Damn it, Danny. All these troops have to do right now is gripe and listen to rumors of how the Cappies are about to be on our doorstep. We need to do something to get them focused!"

—Overheard conversation between Brigadier
General Luis McNamara and his aide

PROVING GROUNDS
NORTHWIND MILITARY ACADEMY
NORTHWIND
REPUBLIC OF THE SPHERE
28 OCTOBER 3150

We are going to lose.

No matter how many ways Declan Casey tried to spin it, the conclusion seemed as inescapable as the event horizon of a black hole. Despite the bitter chill of the cooling vest he wore, he felt a bead of sweat trail down his back from his hairline, just one further annoyance in a day that refused to get better.

His radio crackled with static over the master command line, with reports coming from various units already under fire:

"Gladius Four is engaged with an enemy *Phoenix Hawk,* requesting assistance."

"Three, watch your flanks! Demon tanks incoming!"

"Gladius One is down! Repeat, Gladius One is down!"

Declan swore lightly as he fought to keep his hands off his *Marauder II*'s joysticks, his eyes locked to the battle unfolding on his secondary monitor. His ad hoc company had been ordered to hold position in preparation for a push against the opposition's main battle force that would probably never come, but he was eager to provide support for the rest of his unit.

The exercise had been simple. Each battalion of the New Lanark garrison of the Twelfth Hastati Sentinels had selected two mixed companies of units to represent their respective battalions, with the two teams pitted against each other in a low-power war game in their actual units. The Twelfth's commander, Brigadier General Luis McNamara, had thought a little good-natured competition would both burn off extra energy and distract everyone from the rumors running wild all across the planet.

Like every other Twelfth Hastati member, Declan had heard that a special envoy from the Republic of the Sphere was en route, bringing news and some new equipment from the Exarch as special thanks for the Highlanders' continued defense of Terra. While that would be excitement enough, there were also darker whispers that the arrival was only due to the recent Capellan strikes on the Republic's borders. Even with most of the HPG net being down, rumors always flew on the solar wind, and everyone on Northwind had heard stories that the Capellan Confederation was planning a strike at the Highlanders' homeworld. Most of the inhabitants had been expecting just such a retaliation since the Fourth Succession War, but with the recent deep strikes into former Republic prefectures, Capellan forces were finally within range to take their revenge. This exercise would serve to sharpen their skills and hopefully reduce some of the tension all around.

At least there was a small silver lining in the rumors of new equipment en route to the Twelfth Hastati. While the equipment they were using was already considered top of the line for the Republic, stories of new developments from Republic-sponsored research and development programs abounded throughout the prefecture. In true Northwind fashion, it had not taken very long for several company commanders to make a friendly wager to see who would get first pick of the new equipment, which coincided nicely with the upcoming war game. It seemed like a good opportunity for the troops to sharpen their skills and focus on the mission at hand. Declan himself had been ecstatic when his commander, Colonel Thomas O'Hara, had personally offered him command of a mixed company for the purposes of the exercise, to "show me what you can do." It seemed like an excellent opportunity to gain valuable command experience.

At least, that was the plan.

They are getting torn up out there." From his headset, Ellie Taggart didn't bother to conceal her concern. The newest member of his lance and the regiment, she had recently graduated from the NMA, and had come to see this first exercise as the chance to prove her worth to her new lancemates. A native of Northwind, she was devastated that she had missed the call to join the newly re-formed Highlanders in the wake of Gray Monday, and had worked twice as hard as anyone else to earn a spot in the Twelfth Hastati Sentinels, which was the next best thing.

Unfortunately she wasn't wrong on either count.

First Battalion's tactical plan for this exercise had been sound. The colonel had sent scouts along the perimeter of the engagement area, quickly finding the recon elements from Third Battalion and neutralizing them in a carefully planned blitz. The first meeting between the two forces had ended as a nice technical victory by First Battalion, and everyone had been riding high on their initial victory.

Unfortunately, battle plans rarely survived contact with the enemy. One of the other scout lances from Third Battalion had come on the First's mobile command center during a deep-range probe, forcing the colonel onto the defensive on the eve of his next strike. While he had repelled the initial attack, he had been forced to call up his reserves to ensure he was not overwhelmed, now that his command center had been discovered.

It also meant that it only left Declan's company of mixed forces to eke out a victory.

A light flashed on his console, and he hit the control without conscious thought. "Centurion One, go."

"Centurion One, this is Gladius Actual," the colonel replied, his voice cutting through the din of combat in the background. "We are under attack by Third Batt forces, pulling back to Rally Point Zeta. We believe there is a flanking force driving in our position. You are ordered to intercept immediately and give us time to regroup."

"Confirmed, we're on it," Declan replied, quickly switching back to his lance's channel and bringing his company up to speed. "We've got the call, team. Form up on me. We are moving to support Gladius."

Over the lance channel, he could hear John Oedhe, Centurion Three, throttle up his *Lament's* speed. "Chuckie, any idea what we're up against?"

As usual, Sergeant Charlene Fairchild ignored Oedhe's use of her nickname, too busy bringing her *Ostsol* into formation on Declan's other flank. "From the data I've been getting, Joe Donnelly's lance just broke against Gladius, and our reserves are doing cleanup as they pull back to a new defensive position. If I am tracking right, that means they're going to be letting the Bulldog off his chain."

Oedhe swore lightly, and Declan couldn't blame him. Captain Murray "Bulldog" Garrett was a former Highlander who had signed on with the Twelfth when they had been formed. A hard-charging, brash man whose bark was most certainly not worse than his bite, he had carefully built a lance of powerful striker 'Mechs that had a reputation for hitting targets hard and fast. It also didn't hurt that his lance had a lot of Clan 'Mechs that had previously belonged to Stirling's Fusiliers and the Northwind Hussars—former Northwind Highlanders regiments. While Republic 'Mechs had done wonders in evening the playing field between Inner Sphere and Clan tech, Clan-made equipment was still an impressive force multiplier.

All of which meant that Garrett's lance not only outweighed Declan's, it also had an impressive technological profile.

As he expected, it was Oedhe who broke the momentary silence. "What's the play, Boss?"

Declan smiled: "The cavalry comes riding to the rescue."

Hobbled by the various speeds of the lance, Taggart's *Osprey* reached the battlefield before anyone else, transmitting a bleak picture of the situation.

What remained of Gladius had been forced to pull back in the shadow of a hillock, desperately trying to gain cover from the encroaching Third Battalion forces approaching from the east. Two BattleMechs, a *Hunchback* and the colonel's *Black Watch*, held a rough defensive line with a Marksman tank as they interposed themselves between the hillock and Third Battalion, lighting the air with bursts of bright laser fire and autocannon tracer rounds.

The *Hunchback* struck a Third Battalion *Panther* in the chest with its heavy autocannon, staggering the light 'Mech and dropping it to the ground like a shattered child's toy. While all of the weapons fire had been throttled back to nonlethal levels, the umpire computer at the NMA was controlling the simulated damage, causing falls and registering damage throughout the linked network of units.

Taking a position within a copse of trees on the hillock, Oedhe laid down a withering array of fire at the first of the Third Battalion forces to come into range, a pair of Regulator tanks attempting to skirt the far side of the hill. His fire kept them from closing too quickly, but their speed made them troublesome targets at range.

Declan heard him curse as one of the Regulators narrowly avoided being struck by a particle projector cannon's blast. "These little boggarts are fast as the dickens... Ellie, anything that you can do about that?"

Taggart laughed, and her *Osprey* twisted its torso toward the nearest Regulator, its Gauss rifle tracking the speeding tank. "Just watch me."

Declan clicked the mic twice. "Keep close, Four. I don't want you haring off on a snipe hunt."

When she responded, he could hear the chagrin in her voice. "Yes, sir."

Raising his *Marauder II*'s arm, Declan sent a PPC shot in front of the lead Regulator. While it also didn't hit, the attack forced the tank to break off as it suddenly found the neighborhood hotter than expected.

"Three, hold the hill, keep them from getting too fancy. Centurions Five and Nine, take your lances to link up with the mobile command center. We will support the battle line here. Two, Four, on me." He clicked onto the command channel, bringing up a link to the *Black Watch*. "Gladius Actual, we are onsite."

There was a burst of static on the channel from a near-miss of a PPC, and the colonel's voice was filled with tension. "We're holding for now, C-One. Just take out anyone who wants to join the party."

Declan didn't get time to respond, as the party-crashers chose that moment to finally made their own presence known. As expected, the Bulldog led the way in his Clan-built *Gladiator*, followed by a *Vulture Mk. IV*, a *Tempest*, and a *Griffin IIC*. From their positioning they had clearly been in contact with the units still harrying the First Battalion 'Mechs, and they had known exactly where to appear to cut off any attempt to escape around the hill, moving between the Declan's approaching lance and Gladius's line.

Glancing over at his secondary monitor, he watched the threat count slowly rise. "Charlene, any news?"

He could hear barely concealed frustration in the sergeant's voice. "Not yet, sir. There's a lot of heavy metal moving through the woods. I'm guessing this is where they intend to make their stand."

As she spoke, the attacking lance broke into two elements; the *Gladiator* and *Tempest* moving toward the remaining Gladius BattleMechs, while the *Vulture* and *Griffin IIC* imposed themselves on Oedhe's *Lament*.

The *Gladiator* took point, blazing at the larger of the two targets with its heavy large laser, scoring a virtual wound high on the 'Mech's torso. The computer showed much of the torso armor stripped away in the single hit, although the 'Mech itself remained pristine.

The *Hunchback* immediately stepped forward to assist, but a light Gauss-rifle round from the *Tempest* landed dangerously close to the *Hunchback*'s cockpit, forcing it back a step. Even though it was a simulated round, Declan had been on the receiving end before, and knew their tendency to ring a cockpit like a bell.

They were out of time.

"Four, you are cleared for independent action. Two, you're with me!"

Ellie didn't bother to reply, her *Osprey* ramping up to full speed as she cut past the grove of trees, firing a shot of opportunity at one of the passing Regulators.

Pumping its immense fists, the *Ostsol* ran up beside him, firing a larger laser downrange at the *Griffin IIC* that had struck it in the shoulder.

"Three, get their attention."

"With pleasure." Declan could hear the grim humor in the response. Oedhe wasted no time in lighting up his *Lament*'s PPCs again, sending twin flights of death winging downrange at the *Vulture MK. IV*. One of the PPC shots missed, but the heavy PPC splashed brilliant sapphire lightning against the nearer 'Mech's arms, virtually stripping it bare.

Realizing the new threat, the *Vulture* whirled on the heavy 'Mech, sending a brace of advanced tactical missiles and pulse-laser fire his way. While the laser wasted itself against the side of the hill, the ATM warheads pockmarked the top of the 'Mech's hunched profile, letting it know it had been hit. Despite the evolving tactical situation behind him, the *Gladiator* remained laser-focused on the *Black Watch*, eating up the kilometers with every long stride. Suddenly realizing the danger, the *Black Watch* attempted to loose an alpha strike of its full weapons complement, but the Gauss rifle shot wide at short range, and the blast of ionized particles was not enough to turn the Bulldog's 'Mech from its goal. Backpedaling, the colonel desperately attempted to gain some space to deal with the new threat as the *Gladiator* retaliated with its heavy large laser at point-blank range.

Whether intentionally or by accident, the immense weapon struck the *Black Watch* across the head, momentarily blinding the MechWarrior and locking up the 'Mech mid-motion as the umpire computer registered a killing blow. While the safety governors were supposed to prevent a 'Mech from suffering actual damage during an exercise, there were moments when the sudden loss of signal could have unexpected consequences.

This was one of those moments.

The *Black Watch* lurched backward, frozen halfway into a running step, crashing to the earth in what felt like slow motion. For a moment, things froze in place, everyone instinctively waiting to hear if the umpires would call a halt to the exercise.

Everyone that was, except for Declan. For him, the world stopped moving.

His vision narrowed to a single point on the falling 'Mech's chest, the Republic crest painted over a Highlanders tartan, seeing it waver as the BattleMech tumbled. His eyes remained locked, his lips twisted in silent prayer that the 'Mech would somehow catch itself at the last moment, desperately hoping beyond logic that the laser had not done that much damage. For a moment, the tableau froze in his mind, the moment beginning to pixelate like bad gun-camera footage. He watched the 'Mech drop hard to the ground, his breath ragged as he fought through the sight.

"Lieutenant!" Fairchild's voice forced its way through Declan's haze, the urgency in her voice unusual for the sergeant. "Gladius One is down."

Declan was about to bark at her for stating the obvious, but something in Fairchild's tone forced its way through his mental fog. Slowly, as if surfacing from a stagnant pool, Declan once again began connecting the data. With the colonel out of the action, he was senior.

I am in command.

Taking a slow breath, he quickly surveyed the battlefield. Without the *Black Watch* assisting him, the *Hunchback* pilot was desperately trying to close with the Marksman for protection, but the *Tempest* was pressing it hard to divide and conquer. Oedhe had backed himself behind a heavier stand of trees, but continued to take heavy fire from the *Vulture* and the *Griffin*.

This was exactly the wrong type of fight to be having against the Bulldog, whose tenacity and focus were slowly wearing down the defenders. The other man knew the disparity between the two forces as well as Declan did, and knew ending the threat here would put him in a prime position to move on the mobile command center.

It took Declan only a moment to make a decision, clicking over to the unit channel to give orders. "Two, form up with the *Hunchback* and the Marksman, and hold that line." While it was far from the ideal use for the *Ostsol*'s firepower, Fairchild had the only 'Mech quick enough to capitalize on the enemy's momentary separation. "Four, stay on mission, I'll backstop Three."

He heard their quick acknowledgment, and Fairchild sped past him, firing another flurry of lasers at the *Vulture* as she passed. The other 'Mech turned to cut an ugly weal across the *Ostsol*'s leg, but did not pursue, especially as Oedhe took that moment to strike the *Vulture*'s other leg with a PPC blast.

Ahead, two Condor hovertanks had joined the *Tempest*, and quickly moved to flank the hillock, hoping to get shots at the larger *Lament*'s vulnerable sides and rear. With practiced precision, he shifted his own targeting reticule, sending a burst of cerulean lightning into the trailing Condor as soon as the crosshairs flashed red. Unlike his early shot at the Regulator, this one took the heavy tank in the lift skirt, causing it to trail a stream of sparks as the umpire brought it to a screeching halt.

While it wasn't dead, its lack of mobility made it little more than a pillbox.

The *Tempest* tried to whirl on the new threat, but a pair of PPC strikes took it in the arm and rear torso. On his secondary monitor, he saw a flash of heat from the other 'Mech. "Three, I think you tagged their engine. Hit 'em again!"

Ignoring the heat that momentarily turned his cockpit into a sauna, he fired his own Gauss rifle at the other 'Mech while Oedhe sent another complement of PPC fire.

The heavy PPC did little more than vaporize the leaves on a nearby tree, but his remaining PPC and the Gauss slug took the *Tempest* high in the chest, breaching the armor. The 'Mech instantly froze in place, the umpire shutting it down as the sensors read that its engine had been cored.

Seeing its two companions taken out of action, the second Condor broke off, but not before firing an LB-X autocannon shot that sanded armor off Declan's arm and leg. He instinctively shifted his aim to finish off the nimble tank, but Fairchild's voice came over the radio before he could take the shot.

"Three's in trouble!"

Declan quickly shifted his gaze back and took in the situation: having finished the *Black Watch*, the Bulldog had ignored the remaining *Hunchback*, leaving it for the other three 'Mechs slowly closing in on it and going for larger prey.

Oedhe had already taken significant damage from his two lancemates, and Declan watched the *Gladiator*'s Ultra-class autocannon connect, cutting deep into the hip and making the 'Mech stumble. The second shot burst through the previously damaged left arm, simulating the energy release from the PPC that had been pent up for his next shot. The resulting feedback shifted the connection to his neurohelmet for the few vital seconds he had needed to compensate for the simulated actuator damage, and he listed to one side.

This time, Declan didn't bother waiting for the umpires, and fired a PPC at the *Gladiator*, striking it's leg.

The larger 'Mech turned toward him and began descending the hill, murder telegraphed in its gait. The *Vulture Mk IV*, not wishing to remain idle, launched another flight of missiles that rained over his 'Mech, one of the warheads rattling his cockpit like a giant bell.

"Well, you wanted to get his attention..." Declan muttered, and accelerated his *Marauder II* into a run directly at the *Vulture*.

Aside from wanting to negate some of the other 'Mech's range advantage, he wanted to get close enough to make the Bulldog wary of hitting one of his own lancemates.

"One, Four thinks she's close!" Fairchild reported.

Declan released a brace of medium lasers at the *Vulture*, trying to cool his overheating 'Mech. "Tell her to move it, we need her help here!"

"Don't I know it..." the sergeant responded just loudly enough for her mic to pick it up. Declan saw Fairchild heavily engaged with a pair of Third Battalion 'Mechs, trying to hold up more than her share of the battle as the *Hunchback* attempted to close the range and take advantage of its heavy autocannon.

Declan knew he had to end this now. Third Battalion's commander was clearly trying to get enough mobile forces in line to flank their defense, correctly assuming that the mobile command center would be protected by whatever little they had left. With the sheer amount of damage they'd already taken, the loss of the C-and-C center would surely mean the end of the scenario for First Battalion, and certain defeat.

Heedless of the immense assault 'Mech bearing down on him, Declan concentrated his fire on the *Vulture*. A PPC struck the left torso, while his Gauss rifle struck like a massive fist along the 'Mech's centerline, squarely hitting the beaklike protrusion. All of his medium lasers cut deeply into the torso armor, but one slipped through to trigger a simulated ammo explosion that caused the *Vulture* to slump forward, out of the fight.

He had no time to register his minor victory as his world shook to the core with all the force the 'Mech's force-feedback program could muster. The armor over his left torso went straight to red as the *Gladiator*'s autocannon cut a line of fire across his 'Mech, and the large laser finished the job by ripping off the torso and the arm that went with it.

The damage was too much for the *Marauder II*, and he fell backward onto his rear armor, rattling his teeth as he fought to keep from tensing against the impending fall. He swore as his neurohelmet bounced against the back of the headrest, knowing he'd have a painful bruise in the morning, but he was already moving to get his 'Mech back on his feet.

He'd managed to rise to one knee when the *Gladiator* stepped into point-blank range, aiming its large laser at his cockpit—

"All combatants, cease operations," the umpire channel burst over the comms. "Endex. Repeat, Endex. Cease operations. Third Battalion C&C has been captured. Endex."

Declan closed his eyes tightly for a moment, his breath coming easier despite the temperature of the cockpit. It had been a risk, sending off Four in her *Osprey*, but her Beagle Active Probe was one of the few pieces of tech that could have found the enemy's mobile command center in time. Knowing the Bulldog as well as he did, he knew that by keeping him engaged, with victory so close, he would not have the time to think about what he should have been defending.

Declan smiled wanly, rubbing the bruise on his neck idly.

I always knew we could do it.

Declan rushed out of the hangar, desperately looking for any sign of a cab or a vehicle he could commandeer. Thinking he had plenty of time to get to the Warrior's Cabal, he had not brought his own vehicle, counting on riding out with one of the others. Unfortunately, the chief tech had needed him to sign off on some repairs from his *Marauder II*'s fall, and he had told the others to go on ahead, not realizing it would take so long to get out.

The Warrior's Cabal was a Northwind tradition, a place where warriors could debate major issues affecting the Highlanders and occasionally call for a full Assembly of Warriors to be summoned in times of dire need. Such Assemblies had occurred at the onset of the Fourth Succession War and the FedCom Civil War, and both times had portended major changes for Northwind. If such upheaval was once again on their doorstep, he knew he had to be present.

"Need a ride?" a familiar voice asked. Declan couldn't help but smile at the sight of his grandfather, Major Seamus Casey, his muscular arm half out of the window of his old pickup. The truck was older than he was, but between Seamus and one of his old tech buddies, they had kept it running long after its contemporaries. Declan was always happy to see his grandfather, but now he was a godsend.

"If you're going my way," Declan said with forced casualness, but he didn't wait for a response to climb into the cab, instinctively relaxing in its familiar atmosphere of old leather and good tobacco. As soon as he was inside, Seamus gunned the engine, sending them speeding toward the main gate.

"You heard about the exercise?" Declan asked, careful not to look at the illegal scanner perched on the truck's dash. Both it, and its twin at his grandfather's house, always seemed to be up to date with all of the current Highlander and Republic codes, despite his grandfather not having been on active duty for years. He supposed it was just another example of his grandfather's many friendships at work, but he didn't want to start an argument about security concerns.

Again.

Seamus nodded and glanced over at Declan. "Heard you had to step up when the colonel went down. Nicely done."

Declan shrugged off the compliment, but couldn't help feeling a warm glow of pride in his chest. His grandfather was, like him, from a long line of Highlanders MechWarriors, and his praise meant a lot. Glancing over, he decided to change the subject before the other man could see.

"So, any idea of what sort of envoy the Exarch supposedly sent?'

"From what I heard, it's a Knight of the Republic," Seamus replied, and glanced over at him. "Least it's not another Paladin, eh?"

Declan spared a look at his grandfather, but declined to respond. The two men had argued over Ezekiel Crow, the Black Paladin, and his crimes against the Highlanders far too often to open that particular can of worms again. Still, he agreed with his grandfather on one level: the Highlanders had traditionally mixed results with foreign envoys. The Highlanders of Northwind always trusted in themselves first and foremost, and the family had never let them down when it counted.

When Seamus spoke again, his voice was gentle. "You were thinking of Jimmy when Tommy O'Hara went down, weren't you, lad?"

Declan didn't trust his voice, so he just nodded. Time had been good to him: he could go a few days in a row without thinking of his elder brother James, lost during the second Steel Wolves attack on Northwind in 3134. Unfortunately, it rarely lasted. Every time he looked up at a BattleMech, he would think of how often the two of them had played at being MechWarriors, and how they were going to be as famous as the Kells one day.

When he was able to speak past the lump in his throat, he made an effort to keep his voice light. "Just how much did you hear on that thing?"

"Hear?" Seamus smiled thinly. "I saw every blow. I thought they nearly had you there when you sent Chuckie into the battle line, but it was the right move."

"You were in the training center." It was not quite an accusation.

"Veteran's prerogative," Seamus replied, smiling. "You should have heard the Bulldog swearing a blue streak when they shut down the exercise. I don't think you should ask him for a ride anytime soon."

It was clear Seamus wanted to say more, but as they saw the tree line approaching, Seamus simply concentrated on driving. Declan knew his grandfather understood his concerns about operational security, but the elder Highlander was not about to change the way he did things.

Despite the delay, the truck got them there quickly enough that they were not the last to arrive, with the bonfire well and truly in full swing as they parked on the outskirts of the woods. Still a little peeved by the discussion, Declan curtly thanked his grandfather, then quickly headed toward the center of the clearing. Seamus, undeterred, kept up with him easily, and Declan believed that, despite his age, the man could still pace him from one side of the woods and back. They walked through the trees toward the flickering firelight, and eventually broke into the clearing to see the raging bonfire at its center.

The circle of cabers seemed smaller than usual, with only several members of the various Highlander Clans present, most from the Clan Elders. All of the Highlanders who had families here had tried to send a representative, but most were on Terra in the hopes of deterring another attack, leaving few warriors to act in their stead.

Declan glanced around the fire, seeking out the gray uniform that would indicate a Republic Knight, but didn't see it at first glance.

With the eagle-eyed nature of one used to sizing up a room quickly, Seamus gave a small nod towards the fire. "There she is."

Declan followed his grandfather's gaze, and found Brigadier General McNamara deep in conversation with a tall woman with raven-black hair. She had her back to him, but it was clear that she was wearing not a Knight's uniform, but rather the kilt and kit of a Highlander.

"That's the Exarch's envoy?" Declan asked, watching the other woman as she spoke. Her lithe form seemed familiar, but he couldn't place it from his angle.

Seamus smiled. "More than that, lad, much more. Let's go introduce ourselves, shall we?"

Declan looked over at his grandfather curiously, but Seamus was already in motion. Apparently sensing the mountain of a man approaching, the young woman turned, and Declan saw her clearly for the first time. Two catlike blue eyes glowed under her dark hair, and an expression of delight crossed her face as she saw his grandfather.

"Seamus?" The Knight's face lit up, and it made her seem even younger. To Declan's shock, she wrapped her arms around his grandfather tightly, and while it may have been a trick of the firelight, it looked like his grandfather was actually blushing. "As I live and breathe... I doubted you still did either."

"Aye, lass. 'Tis good to see you." Turning to Declan, he smiled grandly at him. "My lady, may I introduce my grandson, Declan Casey. Dec, this is Lady Maeve Stirling, Knight of the Republic of the Sphere."

Instantly, everything became crystal clear, and Declan applauded Devlin Stone on his choice of envoy. Andrea Stirling had been one of the colonels of the Northwind Highlanders and later Paladin Exemplar of the Republic. The Stirlings had been a part of the Highlanders for as long as the Caseys, and their words would carry a great deal of weight with the other Clan Elders.

"A pleasure to meet you, Declan," she responded, giving him a bright smile. "Your grandfather was one of the first people to ever let me try out a 'Mech simulator." She smiled wanly at the elder man. "You got ripped up and down the yard for it too, if I remember. "

Seamus laughed, his accent coloring his response as he thought back to better times. "Yer muther thought you were a bit too young to be training, yes."

"I was eight!" she replied, although whether she agreed was unclear from her indignant tone.

General McNamara cleared his throat lightly, and Maeve gave them both a sorrowful smile. "I'm sorry, we've got to start. I do expect to buy you a drink later though, Seamus Casey."

"I would not be missing it, lass," he replied, and the two Casey men stepped up to their preferred area to watch the ceremony.

As the crowd naturally settled down in expectation, the general raised his arms, his deep voice resounding through the clearing. "Ladies and gentlemen, while I am not a senior member of my Clan, my dear brother Thomas has asked me to speak for him tonight." Thomas McNamara, unlike his brother, was still an active Highlander, the highest ranking one still on planet. Unfortunately, he had been struck with a vicious bout of the flu and had been bedridden for days, causing his brother to step forward in his place. Despite technically being an officer of the Republic rather than a serving Highlander, Luis was still of the Highlander Clans first and foremost. "Many of you may recognize our guest, Lady Maeve Stirling. Stirling's Fusiliers were one of our most feared regiments, and it is our good fortune to have her standing with us once more today."

A rumble of approbation came from the assembled Highlanders, and the Republic Knight waited for the applause to die down before stepping up before them. "Brothers and sisters, I thank you for your warm welcome. I wish it was with better news that I return home, but I have been sent here with a message from the Exarch himself, giving me leave to place it before the Clans as a whole."

Her blue eyes swept the assembled warriors, taking them all under her thoughtful gaze. "As many of you know, the Republic finds itself besieged from all sides. While the Fortress Protocols have kept us safe, it has only been through the devotion and sacrifice of the Highlanders regiments that we have been able to drive back the invaders for so long.

"Unfortunately, there are those who wish to take advantage of your loyalty, and to threaten a valuable target at the same time. Ladies and gentlemen, as I am sure you have all suspected, I bring credible intelligence that there is an impending attack bound for Northwind."

An angry rumble came from the assembled crowd, but Declan noted very little of it sounded surprised. The Highlanders had known this day was due to come again, and they were prepared to make whatever sacrifices they must to protect hearth and home.

"Capellans," Seamus muttered, and Maeve nodded, clearly hearing the same consensus around the fire. The Capellan

Confederation had done its part to destabilize Northwind since the Highlanders had left the nation's service during the Fourth Succession War, and the Highlanders' memories were long.

"From a strategic standpoint," Maeve continued, "this planet's working HPG makes you an ideal target, even if the Capellans had somehow forgotten how much they hate us for all that they lost in the Fourth Succession War. When you combine the two, I have no doubt the temptation has finally proven irresistible.

"I have come today to help you prepare, and to fight with you. With all of the threats that have beset the Republic, we have little to spare in the way of additional warriors, but we have brought some new BattleMechs to help even the playing field when the Capellans come to call. The Exarch knew that if there is a fight for Northwind, he wanted you as well equipped as he could make you."

There were some small nods in the crowd, but Declan was also very conscious of the number of grim faces that shone in the firelight. As he let his gaze roam over the assembled warriors, someone stepped out from the middle of the crowd, a venerable woman with two piercing brown eyes under a short mop of gray hair. Much like his grandfather, he had known Lieutenant Colonel Cadha Jaffray since infancy, and he listened carefully to what she had to say.

"Why such a small force, Lady Maeve? The Exarch couldn't spare anyone else?"

If the Knight thought the question impertinent, she was careful not to let it show. "The Exarch specifically ordered me here to do what I can, Colonel. I brought my own company and as much equipment as my DropShip could hold to assist in the defense of Northwind. Unfortunately, between the Capellans, the Falcons, and the Wolves, we are beset on all sides. One should not imagine for a moment that Northwind is not a vital part of the Republic's defense, but we also need to cover other planets that do not already have as powerful of a defense as the Twelfth Hastati."

Jaffray nodded, more out of acknowledgment than agreement, and Declan was tempted to speak as well. He was getting that same uncomfortable feeling he'd gotten after hearing of Maeve's arrival: once again Northwind would be receiving the short end of the stick for the sin of being able to maintain its own defense.

To his surprise, Stirling shook her head. "When it comes down to it, however, it is true that this is being done because it must be done. Before I left for Northwind, I had the opportunity to speak to Countess Campbell, an opportunity I will treasure for the rest of my days. I had many of the same questions you do, and I was concerned that I was not doing all I could to uphold the promise the Republic has made with our Clans. To my relief, she reminded me of the bonds between us, and of the mutual covenant we all share, setting my mind at ease as little could. She also reminded me of the realities of the situation: while we believe there is a credible threat to Northwind, the same forces we know are en route could easily redirect to any of a half-dozen other targets, all of which must be protected. Northwind has managed to maintain its freedom throughout the centuries by being tougher than those who wished to take it from us, and this time will be no different. If called on, we shall fight to protect the ground our families have fought for since we settled here, and we will show anyone who threatens Northwind the blood price they will pay."

A murmur of agreement went through the crowd, although it was far from unanimous. Once again, Declan took a mental tally of the expressions on the faces of the various Clan Elders, and while there seemed to be no one openly hostile to the Knight's message, there were still some carefully neutral faces. It didn't mean they wouldn't fight, but some of them were clearly not as pleased with her answer to the colonel's question as some of the younger warriors.

Turning back to the crowd, she said, "Over the next few weeks, I will be meeting with all of the Clan Elders, and working with General McNamara to plan a defense of Northwind that will drive the Capellans back to their lines. Until Northwind is secure, I am here to serve and provide the respectful support of the Republic."

Once again there was applause, and the various Clan leaders began discussing the Knight's message among themselves.

Turning toward where his grandfather had been sitting, Declan was surprised to see he was gone. As large as Seamus was, he could move as stealthily as a Nekakami assassin when he wished, and he had apparently stepped away sometime during the Knight's speech.

Declan glanced around, finally finding his grandfather near the tree line, deep in conversation with someone Declan could not see. For the briefest of moments, flickering firelight outlined a shadowy figure, but he could not tell the person's identity, despite an absolute surety that he had met the person before.

Any further consideration of the figure was cut off by the voice of Lady Maeve Stirling behind him, and he turned quickly. She smiled at him, and he was startled to note how light her eyes seemed to be up close.

"Well, Lieutenant," she said, "it seems your grandfather is otherwise engaged at the moment, so would you care to join me for a drink?"

"It would be my pleasure, my lady," Declan replied formally, and she gave him a small grin. She led the way over to where several kegs had been carefully placed away from the fire, but he couldn't help but glance back at his grandfather one last time.

Seamus, as if sensing his grandson's gaze, looked over at him, and in the reflection of the fire Declan was quite sure that his grandfather's expression was grim, and held an expression he had not often seen on Seamus's face.

Guilt.

CHAPTER 3

"I dinnae doubt that the Exarch wants us to succeed, if only to cover his own wrinkly arse, but where is the countess? Surely she knew one of these damned vipers would come for us at some point. What is she doing fighting on Terra when we are at risk?"

—Padraig Houlihan, Elder of Clan Houlihan, editorial, *Northwind Today*

CAITHNESS WOODS
NORTHWIND
REPUBLIC OF THE SPHERE
28 OCTOBER 3150

Having acquired their ale, Lady Maeve led back to the fire, with Declan taking a seat across from her on two spare cabers set out for just such a purpose. The bonfire was still going strong, the sweet odor of burning pine bringing him back to quiet nights in front of the hearth, reading and listening to his mother singing as she cooked for the family. He watched the Knight as she admired the contents of her cup for a moment, letting the cool winter breeze blow her raven hair over her shoulders. "It's been a long time since I had a Northwind ale." She sipped and closed her eyes in pleasure. "For some reason it never really caught on off-world, and I don't get back here as much as I would like."

Declan had sipped his own as she spoke, and nodded. "When were you last back?"

"Four years ago," she replied without hesitation, clearly having given the matter some thought. "My grandmother had returned here for a funeral, and I took the opportunity to look up some old friends." She looked solemn for a moment. "There always seem to be fewer than I remember."

"For all of us," he said carefully, not trusting himself to go too far into that train of thought. "Is that when you last saw my grandfather?"

"It's been quite a while," she replied, and he noted that she had not actually answered his question. "I saw your competition today...very impressive." She smiled playfully. "I especially liked the part where you took on a lance by yourself."

For a moment, Declan considered grand-patricide, but she gave an airy laugh and waved off his concerns. "Forgive me, the brigadier was kind enough to pipe the feed up to my DropShip at my request. I was eager to see what the Twelfth was capable of, and it helped keep everyone entertained." She narrowed her eyes slightly while looking at him. "You owe me fifty stones, just so you know."

"Consider it an investment," he said, again noting how deftly she'd changed the subject. "A good reminder to never bet against me."

She raised her cup in acknowledgment of his point and drank again. "Well, I hope you use the equipment I brought in good health... I think you may find something to your liking. What did you do before you joined the Centurions?"

"I was seconded to the command staff," he responded, the first stirrings of suspicion coloring his reply.

"Counterintelligence, isn't that right?"

Declan took another drink to hide his expression. That information would have only been in his personnel dossier, which meant she already knew the answer. "That's right, ma'am."

"What was your area of specialization?"

"Being especially good at knowing when I'm being lied to."

Her eyes narrowed at his curt response.

Without another word, he gave her a small nod of farewell, stood, and headed toward the tree line. Anyone watching could have easily mistaken it as the natural ending of a friendly conversation. Careful not to look back, he proceeded to take a half-remembered trail deeper into the woods, the firelight flickering into nothingness as he passed deeper into the emerald curtain of trees. In a second, smaller clearing, he turned, the area lit only by moonlight.

To his complete lack of surprise, Maeve had followed him at a careful distance, holding just inside the trees at the edge of the clearing, her gaze now deadly serious. The stony look in her eyes showed she was not used to being dismissed, and while she made an attempt to look casual, he noted that her open stance could become defensive in an instant. She had left her cup behind, and her hands lay loosely out to her sides, ready for anything he might attempt. They were now truly alone, and although the Highlanders were within range of a full-throated yell, he knew neither of them would call for help if the other proved to be a threat.

"If you wanted a walk in the woods, you could have just asked," Lady Maeve began, her eyes never leaving Declan's face. "There's no need to worry about my reputation."

"It's not your reputation I'm concerned about," Declan replied. "I'm far more interested in your intentions."

"For the Highlanders, or for you?" She took a careful step toward Declan, and he wondered whether he had misjudged her. "Perhaps it would be best if we both just spoke our minds, *Lieutenant.*" She still refused to break eye contact. "I am not used to my intentions being misread."

He locked eyes with her, his voice harsh. "My point, *my lady,* is that I've heard this story before. Tell me if this sounds familiar: With an invader bearing down on Northwind, the Exarch sends a token force to help us with our own defense, leaving the people of Northwind to fend for themselves, and then expecting help when the Steel Wolves are at his own door. You'll forgive me if I don't put much stock in how that story ends."

She raised her chin in challenge, something dangerous flickering in her icy blue eyes. "Are you comparing me to Ezekiel Crow?"

"That depends," he replied, taking his own careful step toward her, noting how she did not shift her own stance in response. "Has the Exarch sent an envoy to the Highlanders for the express purpose of buying time for him to plot his own schemes? *Again?*" He paused to consider for a moment. "Or perhaps a better question might be, 'Which Exarch?'"

The words were barely out of his mouth before she was on him, a gravity knife against his throat. For several moments they stood frozen in place, his own blade pressing against the fabric of her uniform directly over her kidneys, her off hand locked tightly around his wrist. She pushed forward, as if daring him to pierce her skin. Instead, he came to a sudden decision and pulled the blade away slowly until he held directly out to his side. Matching his movements, she shifted her own blade, and they took a mutual step back, which left Declan with a slight moment of regret he couldn't identify.

"How did you guess?" she asked. "The countess?"

He bowed his head in acknowledgment, careful not to take his eyes off her. "You have clearly spoken to her recently, and it sounds like she took you into her confidence. Coupled with the reality that Devlin Stone does seems disinterested in our circumstances right now, it doesn't take a leap of logic to know where you two would've met. You were on Callison, weren't you?"

Word of the fight between Jonah Levin's forces, working on behalf of Devlin Stone, and the forces of former-Exarch Damien Redburn had gotten back even to Northwind, especially when it was revealed that Countess Campbell and some of her Highlanders were fighting on the side of the Remnant against Levin's loyalists. Campbell and her Highlanders had returned to Terra following Redburn's arrest, but there were still a lot of unanswered questions about what had happened during the battle on Callison.

"We did meet there," Maeve replied. "She thought I might be ordered back to Northwind, considering my family history, so I came here to prepare for several different eventualities."

"Quite some time ago," Declan replied. Her eyes narrowed again suspiciously before he raised a hand to forestall her. "You're breathing too easily. After four years away, the thinner air on Northwind should've affected you. Either you practiced an expensive oxygen-reduction therapy on the way in, or you've been on planet for longer than you let on. I'm going to bet that if I checked the system-patrol records, I'll find that a DropShip or shuttle from Northwind rendezvoused with the incoming DropShip today, before you landed at the spaceport."

A thin smile crossed her face, and she seemed to make up her mind about something. "As you said, I should learn not to bet against you." For a brief moment, she stared at him in appraisal, then gestured to his knife. "You any good with that thing?"

Declan gave a thin smile and hurled the knife toward the nearest bole with practiced ease. While not balanced as a throwing knife, the sturdy blade bit deeply into the bark, shivering as it buried itself partway into the wood.

The Knight gave a small nod and then tossed her own, burying her knife neatly beside his. For a brief moment, the two of them watched the moonlight glint off the two blades, and then she looked at him squarely. "You're a soldier in the Republic Armed Forces, and have sworn yourself to the will of the Republic. Regardless of your personal assumptions for my reasons for being here, it is your duty to support all lawful orders from a superior officer. Do you agree?"

He straightened to his full height. "I am a Highlander of Northwind and a loyal subject of the Republic. If you treat fairly with me, I'll treat fairly with you."

"Good," she replied. "I want you and your lance seconded to my company. I am detailing one of my own lances to provide security for the supplies going to Fort Barrett, and I don't want to risk going into battle short. I could use someone with your current knowledge of the terrain and your willingness to think outside the box. Are you up to the challenge, or are ye only fit to whinny and neigh?"

He first instinct was to decline, preferring to go into battle with his own unit, but her last words stopped him in his tracks. For all his flaws, he had never backed down from a challenge. For what seemed like the tenth time that evening, he warned himself to not underestimate the Republic Knight.

"I'd need to get a special dispensation from the general, ma'am," he replied coolly, countering her dipping into the dialect of Northwind with a careful formality of his own. "He is my commanding officer."

"Leave that to me," she replied. "I already told him what I needed, I just didn't know it was you until a moment ago."

"Certainly, ma'am. Until then, however, perhaps you can tell me exactly what you need me for?" He cut her off before she could respond. "What you *really* need me for."

This time, her smile seemed genuine. "Are you always this suspicious?"

He smiled back. "You've clearly looked up my dossier, so you tell me. All I know is you're after something, and the terrain hasn't changed enough since your last visit to warrant a liaison solely for that. I'm guessing from the mention of my counterintelligence work that you need a spook, and the liaison position is a cover."

She nodded. "You seem to have most of it figured out. Care to go for the gold?"

He shook his head. "You're either going to brief me or not. I have a more important question."

For a moment, it seemed she was going to ask, but a slow smile blossomed on her face. "Why you?"

He nodded, and she silently appraised him again. He knew she could have given him another glib reply, but she surprised him by responding sincerely. "I have known your grandfather a long time. He's an honest man, and a damn good one to have at your back in a fight. If he were still on active duty I would probably use him, but he would be too conspicuous. I'm just going to trust that you are half the man he is."

"I try to be."

The Knight gave him an appreciative nod. "Good. You wanted the raw scoop, here it is: I have credible intelligence that someone may be transmitting classified data from Northwind."

"A spy?" Declan asked, attempting to wrap his head around the concept. For a Highlander to betray their unit, their family? It was inconceivable.

"I don't know," she replied honestly. "I know how impossible it sounds, but if it is true, it will compromise our defensive planning. We're trying to compartmentalize as best we can, but without knowing the source of the threat, we don't know how effective our measures will be."

He nodded. "That's why we split our forces to cover the two continents. You're trying to ensure we aren't destroyed completely in a sneak attack."

"The last thing I want to do is to split our forces in the face of a numerically superior foe, but I know better than to trust in the Capellans' better angels if they have our deployment plans. The one thing we truly can't risk is having our defenses shattered in the initial strike."

Declan paused for a moment. Such a plan was ideal if she was concerned that Northwind's defenders might need to prosecute a guerrilla campaign against the incoming Capellan forces, but it would put them at a significant disadvantage in a straight-up fight. "If you already had this intel, why bring your troops in at all? You could have sat at a pirate point and dropped in behind anyone who chose to take advantage."

"But I would still only have a company," she said, staring up at the cloudless sky, the stars overhead clearly visible this far from light pollution. "I tried to bring more, but I was lucky the Council of Paladins allowed me to bring this much. We would have been playing catch-up from the beginning, and without other forces we would be of limited benefit."

He looked at her curiously. "They don't think the Capellans are a threat?"

"They don't necessarily think the Capellans are the *greatest* threat." She moved past him to the tree where the knives had finally stilled. "The weight of history can sometimes blinker even the best of minds. Many in the Republic command structure remember how quickly the Capellans were defeated during the Capellan Crusades, and still more remember how deadly a threat the Clans can be to any who oppose their goals."

She glanced back at him, and he caught a flicker of regret in her eyes. "I heard the same mutterings you did tonight: people wonder why the Republic bothered to send anyone at all if we're going to send such a small force. Unfortunately, it's a question of resources: Northwind is one of the few planets with a full regiment on-planet. Hell, we both know if the Highlanders hadn't pulled our asses out of the fire during the Steel Wolves' attack on Terra, nothing would've been sent at all."

Declan nodded, understanding all too well the picture she was painting. "So once again we are pawns for power plays."

"As soldiers have always been," she replied quietly, as her gaze again slid upward, toward the stars.

For a long moment they stood there in mutual silence, considering the state of their mutual homeworld before Declan spoke up again. "What do you need from me?"

"Two things. First, I need you to be my liaison with the Highlanders. Too many are suspicious of me, and raising concerns that someone here is working against the Republic's interests is not going to win me any friends."

"You want me to spy for you?" Declan's eyes narrowed instinctively as his suspicions flashed back full-force.

"I want you to keep an eye out for those who might be working against the Highlanders and the Republic," she replied. "We may not agree on everything, but I think we can agree the Capellans retaking Northwind is in no one's best interests."

Declan nodded solemnly. "Aye, we can agree on that much."

"Good." She pulled both knives from the tree effortlessly. "I'll give you everything I can to help you do your job, but I'm going to rely on your judgment. Both of us will have enough on our plates soon enough to ensure that I'm not micromanaging." She glanced at him, seeing something in his expression. "You have a concern?"

"Many. Luckily for you, none of them are going to keep me from doing my duty. You did say you needed two things from me, however."

She nodded, weighting the blades in either hand. Declan said nothing, merely watching her carefully as her gaze dropped to the blades.

"I am going to need your help to find a way out of this," she finally responded, looking up at him. "You know the situation the Republic is in. We keep getting pushed back on every front, and many of our people are suffering."

"Suffering from the Capellans, you mean."

"Among other things."

For a moment, it seemed she would say more, but Declan sensed they were not alone. A soft rustling came through the trees, and both of them looked up to see Seamus entering the clearing.

"Well, there the two of you are. I hope I dinnae interrupt anything."

Declan glared at his grandfather, hoping the darkness would cover his blush, but Maeve just laughed.

"You've found our little grove far too quickly for it to have been the first time, Seamus Casey. I've no doubt that you brought a girl or two here in your youth as well."

Seamus made a point to look like he was thinking about it for a moment, then gave her a smile. "As a matter of fact, that tree does look slightly familiar..." He turned to Declan before the conversation could grow even more awkward. "I was heading back to the base and wanted to see if you needed a ride. My lady, can we take you anywhere?"

She shook her head. "No thank you, Major. The brigadier was kind enough to provide me with a vehicle. I hope you'll still have time for us to get that pint soon, though."

"Whenever is convenient, ma'am," he replied. "We retirees have plenty of time on our hands, although I have no doubt you'll be very busy."

"We shall have to see." She turned back to Declan and offered him his blade. "I hope I will see you tomorrow, Lieutenant?"

He looked down and saw the blade she was offering him was in fact her own. He raised his chin, reading the message all too clearly. Like his own, the blade was a clearly a family piece, the Stirling crest artfully cut into the handle. By giving it to him, she was entrusting him with something precious to her...while also ensuring that she kept something precious to him. It was either a sign of trust or a careful warning, and he received both messages loud and clear.

He nodded and took the blade carefully before placing it into his sheath. "Of course, ma'am."

She led them back through the woods. Seamus held back slightly, making sure he kept even with his grandson. Once she was far enough ahead, he gave Declan a sly smile. "A chip off the old block, lad."

"Grandpa?"

"Yes, sonny?"

"Shut up."

The elder man laughed heartily, and the trio headed back toward the fire.

From behind the thick bole of a fir tree, a shadowy figure watched the trio leave the clearing. For a brief moment, they considered whether to continue following, but the risk of discovery was too great. Sliding stealthily back among the greenery, they merged back into the darkness.

CHAPTER 4

"Once again, we have reports of multiple Capellan JumpShips jumping through the Epsilon Indi system. When questioned, the legate stated that his priority must be the protection of the planet itself, and that no aerospace forces can be spared to interdict intersystem traffic. But where are these JumpShips going, and what do they intend to do when they get there?"

—Amber Sodderburg, *Indi Today*

FORTRESS-CLASS DROPSHIP *TALON ZAHN*
OUTBOUND, EPSILON INDI
CAPELLAN CONFEDERATION
2 NOVEMBER 3150

Sang-shao Lindsey Baxter glanced down at herself as she waited in front of the hatch, ensuring that her dress uniform was immaculate before pressing the small stud to ring for admittance.

Following the meeting with *Sang-jiang-jun* Fisk, things had moved at a breakneck pace. With orders in hand, the Fourth had readied for deployment, loading up all the required supplies and finishing whatever maintenance that could not be done underway before burning toward the jump point. As usual, Baxter quickly found herself consumed with the onslaught of minutiae that was standard for the deployment of an entire regiment.

So it was with considerable surprise that upon the eve of their second jump, she received a visitor while discussing some adjustments to her proposed deployment schedule with her lance in the 'Mech bay.

Kyle Endrin and Evan Palos, two of her lancemates, first noticed the visitor's approach. Although no unauthorized person could walk so brazenly into the bay, they instinctively placed themselves between the new arrival and their commander.

The visitor, a low-ranking Warrior House Imarra aspirant dressed immaculately in a pristine green jumpsuit, stopped in front of the two soldiers, his eyes boring into the space between the two men as he waited to be addressed. Lindsey finished speaking to her final lancemate, Qing Rao, before taking pity on the young man. "Gentlemen."

Her lancemates straightened for effect and flanked him on either side, allowing the young man to approach. Stiffening to attention, the young man stepped up to her with the serious mien of one tasked with a vital duty, and carefully presented her with a golden envelope.

Rao accepted the envelope on Lindsey's behalf, and gave it a quick glance before handing it over. The golden envelope had been sealed with the red-wax crest of Warrior House Imarra, and the paper stock was of the finest quality. She nodded her thanks to the young man and took a moment to read the letter.

As she suspected, the envelope contained an invitation from *Gao-shiao-zhang* Jiang Hui, Grand Master of the Blessed Orders, requesting her presence for a dinner aboard his DropShip now that they were back under gravity.

She sent the dutiful aspirant back to the Grand Master with a respectful acceptance of his invitation—which, like any invitation received from a superior, was no request at all—and immediately returned to her quarters to prepare for the dinner. Her dress uniform had been packed with the rest of her gear, so it took her aide some time to locate it and have it properly pressed. For her first meeting with her new commander, she wished to make the best impression possible, and when she looked in the mirror, she was pleased to see how her white-and-green uniform showed off her trim figure.

After a quick staff briefing, she conducted a cursory walkthrough of the 'Mech bays, where teams of technicians and soldiers went over every centimeter of their equipment, knowing they would soon be entrusting their lives to it. Having finished all of her major tasks for the day, she took special care to leave an hour early for the event.

Unfortunately, despite all of her precautions, she was still the third person to arrive.

To be fair, Commodore Shing Xio, as the nominal commander of the mission's aerospace assets, had chosen to berth on the *Zahn* for its command-and-control assets, allowing him to consult with the Grand Master at length, which gave him the advantage of already being present on the *gao-shiao-zhang*'s DropShip. Unlike the others, he wore an immaculate green jumpsuit, eschewing a dress uniform to maintain readiness while underway. His close-cropped hair and dark eyes made it difficult to judge his age, but his competent air and the careful way he moved hinted at a seasoned spacer who had spent a lifetime on the black ocean.

In contrast, Colonel Valeria Centrella-Tompkins of the First Canopian Lancers had joined the *gao-shiao-zhang* when they departed Sian, so her DropShip was docked closer than Baxter's. The colonel was even taller than Baxter, her long blond hair plaited in the tight braid that was traditional for many Magistracy commanders, and her pristine white dress uniform with black leather accents was a noticeable departure from the CCAF uniforms the others wore. The Canopian commander, in conversation with the commodore and Grand Master, was the first to notice Lindsey's arrival and gave her a respectful nod in greeting.

Jiang Hui, the Master of House Imarra, Grand Master of the Warrior House Orders, seemed more like a monk than the head of one of the most feared units in the Inner Sphere. He was a slight man with a precisely trimmed mustache and a shaved head. His impeccably tailored uniform showed the martial-artist grace of his form, although an incongruous number of laugh lines had settled around his eyes.

"*Sang-shao*, it is a pleasure to meet you at last." His voice was deep and resonant, yet surprisingly welcoming. "It is an honor to have a McCarron's Armored Cavalry regiment with us on such a grand undertaking."

"The honor is ours, *Gao-shiao-zhang*," Baxter replied formally. "It is always an pleasure to work with House Imarra." While traditionally the Second MAC had worked most often with the Warrior House Orders, she knew the mutual respect for both units ran deep.

The hatch opening again interrupted the pleasantries, and she turned to greet the next guest. A tall, striking woman entered the room, her unfamiliar gold-and-black dress uniform standing in contrast to the greens, ivories, and golds of the other commanders. It took her a moment to recognize the other woman, but fortunately the Grand Master was up to the task. "Ah, *Sang-shao* Qiao, it is good of you to join us."

Lifting her own glass in welcome, Lindsey carefully sized up the other woman, whom she had only heard about in whispers. The only other former mercenary commander assigned to this mission, Julie Qiao was the new commander of Laurel's Legion, a unit staffed mostly by women. She was a tall, powerfully built woman with long, pin-straight black hair and dark, hooded eyes that revealed none of her thoughts. Baxter had read of the Legion's recent work on the Davion and Republic fronts, and they were fierce fighters. Unfortunately, the regiment had been heavily damaged fighting the Republic and, like the Fourth, had only recently rebuilt. While she had no doubt the Legion would be stronger for the change, she also knew how green some of their replacements were, which meant regaining the regiment's former glory would require intense work.

"Apologies for my lateness," Qiao replied formally, despite being several minutes early. She made no excuse for arriving last, merely offered the apology, which raised Lindsey's estimation of her another notch.

"Not at all, *Sang-shao*," Hui replied, waving off the formality. "May I offer you some refreshment? The Chancellor gifted me with quite the selection of wines, to commemorate our grand undertaking."

As Lindsey suspected, the other woman accepted a sparkling water, and the group engaged in some obligatory small talk before adjourning to the attached cabin being utilized for the evening as a dining room. Stepping inside carefully, she was unsurprised to find that, despite the cramped conditions, the Grand Master had set a fine table, and she mentally congratulated the *gao-shiao-zhang* for his preparations.

The Grand Master was a surprisingly gracious host, and even the taciturn Qiao benefited from his attempts to bring her out of her shell. Like Baxter herself, Qiao seemed conscious of any impression on how the CCAF viewed her unit's recent reorganization, but if Hui was aware of it—Lindsey was convinced that he was—he tactfully avoided the topic.

They settled into the dinner with an exquisite chicken-and-dumpling soup from St. Ives, and the Canopian commander was inspired to speak, telling them of her recent travels from the Magistracy. Almost despite herself, Lindsey was fascinated by the tale, thrilled to hear of rustic battlefields in the Periphery, a region she would probably never visit as long as she remained a commander of a front-line regiment.

Hearing the Canopian commander speak reminded Lindsey that every command in this task force, other than the Hui's own, was led by women, something nearly unheard of in the Capellan Confederation. While women were not relegated to supporting roles as in some of the other Great Houses, it was a surprisingly rare roster.

As they moved on to the salad course, the *gao-shiao-zhang* steeped his fingers and looked around the room at his guests. "I hope you don't fault me for diverting us, but I did promise that this would be a working meal. I assume everyone has reviewed the intel the Maskirovka provided for us?"

Baxter nodded, as did the other two women. She had been studying the intelligence data nightly since receiving it, and her S-2, her staff's intelligence officer, had been diligent in adding the various updates as they were transmitted from each system they passed through. Each time she thought about the daunting task of keeping such a channel open as they crossed light-years of space—not to mention the exorbitant expense—she was reminded of the Celestial Wisdom's focus on the success of their mission, and how he was clearly willing to use every resource at his disposal to ensure they had the most accurate intel possible before touching down on Northwind.

After a moment, Hui gave Qiao a small smile. "I am especially excited to have you with us, *Sang-shao.* Your unit was founded by several ex-Highlanders, and from what I understand, you are a student of their tactics."

Qiao bowed her head respectfully, but slowly enough that Baxter caught the momentarily stricken expression that flickered across her face. "I'm afraid that I am little better acquainted than the rest of you on the current particulars of the Northwind Highlanders, *Gao-shiao-zhang.* While several of our original members once considered the Highlanders home, they have not been involved in quite some time, long before Countess Campbell reorganized the unit in the wake of Gray Monday."

"Surely you are being too modest," the commodore interjected, leaning forward as he warmed to the topic. "A unit is forged by its history and past service. Only by learning from the past can we seek to better understand ourselves, and our foes."

"Yet past service can only take one so far," Hui replied, saving the Legion commander from having to respond. "As the Highlanders have proven, a long history of service to the state is nothing if not maintained, and it is clear where their loyalties lie. Before all else, our first duty is in obedience to the needs and the will of the state."

Although it was clear she endeavored to not react, Lindsey saw Qiao's shoulders tense. The commodore nodded sagely, but Lindsey saw him glance over at the Grand Master as he did so. Was the true purpose of his statement to check for any lingering sympathies for the Legion's former comrades, or had it been about something more? Of all the units under his command, Laurel's Legion had to be the greatest wild card. While they had risen through the Confederation's list of favored mercenaries for their battlefield prowess, eventually being invested as official members of the CCAF's Citizens' Honored brigade, the unit had been decimated when they attacked a Republic world without authorization. While the former mercenaries had intended to relieve two Warrior Houses under heavy fire, they had arrived too late. The Warrior Houses were already in the process of retreat, and Stone's Lament had struck them like the wrath of an angry god, devastating the Legion in the space of several hours. Most of the regiment's surviving members had been ransomed back to the Confederation, but they had lost nearly the entirety of their equipment.

When Lindsey first heard the story, she had been convinced that it heralded the end of the storied unit, but someone had decided to give it a second chance. While the Legion had not been refitted with the most up-to-date equipment, it had been reborn like the phoenix on their crest, a new fighting force given the opportunity to continue serving the Confederation to the best of its ability.

She tilted her head slightly as suspicion flitted across her mind, and glanced surreptitiously at the Grand Master. *Did he save them from dissolution, potentially in gratitude for their efforts to assist the other Warrior Houses?* As the Grand Master of the Warrior House Orders, he was indirectly responsible for them all, and was a close confidant of the *sang-jiang-jun*. His patronage would count for a great deal.

The conversation continued, regarding the specifics of the data for several minutes before the main course was served, and they took a momentary respite to enjoy the fine roast before them. Seeing Qiao excuse herself, Lindsey begged off a moment later as well, earning an appraising glance from the Grand Master as she followed Qiao into the other room.

Watching the Legion commander approach the appetizer table, Lindsey stepped up beside her, taking the moment to admire the remaining appetizers. "*Sang-shao—*"

"I do not need your pity or your companionship," Qiao snapped. "Please leave."

"As you will, then," Baxter replied calmly, and reached past the other woman to pick up a piece of spanakopita, then popped the luxuriant delicacy in her mouth.

Qiao glared at the table for a moment, then bowed her head in contrition. "I'm sorry. You didn't deserve that."

"No, I didn't," Baxter replied curtly, causing Qiao to face her, but she quickly moderated her tone. "But I don't blame you for feeling it. You are not the only one who has rebuilt their unit from the ground up, and I know how difficult that can be.

Qiao considered that for a moment, clearly not trusting the gesture of peace. "Do you know what they call me behind my back?" Lindsey did, but she allowed Qiao to say it. "Jinx."

"Words," Baxter replied simply, watching carefully as Qiao faced her. She had heard the nickname as well, but put no faith in the concept. "The words of small, petty fools who think they know what you've gone through. They will either learn or they won't, and neither has any bearing on the work you're doing now, of which I am sure the *gao-shiao-zhang* is fully aware."

Qiao held her eyes with a sharp, intense stare. "If that is the case, then why did he bring up my failure?"

"I don't believe he did," Baxter replied simply. "I think he was reminding you of the cost we all must occasionally pay for the Confederation's ultimate victory. Your unit was destroyed because it overreached, but it did so in service to the Chancellor and with the goal of saving two Warrior Houses that are vital to the Confederation's defense. While neither of those was his own, as the senior member of the Warrior House

Orders, he clearly cares about what happens to the units under his command. I don't think he was forcing you to dwell on your losses, but rather to focus on the valuable items you bring to the table."

As Lindsey spoke, her own thoughts were pulled back to a crumbling, soot-covered hill on New Canton, pelted with endless rain and the greasy smoke from burning armor. The heat tearing at her skin as she fired again and again at the approaching Republic forces, her *Pillager* the only thing between the enemy and her fallen commander.

She forced herself back to the present, her voice carefully neutral. "The strike on Northwind might quite possibly be the single greatest conquest in the history of the Confederation. It takes us one step closer to taking Terra, and to validating the primacy of House Liao. I don't believe your inclusion in the mission was intended as a punishment, but rather because you have already proven that your unit is willing to do whatever is necessary to achieve your objectives. That is exactly what the Confederation needs in this moment." She glanced back toward the main room. "I don't know what our commander's aim is, but I trust the Chancellor to take the necessary steps to ensure the future of the Confederation."

Qiao nodded curtly. "I suppose that is what we all must do." She glanced up, her expression lightening as she locked eyes with Lindsey for the first time. "I will admit that I am eager to get out from under my predecessor's shadow."

"As are we all," Baxter replied lightly, and she gestured back to the dining room, taking another appetizer before stepping back through the archway.

The Grand Master nodded briefly at their return, and Lindsey caught a small hint of a smile in his expression. "Welcome back!" he said. "Your timing is excellent. The colonel and I were just discussing the motivations of our enemies."

The two women took their seats, and Qiao leaned forward, glancing between the Canopian commander and the Grand Master. "Would not their motivations be to protect their homeworld?"

"Indeed," the *gao-shiao-zhang* responded. "Yet I believe it is also vital for us to consider what happened next." Seeing the confused looks on several of the faces around the table, be continued. "In 3134, when the Steel Wolves attacked Northwind the second time, the Highlanders fought to preserve their homeworld, but they were also willing to pick up and jump their already-devastated forces to Terra when the immediate threat had abated, despite the likelihood that the planet might be attacked again. Unlike with the Federated Suns, the Highlanders have willingly fallen in with the Republic as little more than one of their house mercenaries, a feat that no Great House had ever managed. Even when they were contracted to the Confederation during the Third Succession War, they hung onto their freedom with both hands, never giving a meter. Such tenacity made them some of the most feared mercenaries in the Confederation, but now it makes them the most implacable of foes."

"You have a theory, *Gao-shiao-zhang*?" Qiao asked, dutifully taking the bait.

The Grand Master nodded. "I think Devlin Stone made a pact with the Highlanders, a recognition of their status as a sovereign nation under the auspices of the Republic in return for their pledge to defend Terra if the need ever arose." He looked around. "We have all seen the recent signal intercepts mentioning 'Stone's Covenant.' I believe we are seeing the results of that covenant right here."

"How would that reconcile with the Highlanders regiments folding into the Republic forces?" Lindsey asked. "The Highlanders jealously guarded their autonomy, yet they surrendered several of their units to the Republic."

"Time, *Sang-shao*, forces all creatures to adapt. For the people of Northwind, as with many other ceded worlds, the Republic was seen as the bringer of peace and enlightenment. For all its flaws, the Republic has maintained a standard of living and education nearly as high as our own blessed nation. That would be incredibly tempting for a people beset by war for decades, first by the Federated Commonwealth, then the Word of Blake."

The Grand Master regarded each of them in turn as he continued. "Also, let us not forget the powerful impact that the Military Material Redemption Program had on the Highlanders economy! Devlin Stone's 'BattleMech Buyback,' supposedly intended to bring peace, only served to vastly reduce the quantity of BattleMechs in the Inner Sphere, a reality that struck the Great Houses and independent mercenaries alike. Even before the program fully came into effect, many local military forces were standing down in preparation for Stone's vision of prosperity and virtue. With so few enemies left to fight, what were mercenaries to do? Moving massive amounts of war materiel through the Republic would have been seen as counterproductive to the foundation Stone was attempting to build."

"So the Highlanders simply gave up their heritage?" the commodore asked, noticeably intrigued by the conversation.

The *gao-shiao-zhang* raised a fluted glass. "I think they adapted in the best spirit of their ancestors. Many of their best warriors joined the Republic, and the others took the opportunity of potential peace as the chance to build what they had earned through centuries of blood, sweat, and toil. While they beat their swords into plowshares, however, Stone doted on those who came over to his way of thinking. In their own way, the Highlanders yet again traded one master for another."

"If that is so, *Gao-shiao-zhang*," Lindsey said, now warming to the topic, "what coin could they possibly be bought with? Stone had no Federated Suns money to steal them away with."

The Grand Master laughed, a surprisingly hearty sound from such a small man. "Don't be taken in by the stories, *Sangshao*! No matter what the Maskirovka propagandists says about the Highlanders, they abandoned the Confederation for the most valuable coin in the world for them: the promise of their ancestral homeland. At the time, the Confederation was not in a place where they could make a similar offer, and we lost that particular negotiation before we even knew we were involved." He stepped forward, his gaze lingering on the stars beyond the porthole. "I posit that Stone made the same sort of pact."

"But wouldn't they be wary of being betrayed?" Qiao asked, although it seemed her question was meant more out of an instinctive defense against the concept of the foolish mercenary who only fought for coin.

A delighted smile crossed the Grand Master's face: he had finally drawn the Legion commander into the discussion. "Ah, I have no doubt that they are! The Northwind Highlanders employed some of the most effective negotiators in the Inner Sphere. However, they were also conscious of strategic necessity: Northwind would lie within a Republic prefecture's borders no matter what the Highlanders did, so they would've been surrounded by hungry neighbors with a powerful joint-military structure. So once again, the Highlanders decided that if they couldn't beat them, they would join them.

"And what a deal they struck for themselves! Yes, they took on the trappings of the Republic, but when you look closer, you see how hollow it was. Yes, they took on the legate, prefect, and planetary governor that the Republic required, but they were all from Highlander families. Even the commander of the Twelfth Hastati is from Northwind. And when the Republic began searching for someone to strike at the Confederation, who better than our former champions?"

"So, you're saying they were bought off with the promise of peace?" Baxter asked.

"Peace...and support," the Grand Master countered. "The Federated Suns wanted something from the Highlanders, but they paid with bad coin. For all of his flaws, I doubt that Stone is so foolish. He knew the only way to win over the Highlanders was to deal with them fairly, and to give them what they truly craved: autonomy and the promise that if attacked, they would not be alone."

The Canopian colonel nodded. "You think they have a mutual defense agreement, something beyond what is in place for the rest of the Republic?"

"Indeed," Hui said softly. "It would certainly explain the strange circumstances in the wake of the Steel Wolves' attempt on Terra. After barely surviving two separate attacks on their ancestral homeworld, the Highlanders brought the brunt of their forces to Terra to fight the Steel Wolves there, leaving Northwind nearly undefended! If that does not speak to a deal, I do not know what would."

Lindsey nodded, finding a great deal of sense in his logic, but she noticed one loose thread. "That sound understandable, *Gao-shiao-zhang*, but if it was a mutual defense treaty, then it seems a particularly poor one. A single Paladin was dispatched in the wake of the Steel Wolf attack, and he eventually betrayed them. Hell, even Jacob Bannson managed to bring a full lance of support to that battle. Why would the Highlanders have gone to Terra at all?"

The Grand Master glanced at her as if to answer, but Qiao answered first.

"Highlander honor," she said, having finally decided to partake of the Grand Master's excellent spirits. "If Stone made a covenant with the Highlanders, they would have honored their part of the bargain, no matter the circumstances. For all his miserly nature in only sending a single Paladin, Stone did send someone, and that would have been enough for them to feel obligated to send forces to defend Terra."

"But the Paladin was deceitful," the commodore said, glancing between Qiao and Lindsey. "Would that not negate the agreement?"

"Not necessarily," Qiao replied. "Once constrained by honor, a great deal of Highlanders would've felt obligated to repay the Republic for the years of peace they had under Stone's auspices." She looked around at the others. "There was also a great deal of compelling evidence that the Republic did not know of the Paladin's duplicity at the time, which likely kept the Highlanders from holding their ally accountable for the actions of another."

"And we should not forget that revenge can be a powerful motivator," Lindsey replied, drawing a small nod from the Legion commander. "The Steel Wolves attacked Northwind twice, leaving only to move on to a bigger target. Whether the Highlanders fought on Terra to negate a future threat to their homeworld or simply wanted to get some payback, they would have been burning to settle the score with the Steel Wolves...and they did."

The *gao-shiao-zhang* nodded, clearly having made his point. "I agree. However, we will need to verify their intentions before anything else." His expression turned serious. "Regardless of our conclusions, when the Northwind Highlanders are involved, you never know what will happen."

CHAPTER 5

"To the people of Northwind, I assure you that the Twelfth Hastati Sentinels, in concert with the forces of Lady Maeve Stirling, have worked diligently to ensure the defense of Northwind. We remain prepared for any threat and strive to maintain our security and prosperity."

—Excerpt from an official statement from the legate's office, 13 November 3150.

PLUNKETT'S TAVERN
TARA, NORTHWIND
THE REPUBLIC OF THE SPHERE
13 NOVEMBER 3150

Heedless of the thick tufts of snow clinging to the heavy sweater that was his only defense from the cold, Declan waited for a nearby truck to pass before crossing the street to the noisy tavern on the corner.

Plunkett's Tavern was a relatively new establishment when compared to many of the decades-old pubs that lined the streets of Tara, but it had quickly become a Northwind institution. The famed bartender had been a contemporary of the great Loren Jaffray, the Capellan Death Commando who had reclaimed his ancestral place with the Highlanders and eventually led a series of daring raids into Clan-occupied territory. His granddaughter, Cadha Jaffray, had been one of the final colonels of the Northwind Highlanders before the various regiments had been disbanded or transferred to the RAF. Sergeant Major Plunkett had been well compensated for his work during the difficulties with the Federated Suns, using his own money to eventually open his own place in his waning years. While Plunkett was long gone, his memory lived on in the tavern that bore his name, a place where the people of Northwind could forget their problems for a while. Unlike the Pub, the Highlanders-only tavern where Plunkett had tended bar, this was a place where all of the people of Northwind could gather and find comfort. It was especially valued by the non-Highlander ranks of the Hastati, where a soldier could always find a drink or a hot meal without having to worry about getting to the next pay cycle.

While not much of a drinker, Declan was privately convinced that the food was second to none, and after the day he had endured, he was more than happy to take a break. His work with Lady Maeve in preparation for the potential Capellan attack consumed a great deal of his time, and he had maintained a grueling training schedule with the rest of his lance, wanting to make sure they were prepared for the impending threat. Unfortunately, that didn't lend well to relaxation, and his exhaustion had gotten so bad that Fairchild commented, nearly throwing him out of the Bachelor Officers Quarters to get some real food.

"Can I buy you a drink, stranger?"

His reverie broken, Declan looked up at the familiar voice and smiled. Bianca Haller smiled pleasantly down at him, and placed a perspiring stein down before him as she settled on the other side of the table. As usual, the young ComStar researcher had traded her pristine white jumpsuit for a long, flowing skirt with a floral print and a dark blue blouse, standing out brightly like a breath of springtime against the backdrop of the wintry highlands. While ComStar was no longer the theocratic institution it once was, having adopted a more secular outlook in the wake of the Word of Blake Jihad, it never failed to make him wonder how she could have survived under either regime.

She sat down carefully, her bright eyes taking in the haggard expression behind his smile. "You look like you've had a rough day."

"I bet," he said, sipping from the frosty mug of Northwind ale. He sighed despite himself and gave her a grateful nod. "I needed this."

"Well, you've been working eighteen-hour days for the last two weeks straight." She said, tucking a loose lock of platinum blond over her ear. "Luckily I know the feeling. We have to keep up on our research while preparing all of the security protocols to secure our data if the Capellans do manage to take the HPG."

Declan nodded, understanding the threat all too well. Bianca was one of several specialists from Project Sunlight, a joint ComStar-Republic initiative created by Tucker Harwell, the only person who had successfully managed to reactivate an HPG in the wake of the Gray Monday blackout that had knocked out over 80 percent of the Inner Sphere's hyperpulse generator network, the key to interstellar communication. Like several of her teammates, Bianca had been assigned to Tara to research the reason that the Northwind HPG still functioned while so many of its contemporaries were still down. Unfortunately, she and her entire Project Sunlight team would be at ground zero should the Capellans attack, as the HPG would be the primary target for any would-be conquerors. With the ability to send HPG messages at will and deny the easy transmission of RAF communications, anyone who could claim Northwind's HPG in Tara would have a definitive strategic advantage.

"I mean, what do they expect us to do?" She shook her head. "They tried giving us emergency training the other day, did you know that? I went in thinking it would be the standard evac drill: know your areas of egress, your rally location, the usual...but hell, if this constabulary guy did not come in and tell us how to get to the building's armory, how to properly choose equipment to ensure our safety." She shivered, and Declan couldn't help but reach out and place a reassuring hand over hers for a moment. "I know it must seem silly to you, but I'm a researcher, not a warrior!"

"No one expects you to be," Declan said, hoping his tone was soothing as he squeezed her hand. "Some people just believe the best defense is a good offense." He saw the look on her face and immediately regretted it, trying another tack. "Not to mention, that's what you have people like me for. We're the ones who run into the burning building so you don't have to."

"And how is that supposed to reassure me?" she demanded, pulling her hand back. "All that does is to make me worry about you even more than I already do!"

He smiled at the playful light returning to her eyes. Nothing had ever happened between them, but her eyes never failed to captivate him. Taking a deep breath, he pushed the thought away, leaned forward, and took both of her hands in his. "May I ask you a question?"

She smiled up at him, narrowing her eyes playfully. "That depends. Is this a personal or work question?"

"A little of both," he replied honestly. "If someone wanted to send messages from the HPG, how would they do it without being caught?"

"Easily," she said, surprising him by not hesitating for a moment. "Every day we get hundreds of thousands of outgoing messages from across the planet, not to mention countless more incoming messages whenever a Pony Express JumpShip or local trader comes into the area with a mail call. Depending on where it's coming from, the message could be routed to most planets, it just might take them a while to get there."

She paused for a swallow of ale. "Still, even when it reaches its destination, there aren't enough human beings to check all of the traffic, so most items go without human verification at all, just the standard automated safeguards that are controlled by the system itself. The best bet for anyone trying to sneak out clandestine messages would be to pass out something in code, preferably in a standard, seemingly innocuous message, and then send it to an independent third party to make sure it can't be tracked."

She used her hands to demonstrate the path of the message in front of him, her drink forgotten. "Let's say you want to send a message to your secret contact in Geneva. The surest way to do it is to send the message to some random salesperson in a completely different city than your contact, which is only passed on to Geneva from there. Sometimes the intermediary might not even know what they are doing, or it will go through multiple people." She shook her head sadly. "If you don't know who is sending the messages, it'll be nearly impossible to backtrack without some data on the sender, content, or destination." For a brief moment, she looked disappointed. "The days when ComStar had that level of control over all aspects of interstellar communication is far behind us."

"Thanks anyway, B," he replied.

If she noticed his crestfallen look, she was kind enough to ignore it. He had known it was a long shot, but he didn't realize just how difficult it would be to track down an intelligence leak when he couldn't even verify one existed.

Glancing over Bianca's shoulder, he saw a pair of familiar figures coming from the back room of the pub, a private meeting space traditionally dedicated to the redistribution of wealth through games of chance. His grandfather and Lady Maeve were both smiling, and he turned back to Bianca with his own apologetic grin. "Are you going to be here for a while? I want to make sure my grandfather isn't saying anything too embarrassing about me."

Bianca's eyes widened as she glanced at where he was looking, then turned back with a playful smile. "Is that her? The Knight? Wow. Now I understand why you've been so devoted to your training."

"*Et tu, Brute*? It's bad enough I get enough of that from Oedhe." His cheeks heated slightly, and he gave her a mock-withering glare. "Besides, I still haven't figured out her angle yet, and I try not to get involved with anyone I don't trust."

To his surprise, her face suddenly became uncharacteristically serious. "That's a bit of a problem when you don't trust anyone."

For a moment he just stared at her, unsure what to say, but her expression reverted to its usual impish nature as she gave him a wry grin. "Seriously, though," she said, "make sure your grandfather saves some of those embarrassing stories for me. I'm going to run back to the HPG for a bit, but I'm good for at least another drink. Come and find me if you get time."

"Gladly." He momentarily considering whether to say something else, but she made the decision for him as she returned to the bar.

Declan walked over to where Seamus and Maeve had taken a seat by the fire. "My lady, Major."

"Come and have a seat, lad. I was just leaving."

Declan tried to protest, but Seamus was already standing, putting a heavy hand on his shoulder. "Tommy Finnegan asked me over to his place for a poker game, and the old sod owes me sixty stones as it is."

"Yes, Lieutenant," Maeve said. "Please join me."

Outnumbered, Declan nodded respectfully, and took his grandfather's seat as he departed. "I'm glad you had the chance to catch up with the major. Was it everything you hoped for?"

"And more," she replied. "Your grandfather is one hell of a storyteller."

Declan nodded. "Some of my most vivid memories as a child were when he read to me or told me the stories of the battles he'd been in. My mother hated it, but I couldn't wait for him to come tell me one more story." He shook his head thoughtfully. "To this day, I always wonder which ones were real."

She chuckled. "I know the feeling. When taking to your grandfather I always wonder whether I just missed an episode of *Immortal Warrior*."

"You're not the only one."

Maeve smiled at him briefly before lowering her voice, careful to keep her back to the crowd. "Have you learned anything?"

"Nothing definitive," he replied. "Everything I've heard so far just raises more questions. I spoke with some of the people I know over at Intelligence first, but there's no sign that any of our data has been compromised. I even ran a quick scan of my own, and there's no trace of unauthorized entry into our secure servers. If someone is accessing our data, they have the authority to access the servers without raising suspicion. If that's the case, the only way I can be sure is by taking more active measures, and there's no way I'll be able to keep that quiet without bringing more people in on our suspicions. Beyond that, I just spoke to a friend over at the HPG compound. If any information has gotten out, there are countless ways it could get transmitted out of the system, and we'd never know in time."

"Damn," she replied, but there was no heat in the statement. From her resigned tone, she had clearly expected as much.

For a moment he wondered whether she had sent him off on a snipe hunt, but even if she had just used him to confirm her own take on the situation, it was still helpful to both the Highlanders and the Republic forces.

"Have you taken additional security precautions?" Maeve asked.

"Not beyond putting some subtle flags in the system," he replied. "Anything more blatant would warn the spy we may be on to them, and it would be closing the barn door after the horses are gone. If everything I learned so far is correct, our leak is not getting the information from the system. That means that they're most likely somewhere within the Republic command structure, or immediately adjacent." He was careful not to mention the Highlanders by name. "For now, the best we can do is stay the course—compartmentalize our plans as much as we can, and try to backtrack from there."

"Well, I appreciate you looking into things for me. Keep me apprised if you hear anything else." She began to stand, but stopped partway. "Anything else I can do for you?"

"Well..." He allowed some of his annoyance to seep into his voice. "The more I think about it, the more I wonder what makes you think there's a leak somewhere in the system. It's a pretty extraordinary claim."

She sat back down carefully, and for a moment he thought he'd gone too far, but she just gave a shallow nod.

"Do you know the name Nicholas Borden?"

Surprised by the non sequitur, Declan raised an eyebrow. "Borden was the former commandant of the Northwind Military Academy." He tried to remember his own academy days, but the commandant had changed four years after his graduation. He did remember hearing about Borden's death, however. "He died in his office, didn't he? Slipped and bashed his head against his desk?"

"That's how the official story goes," she replied carefully. "However, a few items caught my attention. First and foremost was the timing. It was during the second Steel Wolves invasion of Northwind."

"You think the Wolves had the commandant killed?" Declan asked. "That doesn't sound like something they would do."

"Don't underestimate Anastasia Kerensky. She's able to do all sorts of things no one else would expect. But no, I don't think it was her. We do have proof that One-Eyed Jack Farrell and his people were on-planet during the battle, and he would've had no compunction killing someone if it gave him an advantage, honor be damned."

Declan nodded, seeing where the Knight was going with this. While the Steel Wolves would at least pay lip service to their concept of honor, Jacob Bannson focused solely on enhancing his personal power. If killing the commandant of the Northwind Military Academy would benefit him, he would do it without a second thought, especially with the rumors that he had recently moved much of his business interests to the Capellan Confederation.

Declan watched Maeve carefully. "That's all very interesting, but what does this have to do with a leak?"

"You're the trained investigator, you work it out."

He was tempted to snap back at her, but the wry twist of her lips immediately identified it as another challenge. Taking a deep breath, he considered everything she'd told him so far.

"The second attack by the Wolves was a sneak attack, but Countess Campbell was prepared for them to return. The NMA would've been on a secure footing, with heightened security measures throughout the building." He remembered well the long nights of double patrols and full-unit maneuvers when security drills were called.

"Correct," Maeve replied. "In fact, the commandant ordered the measures after the first battle and never relaxed them. The compound had been under secure conditions since the first attack."

"And there was no sign of a break-in?"

"None that the investigators could find."

He nodded, seeing her point. "That means there was either no assassin, they were very good, or..." He glanced up at her.

"How did you put it? 'Within the Republic command structure, or immediately adjacent.'"

For a long moment, he just stared at her, attempting to read her expression, his thoughts whirling with the new revelation. "You think he was killed by a Highlander."

She glanced down at her empty glass for a moment before looking him straight in the eyes. "On the day of the Steel Wolf attack, the commandant sent a message to Michael Griffin, Countess Campbell's head of intelligence, seeking an emergency meeting, citing an urgent matter he could only discuss in person. Three hours later, the commandant was dead."

"Did Griffin know anything about it?"

She shook her head. "The colonel was already in the field. He didn't get the message until after the Steel Wolves had retreated. With the commandant dead and the Highlanders preparing to support Terra, no one could find out exactly what he'd wanted to discuss."

Once again, Declan considered what he was being told, searching the Knight's face for any sign of duplicity. "You think the two items are connected."

"I do," she replied.

Declan nodded as he grappled with the horrific thought. "You think someone sold out the Highlanders, and the commandant caught on, which marked him for death. You truly think a Highlander would betray Northwind?"

"I know, I can barely consider the possibility myself, but we both know the NMA has one of the highest staff-retention rates in the Inner Sphere, many of whom are from the Highlander Clans. If our killer or our spy is a member of the NMA staff, the odds are excellent that they're still here."

Declan nodded. "You needed someone the Highlanders would trust to investigate, which means an active Highlander or a family member. You are seen as too close to the Republic, and on some level you would be seen as an outsider. Not only that, you need someone beyond reproach: I wasn't stationed anywhere near the NMA at the time, and if I was caught asking too many questions, I wouldn't be thought of as anything but a curious Highlander." He glanced in the direction his grandfather had departed, his lips thinning. "I don't suppose it hurts that I'm the grandson of Seamus Casey, the man with friends at every station on the planet."

Maeve shrugged, but her expressive eyes told him this wasn't the first time she had considered the point. "I won't lie to you by telling you it wasn't a consideration. Let's be realistic, however. With what you've already uncovered, it looks like your grandfather isn't the only one with friends in high places."

Declan's eyes slipped to the bar, where he saw Bianca laughing at something her neighbor had said. He shook his head and casually looked around to make sure no one was within earshot as he turned back to Maeve. "Something still bothers me, however. If you're certain there's a leak, why have you let your movements be so public? Everyone knows you're here, and your lance is watching over the equipment at Fort Barrett..." The realization struck him like a PPC blast, and he shook his head ruefully. "It was never about the supplies, was it?"

Maeve smiled. "No, it was not."

He leaned forward, his eyes intent. "What's really in those containers?"

She shrugged, glancing toward the stone fireplace. "Spare parts mostly, but some of those 'spare parts' happen to be eight light 'Mechs, crammed in as tightly as we could fit: a pair each of *Jackalopes*, *Crimson Hawks*, *Spiders*, and *Wights*. Together with my lance, they can deploy as a fast-attack company wherever needed."

Declan nodded. "All jumpers, as were the larger 'Mechs you left behind. You've essentially created a mobile fire brigade."

"And ready to move out on my command, still loaded on the DropShips. As for the boxes of supplies currently sitting out on the tarmac, those are loaded full of scrap metal, to fool anyone who scans them."

He nodded, understanding at last. "That's the real reason you wanted additional lances to train with you. It'd look suspicious if you went into battle with a short complement of 'Mechs, especially if you didn't wind up recalling your security lance."

She nodded, and he merely tapped the tabletop for several long moments.

Leaning forward, he locked his gaze with hers. "One more question. Have you roped my grandfather into this?"

For the first time since the beginning of the conversation, her smile looked completely natural. "If you think anyone in the world can convince Seamus Casey to do something he doesn't want to do, you don't know your grandfather at all."

Declan nodded, accepting the statement, before realizing she hadn't truly answered his question. He was about to speak when his communicator buzzed, and he was unsurprised to find that he wasn't alone. Nearly every other soldier in the bar was looking down at their own devices, with the majority apologizing to their companions and heading for the door. Declan had just enough time for a quick glance at a nervous Bianca before looking back at the Knight, who now regarded him with a raised eyebrow.

"An all-call," he said. "I think our wait is finally over."

CHAPTER 6

"Citizens, we stand here on the cusp of an auspicious day! Not only do we have the opportunity to strike back at Stone's Republic, but we can administer a lesson on loyalty that has been decades in the making."

—*Gao-shiao-zhang* Jiang Hui,
in a message to Task Force Clarity

UNION-CLASS DROPSHIP *YUAN GUI*
PLANETARY ORBIT, NORTHWIND
REPUBLIC OF THE SPHERE
19 NOVEMBER 3150

As the DropShip began its descent, *Sang-shao* Lindsey Baxter clenched her hands into fists, careful not to wrap them around her joysticks or any of the handholds placed around the cockpit. While she knew her *Pillager* was secured to make sure she didn't accidentally punch or shoot through a bulkhead as they descended, years of best practices made sure that McCarron's Armored Cavalry kept all 'Mechs ready to move at a moment's notice while in hostile territory. Her BattleMech was fully powered, as were all of the others in the bay. If something were to happen to the DropShip, Lindsey and her MechWarriors might be required to escape in a hurry, which mandated all systems be powered during a combat drop.

Having run through the test procedures for her 'Mech for a third time, she looked around the cavernous bay, searching for any visible issue with the other BattleMechs, despite the fact that each lance had double- and triple-checked their equipment prior to final decent. She had confidence they were as prepared as she could make them, but she never stopped trying to find ways to keep them sharp.

Having convinced herself there was nothing else she could do, she reviewed the battle plan she had helped the Grand Master develop. In defiance of traditional tactical doctrine, the *gao-shiao-zhang* had split his forces to take on Republic defenses in two theaters at once. The data from the *Zang shu er*—a branch of the Maskirovka known as the Chancellor's Ear—had informed them that at least two battalions of the Twelfth Hastati Sentinels were guarding the continent of New Lanark, while a third had been secretly moved to Fort Barrett, where the Republic DropShips had landed. The move, which the Capellan forces would have missed without their intelligence assets on New Lanark, confirmed the Grand Master's suspicions that the Republic had something in the works on the far side of the planet, hoping to spring it on the Capellan forces when they struck the HPG compound. While Lindsey would have preferred to focus overwhelming numbers on a single location at the onset of the invasion, the risk of having a second mobile force of unknown strength at their back required them to take both targets simultaneously.

She had no doubt the *gao-shiao-zhang* would've preferred to take the city of Tara himself, but he was a strategist first and foremost. The Fourth MAC were expert city-fighters, and their roster was varied enough to excel at the tight, freewheeling battles bound to occur in Tara. Conversely, his heavier Warrior House units would be vital to taking Fort Barrett, a Star League-era fortification the Republic forces would use as a defensive position.

Honestly, Lindsey would've preferred to have Laurel's Legion with her, but she did not blame the Grand Master for wanting to watch over that particular unit personally. Despite all she had seen of the Laurel's Legion commander and her confidence that they would fight when the time came, she could also understand Hui's reticence toward leaving them under someone else's supervision, considering what had happened in the past. That left Lindsey with the Canopians, whose light forces would also work well in the city. While not official members of the CCAF, the Canopians had also been stalwart allies of the Confederation for years, and there was no doubt they would obey her orders to the letter.

A transmission from the DropShip's bridge cut through the silence over her headset. "*Sang-shao*, we have Republic fighters coming up from the planet. Our escort is engaging."

"Can you give me an outside feed?" she asked, activating her secondary monitor. There was no response, but her *Pillager* received a visual signal from the DropShip's command and control. Pulling the visual feed up on the secondary monitor, she saw the small red representations of Republic fighters coming up from the planet to intercept the DropShips, which were in a tight formation to provide maximum overlapping fields of fire. Unfortunately, the Republic were also no strangers to good tactics, and they had waited for one of the most dangerous moments in the landing process to capitalize on their invader's distraction, with two flights of fighters rushing out to meet them.

Settling in to watch the battlespace tactical feed, she found herself engrossed in the dance of the battle, almost forgetting that a single missed shot could end her mission before it began.

Luckily, Commodore Xio clearly knew his craft. Although Lindsey was admittedly far more adept at ground combat than the intricacies of space warfare, she watched with keen appreciation as Xio's fighters kept in tight pairs, moving to engage the Republic forces as they burned toward the task Force. The commodore ordered the assault DropShips pacing them to increase speed and cut in front of the troop transports at a varying angles to block the transports and provide an interlocking layer of defense in three dimensions.

One of the 'Mech transports, a *Union*, found itself bracketed by fire from two Republic *Rapier*s, but the *Lung Wang* trailing it fired its extended-range large lasers, which turned one of the fighters into a trail of debris.

If anyone thought the death of their wingman would deter the second *Rapier* pilot, however, they were wrong. The surviving fighter closed with Lindsey's own DropShip, its heavy autocannon blazing. She felt the hull shudder under the heavy impacts, but the sound stopped as quickly as it began. Knowing the other MechWarriors in the bay wouldn't have the benefits of knowing what was going on outside the hull, she switched over to her company channel. "All Fourth ground forces, we are under attack by Republic fighters, but our aerospace forces are clearing a path for us. All units, prepare for a rough landing or emergency drop. All units, secure for landing and await further orders."

Her lance commanders confirmed her message, and Lindsey refocused on the exterior feed, wishing there was more she could do. On her screen, a pair of ER PPCs fired from the DropShip and eviscerated another enemy fighter, blowing out the cockpit in a momentary flash of fire before the vacuum instantly put it out forever.

As she watched helplessly, two more *Rapiers* burned in, only to face a pair of Capellan *Transgressors*. The lead *Transgressor* lashed out with its heavy PPCs and clipped a thruster of the trailing Republic fighter, sending it into a flat spin that would be its death spiral unless the fighter was recovered before it hit the atmosphere. The *Transgressor's* wingman closed to point-blank range, sliding into the sweet spot above and behind the remaining *Rapier*. PPCs and lasers eviscerated the Republic fighter. Shredded armor plates and a growing line of sparks trailed in the *Rapier's* wake. With clear desperation, its pilot pulled up at a sharp angle to return fire, but the *Transgressor* merely cut power and fired its twin heavy PPCs in a well-timed volley, punching right through the core of the fighter with a blinding explosion.

The battle was over as quickly as it began. Five Capellan fighters were out of action—two damaged, three destroyed— but twelve Republic fighters had been eliminated. Like the task force, the Celestial Wisdom had spared no expense to ensure victory. The DropShips were commanded by some of the best captains the Confederation had, and the skill of their gunnery sections further demonstrated their capability and professionalism.

"We are all clear, *Sang-shao*," the communications tech informed her. "Planetfall in twelve minutes."

With the threat of the Republic fighters negated, the rest of the drop felt anti-climactic. Lindsey measured her breathing, attempting to work through the sudden end of her adrenaline surge. She took a moment to gather her thoughts and focused on the external feed again, which showed the four transport DropShips landing in a tight diamond formation, allowing them to provide overlapping fields of fire as a defensive perimeter once they set down. In a pinch they could put up makeshift walls or barriers to make their own semi-permanent landing area, but she didn't think they would need it. As she watched, her DropShip's sensors verified the lack of threat in the area, and she heard the all clear.

The DropShip settled heavily onto its landing gear, and as soon as the external loading ramps had deployed, the first units began to disembark.

With careful strides, a long-legged *Raven* stepped out onto the plains of Northwind. The venerable scout 'Mech descended the ramp, reaching out with its powerful sensors as it took its first steps onto the planet, then it cut to the left and sank its clawlike feet into the pristine snow covering the plains.

In its wake came a second *Raven*, which broke to the right, followed by a Canopian-made *Anubis*. The final member of the lance, the lance commander's *Agrotera*, jumped from the top of the ramp and glided forward on its partial wings to position itself between the two *Raven*s.

The assembled lance marched toward the tree line, and Lindsey saw recon lances from the other DropShips matching their formation, moving outward in a widening circle as they scanned for any potential threats. Having expanded the outer line of defense, the first of her heavier 'Mechs descended the ramp, led by a pair of brand-new *Catapult II*s. Much like their smaller cousins, these fire-support 'Mechs could put pinpoint missile fire wherever it was necessary.

As the perimeter scouts moved outward, she switched over to the naval channel, where the fighters overhead were still destroying military satellites in orbit to prevent the Republic forces from getting surveillance on their landing site.

"*Incoming!*" a voice cut through on the command channel.

Lindsey's head shot up as the first plumes of dirt and debris erupted into the sky near the foot of the nearest landing ramp. The ground shook as artillery rounds streamed in toward the DropShips, crashing just short of the ramps. The rounds blasted huge divots in the ground, and she saw a *Sha Yu* barely dodge around the hole in time.

She clicked open her channel to the bridge. "Get me tracking on the source of that artillery, ASAP!"

"We have general directional data, but are awaiting confirmation," the bridge replied. "The commodore is redirecting our air cover for counterbattery fire."

Lindsey hated the necessity of redeploying their valuable air cover, but they also couldn't let Republic artillery pick the DropShips to pieces without responding. She tapped her console to switch back to her command channel. "Scout lances, move toward the forest and find out where that artillery is coming from."

"*Sang-shao*, we have reports of contacts in the forest."

Lindsey brought up her exterior feed again and saw that her troops had finally found the Twelfth Hastati's ground forces. As she watched, the *Agrotera* squared off against a Republic *Griffin*, protecting its lancemates from the Republic 'Mech. The Capellan BattleMech struck the *Griffin* in the chest with a PPC blast, burning away armor and causing the enemy 'Mech to step back to steady itself. Still, the damage did nothing to hurt the pilot's aim as they lashed back with long-range missiles, which peppered the *Agrotera* with explosions. In support of its lancemate, a Republic *Lineholder* stepped out from the tree line and scored a glancing blow with its large laser, carving away armor on the *Agrotera*'s torso.

Something is wrong.

Her mind raced as she tried to figure out what was nagging at her. The Republic forces couldn't have known exactly where her forces would land, but they probably had a good idea from the topography of the region. If they had seeded the woods with BattleMechs, they would be able to pick at the DropShips with long-range fire, but they could do that without engaging the scouts out in the open. It only made sense if...

Moving quickly to gain a better position on the *Lineholder*, one of the *Raven*s edged close to the tree line, and a quad BattleMech reared up on four legs, a Republic *Thunder Fox*. Still in motion, the *Raven* lit off its medium lasers at the new threat, but missed wide. The *Thunder Fox* didn't: the light Gauss rifle sent a round into the smaller 'Mechs torso, while a large laser carved away armor on the left leg. A quartet of short-range missiles exacerbated the laser's damage. The *Raven* stumbled plowed beak-first into the ground, cutting a deep furrow into the dirt. The *Lineholder* then fired its large laser into the damaged leg, severing it at the knee.

Suddenly it all became clear. The Twelfth Hastati probably had a few companies seeded throughout the woods, hoping to ambush her forces during their push toward the city. As she watched, a second *Thunder Fox* reared up and took a potshot at the *Anubis*, which luckily missed the fleet little 'Mech.

Glancing around the battlefield, she saw the Twelfth was taking full advantage of her deployment order. With her lighter scouting elements up front, it would take several minutes for heavier support to even disembark, much less move quickly enough to support her recon forces. By the time backup would arrive, the scouts would be routed or destroyed. While the enemy could not hope to stop all of the Clarity forces, it was an ideal time to whittle down her scouts and keep her forces close to the DropShips until they were fully deployed. The majority of the 'Mechs she had seen had been equipped with long-range weaponry, and they had a plethora of targets as the Capellan forces slowly disembarked.

Switching to her company channel, she ordered the ranks to make a hole, and her 100-ton *Pillager* stalked down the ramp at a full run, the reinforced structure shivering in response to each heavy footfall.

"*Sang-shao*, wait for us!" Endrin shouted, as she had accidentally blocked her lancemates from descending the ramp in her urgency to get onto the field. "You can't engage without support!"

She understood what he was trying to tell her, but she was one of the few heavy units in range that might be able to even the odds. For the moment her light forces seemed evenly matched, but her blood ran cold as she saw an immense black-and-gold form step from the trees. A 95-ton *Banshee*, one of the best-known assault 'Mechs fielded in the Inner Sphere, turned ponderously on one of the *Raven*s and shot a heavy PPC into its torso before it made a desperate break to get out of range.

To draw the *Banshee*'s attention, she fired both of her Gauss rifles from long range, which staggered the 'Mech with twin hammerblows to either side of its chest. Despite losing more than a ton of armor, the assault 'Mech remained standing and returned fire with its own Gauss rifle and heavy PPC. The Gauss slug missed wide as Lindsey sped toward her opponent, but the heavy PPC flayed armor from her left leg.

The *Lineholder* turned toward her to capitalize on the *Banshee*'s strike, but it froze as autocannon fire from her left ripped into the 'Mech's chest, sending up a burst of green smoke from a destroyed heat sink. Although the rest of her lance had not yet cleared the DropShip, she heard Endrin on the command channel, ordering one of the debarked lances to support her.

Having gained the *Banshee*'s attention, she quickly surveyed the field. The remaining *Raven* had pulled back to the DropShip, trading fire with the *Thunder Fox*es while the *Agrotera* and *Anubis* harried the *Griffin*.

Seeking to even the odds, she shifted her aim, letting her targeting reticule settle on the nearer *Thunder Fox*. With a quick pull on the trigger for her primary targeting interlock circuit, two glittering Gauss rounds ripped off the rear-left leg and forced the now-three legged 'Mech to stumble.

Whether the other MechWarrior was defending a fellow warrior or was merely frustrated at being ignored, the *Banshee* fired its weapons again, throwing in a light PPC for good measure. This time all three weapons hit, and Lindsey fought her controls as her *Pillager* reeled under the heavy firepower. While she had only a five-ton advantage on the *Banshee*, the Republic 'Mech had superior firepower at every range.

However, she had her own advantages.

Watching carefully for the right moment, she engaged her jump jets just as the *Banshee* prepared to fire, and leaped in a tight arc that brought her down to her opponent's left. As she closed, the *Banshee* once again lit off its PPCs, adding several medium pulse lasers for good measure. The hits shuddered along her 'Mech's legs and chest as she landed hard, dropping to one knee in an attempt to steady herself.

The *Banshee* turned toward her, but more slowly than before. As she'd expected, the constant use of its PPCs had heated the 'Mech up more quickly than hers had, and the pilot was beginning to see the effect on their targeting system and movement. Smiling thinly, she fired her Gauss rifles, and rejoiced to see her opponent's heat spike as the ferrous slugs cracked its engine shielding.

With greasy black smoke escaping from the *Banshee*'s torso wounds, things were looking bleak for the Republic MechWarrior. The pilot fired off only their lasers while closing range, desperate to take her down before she could fire again. Her own heat spiked as a medium laser seared through her armor and vaporized a heat sink in a flash of green coolant, while the others opened rents in her chest and side torso.

Narrowing her eyes, she watched her targeting reticule turn solid red, and hit the primary interlock's trigger to loose her full weapon complement. The alpha strike dug deep into the *Banshee*'s chest, her lasers stripping the final armor off the enemy's arm and cutting deeply into the myomer beneath.

It was her Gauss rifle that did the true damage, however. While one shot went wide, the other ripped through the *Banshee*'s chest, the slug burying itself deep inside the 'Mech's innards. Her opponent slumped forward, the engine no longer responding as the Gauss round had pierced the fusion reactor's shielding, and the *Banshee* dropped heavily to the ground.

Gasping from the heat, she looked around the battlefield, ignoring the shattered 'Mech at her feet. The support lance Endrin sent her way had finally taken up positions facing the edge of the forest, and they occasionally fired into the trees while still remaining on station. On her sensor screen she saw the first of her heavy support elements pulling up, with the rest of her lance in tow.

Rao's *Ti Ts'ang* arrived first and stepped up beside her, the monstrous machine seeming to gaze down at the shattered *Banshee*. "Looks like we missed all the fun."

"There will be more, mark my words," Lindsey replied. "Casualty report?"

"We have a half dozen 'Mechs down, with another four requiring extensive repairs. Aside from the *Banshee*, two other enemy 'Mechs are salvageable."

She swore softly enough that the voice-activated mic could not hear her. "Task several of our companies for hunter-killer missions into the woods. I don't want to leave any threats at our back." She twisted her torso to take in the whole battlefield. "Keep some of our armor here to support the DropShips. They can catch up with us when we reach the city." Coupled with the elements of the Lancers' Third Battalion and the DropShips' native armament, her troops would have no problem protecting the landing zone.

"And the rest of the regiment?" Rao asked.

"Have our forces form up to march," Lindsey replied. A mischievous smile crept across her face as she spared one more look at the devastated enemy assault 'Mech. "The Hastati were kind enough to come all this way to greet us, so it's only polite to return the favor."

CHAPTER 7

"As a matter of fact, I know exactly how busy the Exarch must be at this moment, but this has been my fourth attempt to make an appointment. It is imperative that I–
"She put me on hold!"

—Countess Tara Campbell, overheard

The immense wooden doors leading into the Exarch's private office had barely opened before Countess Tara Campbell walked the length of the red-and-gold carpet leading to the far end of the room. From the doorway, her aide, Captain Julia Kent, looked hesitant to let her commander go alone into Stone's inner sanctum, but she also knew that, short of dragging Tara bodily from the building, little could be done to stop her.

To be fair, Tara's aide had a right to be concerned. It was not long ago that Tara had disobeyed her recall order by choosing to stand with former-Exarch Damien Redburn and the Republic Remnant instead of returning to Terra, and she was deemed insubordinate to the lawful government of the Republic, despite all she and her troops had sacrificed in its name. Luckily, former-Exarch Jonah Levin had put forth a deal: if the Remnant forces and their Highlander allies returned to the fold, all would be forgiven. It was a generous offer, but also a necessary one, since the Republic could not risk losing any potential allies, and making enemies of the Northwind Highlanders was always a risky proposition.

Tara always wondered how Devlin Stone felt about that.

The massive doors shut behind her before she had made it halfway into the room, her eyes carefully taking in the battlefield before her. Much had changed in just a short time. Most of the greenery from the Redburn years had been removed, and the desk looked spartan without any of Jonah Levin's family photos on the desk. Still, the large office, used for receiving official visitors, looked much the same as it had last time, as if the current Exarch had more pressing things to do than redecorate.

Or was it merely because he did not want further reminders of the past?

What struck her most was she had been invited to the Exarch's public office, not the smaller, more intimate office used on a day-to-day basis. Just another glaring warning that things had changed.

Stone's consultant, Tucker Harwell, gave her a slight nod as she passed. He seemed uncommonly grim by the windows overlooking Memorial Park, but she couldn't tell how much was his actual mood and how much was due to the heavy sheets of rain from the dark gray clouds above.

In contrast, Paladin Janella Lakewood flanked one side of the desk, the intelligence advisor's expression revealing nothing as she gave a respectful nod. On the other side, Paladin Gareth Sinclair offered Tara an encouraging smile; she had recently worked with him in planning defensive deployments on Terra. Although she considered both Paladins friends, she knew where their loyalties lay.

Stopping about two meters from the desk, Campbell locked eyes with the first Exarch of the Republic, Devlin Stone himself. The cryogenic freezing process ensured he looked much the same as he had before his "disappearance," but every year of the Republic was etched into the dark pools of his eyes, easily signifying his true age. He stood straight, his uniform as immaculate as ever, and Tara almost forgot about the ravenous hordes itching to strike at Terra at their first opportunity.

"Thank you for granting me this audience, Exarch," she began respectfully. *Especially since you've been putting me off since I returned to Terra.* "I know how busy you must be with matters of state." Under Levin's administration, she had been a vital part of the Republic's defensive planning, with the Highlanders being used as troubleshooters throughout the prefectures, but Stone had chosen not to take advantage of her talents. Although she previously had access to the wealth of the Republic's military intelligence, she had since become reliant on the Highlanders' own intel resources ever since the Fortress Wall had been activated.

Across the desk, Stone glanced over at Tucker Harwell, and Tara immediately realized that maybe the Exarch had not relented as much as she had hoped.

"I am always here for the Highlanders, Countess," Stone replied, his deep, resonant voice filling the space. "I am just sorry that I have not had the time to meet with you sooner."

"I fully understand," she said, careful to maintain her composure. "However, a serious matter has come to my attention, and it is vital that we discuss it."

"I had guessed as much," the Exarch said in a bemused yet serious tone. "I assume your concern has to do with Northwind."

"Yes, Exarch. The Capellan Confederation has struck Northwind, exactly as I feared. From the intel reports made available to me, it appears the Chancellor has allotted significantly greater forces than we anticipated for the attack, and the Twelfth Hastati will be at a serious disadvantage in the long run."

"A valid concern," the Exarch said. "Still, we accounted for that in our defensive planning."

Campbell nodded, but her eyes did not leave Stone's. "That is true, but all of that planning relied on dispatching a relief force to bolster the Twelfth and drive the Capellan invaders off-world. So far I have seen little sign that any sort of force being prepared."

Lakewood stepped forward and said, "That brings us to an important point, Countess. We've received some troubling reports that your DropShips are preparing to launch."

"That is correct, Lady Lakewood," Campbell replied. "As we speak, every one of the Highlanders' DropShips is preparing for immediate launch, and our JumpShips have been notified to prepare for immediate departure from the system." She took a theatrical glance at the chrono on her wrist, which she had specifically worn for the occasion. "If you check with your staff, you'll see that flight plans have been filed for each of them per Republic regulations, and right now local commanders are receiving notifications that they will need to redeploy forces in the wake of our departure."

Sinclair stepped forward, his tone conciliatory. "Countess, we know how you feel..."

"With all due respect, Paladin, you have absolutely no idea how I feel." The tension in the room ratcheted to a new level from the cold steel in her voice. "My Highlanders came to Terra to help defend against an invading force. We were not requested, we were not supported, and in some places we certainly were not thanked. We came to Terra when the Steel Wolves attacked because we knew the threat they posed to the capital, and we came willingly, without hesitation. When the Fortress Wall went up, we served the Remnant willingly, cut off from our friends and loved ones with no guarantee we would ever see them again. Now our ancestral home is being invaded, and our sisters and brothers die on the soil of my birth. Please understand, Exarch, I have nothing but the utmost respect for the Republic, but this will not stand."

"We have already sent a relief unit—" Lakewood continued, but Campbell cut her off, not wanting the Paladin to embarrass herself.

"A mere company of 'Mechs and supporting units," Tara said, her eyes not leaving the Exarch. "In case you have forgotten, we're no longer in the golden age of the Republic, where a handful of BattleMechs and armor are going to be enough to protect an entire planet. As of this moment, four regiments of crack Capellan troops have grounded on Northwind. That's nearly four hundred BattleMechs fighting against our people, something not seen since the end of the Jihad."

"What more would you have us do?" Stone asked, gesturing to the large screen dominating one wall, and a nod brought up a conflict map of the Republic. "We are being encroached upon by three major factions, with active fighting on a half-dozen worlds. What else would you have me send to Northwind?"

"Nothing," she replied, surprising the Exarch as she shifted her gaze between the room's occupants. "Ladies and gentlemen, with all due respect, you don't seem to understand. I know exactly the dire straits the Republic is facing. I know you sent what you could, and potentially more than that, to protect a planet that is already one of the most heavily defended in the region. I was once part of your planning councils, so many of the deployments you put in place were done with my full support."

She looked around the room, her eyes finally settling on the Exarch. "What you don't seem to understand is that *I. Don't. Care.*" She shook her head, the thought finally out into the open. "Terra may be the birthworld of humanity, but Northwind is my home. If I didn't prepare for us to leave, right now, half of my staff would be on the next commercial transport home. You'd still be without your troops, and there'd be nothing you could do.

"By doing things this way, I'm giving you the opportunity to save face. We ask for nothing. All you need to do is to let us go. The only people who will know we're leaving without orders are you and my officers. They'll understand you cannot just let them go with a wave, but they'll also understand the message by letting me return to Northwind to defend our planet."

"What sort of message would that send?" Stone asked. "If I just let any trooper head back to their home planet, where would the Republic be?"

"It would send a message that you intend to keep your promise," she countered, answering his first question while ignoring the second, and she got a small joy from seeing the Exarch rear up slightly. "When you accepted Northwind into the Republic, you did so as part of a covenant, a promise that leaders before you have made before and ignored. Northwind is our home, inviolate, and will be protected by the Highlanders at all costs. Even when you took many of our 'Mechs, we acquiesced because we understood the necessity of the program, knowing full well that if we did not agree, none of our neighbors would. We even allowed you to fold several of our regiments into your own forces, which we had never let any other government do before."

"But war has now come to Northwind again, for the third time under the Republic's rule. Twice before, we pushed back the invaders and kept our planet safe. After that, we took all we had to Terra, at our own cost, to protect your world from those who would see it destroyed." She took a deep breath, taking another look around the room. "You think we're angry at you, that we blame you for what is happening... That is not the case. We are angry that the dream is being torn asunder, that our people will be forced to fight and die once more to save our world. You did not cause that. In fact, I'm grateful for the decades of peace you have brought to me and mine... but we are coming to a crossroads, ladies and gentlemen. A new era. We are about to face the greatest threat to our very survival since the Word of Blake Jihad, and the Highlanders will be ready for it."

"And if we don't let you go?" Surprisingly, it was Sinclair who asked the hard question, rather than the Exarch himself, and she glared at him, a dark, steady gaze that his eyes turned away from.

"My troops are leaving. If we need to fight our way clear of the planet, so be it. Many of us may be lost, we may be forced to fight those we've stood alongside for decades, yet we will do what we must, as we always have." Her gaze was cold. "You do not want to fight us, Exarch. Let us go in peace, as the friends we have always been."

She turned back to Stone, hands clasped behind her back. "I came to you as a courtesy, Exarch, but do not misunderstand me. I am not seeking permission. The Highlanders are going home."

For a long moment, they merely stared at each other, as if they were the only ones in the universe that mattered.

After what seemed an eternity, Stone gave a single nod. "Would you be so kind as to give me a few minutes? I appreciate your input in this matter, but I must consult with my staff."

For a moment, she hesitated, hating to lose the initiative by being dismissed, but something in his eyes stopped her, and she gave a small nod in return. "Until we meet again, Exarch."

With a final respectful farewell to the others, she departed, careful not to let her gaze linger on Republic crest on the carpet for too long as she strode purposefully from the room.

Devlin Stone watched the Countess of Northwind depart, careful to keep his expression composed until the doors closed behind her.

"Opinions?"

Sinclair, being the most familiar with the disposition of forces on Terra, spoke first. "We can stop them. Many of her people grew up under the Republic, so they will follow your lawful orders."

Stone shook his head. "I wouldn't count on that. Even though they may have grown up in the Republic, they are Highlanders first and foremost. Not to mention, we have enough enemies as it is. Bringing war to Terra is what we are trying to prevent." He purposefully avoided looking at Harwell, as memories of their arguments about the debacle on Callison vividly replayed in his thoughts.

Reaching over his desk, he tapped a button on his console and was unsurprised to see a figure step out of the shadows. Emil, known to many as the concierge at the Hotel Duquesne in Geneva, served primarily as the eighteenth Paladin, the fabled Ghost Paladin, the head of the RAF's Department of Military Intelligence and the men and women who served as Ghost Knights. The tall, thin man gave small nods of greeting to the others, then faced the Exarch. "If it helps, I think you handled that as well as you could have."

Tucker Harwell shook his head, walking back from the window to join their conference. As usual, Stone saw his displeasure and focused on it.

"What would you have me do, Tucker?" Stone asked, his eyes narrowing. "You know she's right. We simply don't have the troops to spare."

"Why are you trying to convince *me*?" Harwell responded, with admirable fire. "You're just going to do exactly what you want to anyway."

Stone made an exasperated sound and turned to Lakewood, who'd kept her own counsel so far. "And what do you think, Janella? Am I wrong?"

"We both know you're not wrong about the state of our military," she responded. "If we send Northwind any additional forces, we would be cutting ourselves dangerously thin on some other front."

Stone flicked his gaze to Sinclair, who answered without being asked. "The Sixth Fides would hurt us the least, unless you're willing to use a regiment from your brigade."

Stone looked back at Lakewood. "You said I'm not wrong about the state of our military. That isn't the same as saying you think I'm right about how to deal with the Highlanders."

To her credit, the Paladin maintained the steady composure that had made her input invaluable. "That's not for me to say, sir. I can say that the countess makes an excellent point. If you were to let them go, she has given you the perfect out to save face. It may not be enough for the Highlanders in the long run, but it is something."

"That's not the issue," Tucker interjected, emboldened by the Paladin's support. "The real problem, Devlin, is that you made them a promise, and it's come due."

Stone ignored the younger man, turning to Emil. "Are we prepared if they decide to leave?"

The Ghost Paladin nodded. "Our contingency planning covered this eventuality, and everything is in place. If they try to leave, we are ready for them."

Harwell shook his head in disgust. "More scheming? More betrayal?"

Stone glared at the younger man, letting his anger blaze into an almost palpable force. Unfortunately, Harwell had been through the crucible of this inner circle for too long and seemed immune to Stone's glare. He no longer feared the Exarch; he seemed merely disgusted by what was necessary for the Republic to survive another day.

Stone turned to Sinclair, who stood with his hands behind his back, missing nothing. "Send the orders," he said, glancing over at Harwell, his lips taut. "We do what we must."

Harwell did not give up. "But at what price?"

Stone leaned back in his chair as he stared out the window behind Harwell and saw the dark storm clouds that had surrounded the office. "The only one a covenant will take.

"Blood."

CHAPTER 8

"By order of the Legate, all nonessential personnel are required to evacuate the city of Tara immediately. For those unable to evacuate, please contact the following number for constabulary assistance..."

—Excerpt from evacuation order for
the capital city of Tara, 22 November 3150

OUTSIDE TARA
NORTHWIND
REPUBLIC OF THE SPHERE
23 NOVEMBER 3150

In her *Pillager'*s cockpit, *Sang-shao* Lindsey Baxter smiled briefly in contentment as she surveyed her assembled forces. The staging area was just over the horizon from the city of Tara, and she could see her patrolling pickets keeping a keen eye on the city outskirts and ensuring that none of the Republic forces disrupted their preparations. As she watched, MechWarriors and armor crews mounted up, with battle armor and conventional infantry waiting patiently to board their carriers. It was always impressive to see the full force of her battalion gathered, and she looked forward to the opportunity to show what her rebuilt unit could do.

In most other situations she wouldn't have placed her staging area so close to the city, but to provide the most up-to-date intelligence possible, the *gao-shiao-zhang* had assigned a *Zhen Niao* surveillance DropShip to the mission; it had sneaked into the system weeks ago as a cargo vessel and quietly left a string of stealth satellites to track the Republic's ground movements. The aerial overwatch, coupled with her forward pickets, allowed her a great deal of freedom in moving on her target. Now that battle was joined, those satellites had been repurposed to serve as secure communications relays between the various Operation Clarity forces.

In fact she had just received a message from Julie Qiao directly, proudly informing her that the combined House Imarra and Laurel's Legion force had struck hard at the Twelfth Hastati's Third Battalion, forcing them back into Fort Barrett and disrupting any attempts at a surprise attack on the Clarity forces on the New Lanark continent. As they spoke, House Imarra was maintaining their siege on the fort, and Laurel's Legion had begun investment to ensure there was no chance of a breakout. While the fort itself hadn't yet fallen, the Republic forces on New Lanark wouldn't be receiving any assistance anytime soon.

With the threat to her flanks largely negated, Lindsey could finally move to the next step of the operation: the seizure of Tara and the HPG compound. Having secured the area around her DropShips with elements of Third Battalion, she had moved First and Second Battalions in as a vanguard and the Canopian forces into overwatch positions around the Northwind Military Academy in preparation for the upcoming conflict. There had been a few probing strikes by Hastati scout lances, but for the most part they had remained quiet, content to let the fighting come to them. While it was certainly not the quickest method of defense, she would have done the same thing in their place. Without the additional forces the defenders had foolishly split off at Fort Barrett, there was little chance they would be able to split her tightly knit forces.

Thinking of the Canopian commander, she opened a channel to Qiao, once again taking advantage of the stealth-satellite network. "Colonel, how goes the preparations?"

On the other end of the line, she heard the confidence in Qiao's voice. "My final units are moving into position above the NMA now. We've seen no sign of recon forces so far, but I don't doubt they know we're here. I've had some of my battle armor destroy some remote sensors we found, but I'm sure more have eluded us."

"They can watch us all they want," Baxter replied confidently. "With your forces in place, they'll have a hard time getting out of the complex. If they want to risk running your gauntlet, more power to them."

The heaviest of the Canopian forces were split between overwatch of the NMA compound and the border of the city, ready to strike at either target as necessary. Conversely, Second Battalion was positioned to strike Tara from the opposite eastern front, forcing the Republic troops to choose between protecting the NMA or the city itself. Lindsey's First Battalion would provide a spearhead into the city to inspire Second Battalion to stand and fight, but she would also be well placed to provide fire support against the NMA in the unlikely event the Republic troops chose to make their stand there. This was the sort of battle she favored, and one in which her forces excelled: forcing her opponent to deal with an abundance of threats, and then taking advantage of a freedom of action that most Capellan line units could only dream of.

She had also intentionally left a single axis open, to the southeast of the city. By allowing the Hastati a clear avenue of retreat, which she had seeded with sensor platforms, she hoped they would try a breakout when things turned hopeless. While the Republic troops would see the trap, it was a Hobson's choice: either they attempt to break out and fight another day or die on their shields within the city. If the Highlanders did as expected and took the breakout, she was confident that Second Battalion would inflict heavy damage on them before they could escape into the trees or try to encircle her own forces.

While it galled her to abandon the potential for a decisive victory, her first priority was to secure the HPG compound. Once she had control over the compound, the Confederation would be able to coordinate strikes all along the Republic front, giving them a significant advantage.

Switching the comm channel, she checked in with her various commanders to ensure they were all prepared. Once she completed her final check, she switched back to the channel for the First Canopian Lancers. "Colonel, we are ready. Would you like to do the honors?"

"It would be my pleasure," Colonel Centrella-Tompkins responded. "Skirmishers, open fire!"

From the ridgeline above the NMA, the Canopian forces laid down a web of fire from extreme range, aimed more at keeping Republic forces inside than causing damage. She knew that right now several jump-capable lances were sneaking around the forest behind the NMA, seeking the opportunity to surge inside the compound itself.

With the battle joined, Lindsey ordered her forces forward, approaching Tara at a steady, inexorable pace. She wanted to give the Republic any opportunity to take the battle to them, outside of the city, but knew they would never take it. While they would do anything to protect the residents of Tara from harm, attacking in the open against a numerically superior opponent would only have ensured their destruction, leaving the citizens of Tara undefended.

She switched back to the Canopian channel and was surprised to hear the familiar burst of electromagnetic distortion from a nearby PPC discharge. "Colonel, is everything all right?"

"Yes, *Sang-shao*," Valeria replied, but there was now a tightness in her voice. "We are taking long-range fire from the NMA grounds, primarily lasers and PPCs. We are adjusting to provide counterbattery fire, but they have placed reinforced redoubts to provide cover for their 'Mechs."

Baxter instantly improved her opinion of the NMA commander for such extensive preparations. By relying primarily on direct-fire energy weapons, the NMA forces could operate without worrying about resupply, thus saving ammunition for when the battle was truly joined. While the Hastati were significantly better supplied than many other Republic units, their resources were still limited.

"Colonel, I am guessing you have spotters in the trees, not just remote sensors." She smiled wickedly although no one could see it. "While you continue your assault, let me see if I can give the Republic forces something else to think about." She switched over to her own unit's channel and gave her people the order they had been waiting for. "Vanguard elements, proceed as planned."

Under her watchful eye, the light elements cautiously entered the city. Led by Alpha Company, they moved on preplanned routes through the outlying city streets, maintaining overlapping fields of fire to strike at any potential threat. In the lead, her light armor, primarily Pegasus hovercraft acquired from the Free Worlds League, moved in a cautious battle line toward the city center, then broke into pairs as they approached the outskirts.

Seeing that the situation was well in hand, she checked in with commander of Second Battalion, *Sao-shao* Paul Handel, whose unit was watching the highway, the most likely route for movement out of the city or towards the NMA. "*Sao-shao*, any issues?"

"No, ma'am," Handel replied, his deep voice coming across the line clearly. "No sign of hostiles."

She was going to press him further, but a bright flash and a burst of smoke erupted to her left. One of the first 'Mechs in her vanguard, a *Vindicator*, had tripped a vibromine, rending armor and internals in its left leg, its crisp camouflage paint marred by ugly streaks of soot and blackened armor. The pilot held position, shifting the 'Mech's weight to the undamaged leg, careful not to move until he identified the threat.

"Contact, contact! Minefield!"

"All vanguard forces, hold!" Lindsey narrowed her eyes tightly in dismay. *I knew the Republic would never cede the city without a fight.* "Bring up the sappers and combat engineers. I want those mines cleared immediately."

She watched the *Vindicator* rear back as if startled, and for a moment she thought that the 'Mech had struck another mine, until she saw the glaring red beam of a large laser strike its shoulder. As she watched, a volley of long-range missiles struck the *Vindicator* across the head and chest, dropping it on its side. For a brief moment, she thought the BattleMech was going to land safely, but another vibromine detonation ripped off the 'Mech's left arm.

"*Sang-shao*, our vanguard forces are under fire from the city. It looks like light armor," reported Alpha Company's commander, *Sang-wei* Hu.

Lindsey nodded, understanding exactly what they had done. Her lighter vanguard units wouldn't trigger the minefield, but her heavier units would; this split her forces so the defenders could pick them apart piecemeal. While she had expected a trick like this, the enemy had timed it to take fullest advantage of the open fields outside of the city. Either she would split her forces to reduce the threat to her uncovered vanguard, or she would have to retreat to cover.

At least, those were the options they wanted for her.

"*Sang-wei*, tighten up and take defensive positions against the outermost buildings until we can break through the vibromines. Can you hold?"

"Yes, *Sang-shao*," Hu replied. "Moving to new defensive positions."

"Excellent. Vanguard armor, proceed into the outskirts of the city in pairs, report any contact you find. We want to move them out of their firing lanes." She had been prepared for this sort of situation, and had several jump-capable 'Mechs close enough to deal with it, but the last thing she wanted to do was to jump some of her lighter 'Mechs into the city when they still hadn't seen any sign of Hastati 'Mechs. "Jump lances, prepare to provide mobile support."

It was time to stop reacting and start acting. "First Battalion, forward on me."

She moved First Battalion forward, ready to break through into the city the instant the sappers had completed their job. As they approached, the occasional shots from within the city grew in both frequency and intensity, but the well-trained members of her unit maintained fire discipline and focused completely on the task at hand. As she monitored Alpha Company's channel, she received a report of a Republic Demon tank that had moved too slowly, and a PPC blast from her battle line eliminated the threat.

Suddenly, something occurred to her, and she turned back to Alpha Company's channel. "*Sang-wei*, any sign of civilians in your area?"

There was a long pause.

"No, ma'am. It seems most of the area has been evacuated."

She tightened her eyes slowly, swearing loudly as she muted her microphone. "*Sang-wei*, as soon as you have disengaged, have your people search the area. I believe our Republic friends may have evacuated this portion of the city to provide us with some additional surprises."

"Yes, ma'am," Hu responded.

She gave a small nod of approval, and then returned to the channel for the sappers. "Engineering teams, we need you to make a hole right now!" She didn't wait for a reply before reaching out to Centrella-Tompkins. "Colonel, any success with the NMA?"

The Canopian commander's reply was tight with tension. "There are at least two companies of heavy and assault 'Mechs on the academy grounds, all heavily entrenched. Nothing short of a frontal assault with a full battalion will be enough to shake them loose, but our flanking force is still en route."

Baxter nodded appreciatively as she recognized the choice Brigadier McNamara had forced on them. While the Republic forces at the NMA were not currently mobile, their force-composition analysis was based on only what they had allowed the Clarity forces to see so far. If Centrella-Tompkins sent in too weak of a force to assault the academy, they would be picked apart in detail. However, if her Canopians made a full strike at the academy and there were too many unseen forces, she risked facing a full battalion of Republic forces, entrenched and fully armed. If that happened, Lindsey would have to break off from the city to support the Canopians, or risk losing them entirely.

"Colonel, hold position, and keep them bottled up in the academy. You are cleared to engage only if they try to break out. Do you understand?"

"Yes, ma'am," Centrella-Tompkins replied, and Baxter caught a hint of relief in her voice. Striking at an entrenched enemy was never an ideal command choice, especially when going up against an elite force like the Hastati Sentinels.

Focusing back on the current problem, Lindsey finally received a message from the sappers, informing her that they had cleared a lane into the city. While she wasn't thrilled to send her units through a death funnel, she needed to get forces in position as quickly as possible.

Switching back to her command channel, she brought Hu on the line. "*Sang-wei,* send in your scout lances, followed by heavy support. Clear out block by block. Leave no blind corners."

She received confirmation and slowly moved her *Pillager* down the lane she had chosen. Behind her, she felt the watchful presence of Rao, whose *Ti Ts'ang* watched her back carefully.

"Contact!" It was one of the Pegasus tank commanders on her channel. "A *Thunderbolt.* Striker Four is down, Striker Four is down. Coming your way."

Glancing at her secondary display, she saw that Striker Lance, a patrol group of Pegasus hovertanks, was several blocks over, a red circle showing Striker Four's last reported position.

"Rao..."

"Understood," the other MechWarrior replied.

Lindsey instinctively raised her *Pillager*'s arms as the Republic *Thunderbolt* turned down the street. Bright red gashes scored its night-black and golden-accented armor, which spoke well for Striker Four's final moments.

Still, the BattleMech was combat capable, and the *Thunderbolt* raised its arm-mounted laser as she came into view. Unfortunately for the Republic pilot, she was a split second faster, sending two Gauss rounds into his right leg and left torso, and the 'Mech reared back under the dual hammerblows. The *Thunderbolt* fired its large laser, which scored her left arm, but the other MechWarrior had taken the worse of the exchange. She quickly moved forward to follow up on the strike, but Rao leapt from behind her on twin jets of plasma and came down behind the *Thunderbolt*. He didn't even bother to fire his weapons, simply swinging his *fu*, the *Ti Ts'ang*'s double-bladed battle-axe, at the Republic 'Mech's thinly-protected back. Lindsey heard the agonizing shriek of rending armor as Rao tore open the left torso, the heavy axe head biting deep into internal structures.

The *Thunderbolt* pilot, realizing they were outclassed by the two Capellan BattleMechs, attempted to pull back around the building, momentarily leaving Lindsey's sightline. Over her external microphones she heard the familiar howl of incoming missiles, and a damaged Pegasus swung around the corner, peppering the *Thunderbolt* with a dozen short-range missiles. The damage was too much for the wounded 'Mech, and it toppled over, scraping its torso against a nearby building as it collapsed.

Baxter had no time to celebrate their victory, however, as additional threat icons popped up on her display. To her right, Rao engaged a nearby Republic tank, and she caught a brief glimpse of additional enemy armor speeding through a nearby intersection, too fast for her weapons to get a lock. From the sounds of battle on her command channel, it seemed they had found the Hastati at last.

Something flickered in the corner of her 360-degree display, and she turned instinctively. A pair of large pulse lasers scored across her arm, sending her damage readout quickly into the red, luckily not cutting in far enough to cause damage to her Gauss rifle. As she turned, a pair of short-range missiles followed in their wake, taking her high in the chest.

She cursed herself for getting distracted and quickly turned on the Republic *Gallant* that had appeared from a nearby alley. With its remote sensor drones, it had probably known she'd been there since the beginning, hoping to capitalize on the opportunity to shoot the larger BattleMech in the back.

Unfortunately for the pilot, they now had her undivided attention. Careful of her heat, she triggered her own laser battery in response. The large laser and one of the mediums missed, but the heat from the other three medium lasers gouged armor from the *Gallant*'s torso and left leg.

Something nagged at her, and she gave a grim smile. *It would come from behind...*

Stomping on her foot petals, she vaulted her *Pillager* into the air on twin bursts of jump-jet plasma, sending it down a side street. She momentarily lost sight of the *Gallant* but was in the perfect position when a Republic *Blade* that sought to ambush her sped down the street and came to a sharp halt as it realized its quarry had disappeared. The *Blade* turned quickly, bringing its autocannon to bear, and explosive shells chattered across her center torso and trailed dangerously upward, toward her 'Mech's head.

Unfortunately for the Republic MechWarrior, her hunch had paid off, and she triggered her primary interlock as soon as she spotted the speeding *Blade*. Two Gauss rounds connected with the 35-ton 'Mech, one taking the left arm, while the other gouged deep into the torso armor. The 'Mech stumbled forward a step. Its right arm and the underside of its torso scraped a nearby building, sending armor shards and concrete raining down on the street below. On her secondary map screen, she finally saw Rao closing in, having finally disengaged from his own enemy.

Despite the devastating one-two punch that the *Blade* received, its pilot had not given up on getting some small measure of revenge. This time the autocannon fire did scrape across her cockpit, the armored canopy cracking dangerously under the onslaught. Her eyes narrowed in barely contained fury. Was this an attempt at headhunting?

Rao advanced to avenge the attack on his commander, but Lindsey pushed her 'Mech into point-blank range. Using one of her *Pillager*'s immense hands to shove the autocannon to one side, she remorselessly punched the armor-tipped spikes of her other fist deep into the smaller 'Mech's chest. The *Blade* shuddered as she stabbed through the weakened torso armor, and she imagined the smell of the burst heat sinks and coolant lines as she clipped the engine with the assault 'Mech's claws.

She felt the 'Mech spasm like a dying man as the delicate gyro in its chest ground itself to pieces on her fist. The *Blade* suddenly went limp, held up only by her arm embedded in its chest. With a contemptuous motion, she dropped her *Pillager*'s arm, letting the smaller 'Mech slide off the spikes and collapse at her feet.

Lindsey turned to survey the battlefield, her rage cooling with the death of the enemy 'Mech. The *Gallant* was gone, its pilot choosing the better part of valor. She took a steadying breath, and switched on the Alpha Company channel. "*Sang-wei* Hu, report."

"*Sang-shao*, we are at seventy percent effectiveness, but we have control of the area. Our armor holds the first set of intersections, and our initial attackers have disengaged. Our battle armor is seeing to our downed enemies." He paused for a moment. "We are seeing signs of more recent habitation in nearby buildings."

She nodded, smiling slowly. She'd known the Republic couldn't possibly have evacuated the whole city, so they would've done what they could to minimize the damage to a small area. Unfortunately, that plan only worked if she was unwilling to do what was necessary. "Excellent, *Sang-wei*. Maintain position, and we will consolidate our lines before we advance. Have your infantry move through the local community under overwatch, and remind the populace that there will be no retaliation if they behave." Such reassurances may sound hollow, but it would be worth it if it kept the populace from getting too rowdy. It would also serve as a pointed reminder of what the Confederation was capable of if they resisted.

Hu confirmed the order, and she moved in behind his re-forming armor line. Rao followed her, his battle-ax swinging menacingly, cautious of each side street despite Lindsey's confidence that they had dealt with any stragglers.

It didn't matter. Tara would soon be hers.

CHAPTER 9

*"While we must answer the call to our honor, we will
never forget our friends and loved ones here on Northwind.
Should we ever be needed, we shall be here..."*

—Farewell message from Countess Tara Campbell,
before her departure for Terra after the second
Steel Wolf invasion of Northwind

THE CASTLE
NORTHWIND
REPUBLIC OF THE SPHERE
23 NOVEMBER 3150

From his place in the command well of the Castle's operations
center, Brigadier General Luis McNamara glared sullenly at
the multiple displays that ringed the room, attempting to stay
ahead of the onrush of information coming from all sides.
The command-and-control facilities of the Castle had been
completely upgraded in the wake of the Steel Wolf attacks on
Northwind, specifically designed for just this sort of scenario,
but he never anticipated he would still feel so helpless among
all this data.

As suspected, the Capellan forces had quickly secured
the city of Tara, intent on taking the HPG compound intact
by knowing his forces would be loath to cause damage to
the city itself. He had planned to overwhelm the Capellans
with a variety of threats, wearing them down and trusting the
Highlanders' command-and-control abilities and home-field
advantage to give them an edge. Unfortunately, while the plan

gave them some early successes, it lent itself to a high level of complexity, which was far from ideal.

A major aspect of the plan focused on the changes to the city itself, which had occurred during the rebuilding efforts after the Steel Wolf attacks. As the people of Tara had put their lives back together, vast swaths of land outside Tara were quietly sold to private investors who wasted no time breaking ground for new warehouses. While most people didn't notice until the first construction crews were called in, they were quick to embrace the new jobs and investment that came to a previously fallow area.

Instead of disturbing the rustic, peaceful look of the inner city, the new warehouses were built on the outlying plains ringing the city, where they would be less of an eyesore and provide a nice definition between the city and the raw beauty of Northwind itself. The warehouses being rented out to local companies at bargain-basement prices only fostered further goodwill among the populace. With all these benefits to the people of Tara, no one dug deep enough to learn that all of the buildings were held through several shell companies owned by the Campbell family.

When it came to defending the city against an invading force, however, the development projects transformed into an impressive fortification. The outer wall was designed to look like normal vacant buildings from the outside, but in the inner courtyard were two blocks of open space, allowing for clear fields of fire that made an impressive kill zone. The inner wall was made up of heavily reinforced three-story warehouses, just large enough for IndustrialMechs or BattleMechs to post inside, and several had reinforced rear doors that would allow easy egress as the enemy approached. Since none of the buildings were zoned for habitability, they had been easily evacuated the moment the impending Capellan landing had been announced, and they now formed the inner boundary of the city's defensive perimeter.

Despite all the benefits, however, cost and secrecy brought their own drawbacks. To keep the plan from being too apparent, the roads themselves had to be kept clear for civilian traffic, which placed several large holes in the wall of buildings. While those approaches were now covered by assault 'Mechs from the Twelfth Hastati, they still served as paths into the city itself. Although another wall of reinforced warehouses at their back partially shielded the city from stray shots, it didn't provide the full defense McNamara preferred.

Unfortunately, the cost of surrounding an entire city with warehouses was prohibitive, even for a group as wealthy as the Campbell Clan. As such, they could only cover the major routes an attacker might take, and mobile forces had to be spared to cover the portions of the line not protected by the warehouse wall. Should the Capellans get past the inner defensive line, the Twelfth would have to depart the city to prevent civilian casualties, especially when one considered how the CCAF traditionally treated civilians in conflict zones. Toward that end, two egress routes covered by mobile forces were left tantalizingly open to the Capellan invaders.

The border where the city met the Great Thames River was covered by the Twelfth's remaining aerospace resources. If the Capellan forces did attempt to ford the river, they would be mired in a killing zone covered by aerospace and pre-sighted artillery, with Third Battalion ready to move in and take advantage.

The other egress route led from the city to the Castle, the Twelfth's main defensive position on New Lanark. If the city's defenders needed to escape, that would be their route. While McNamara loathed the idea of being that obvious, he secretly hoped the Capellans would choose to engage there: it was far enough from the city to ensure a lack of collateral damage, and it would allow Third Battalion to engage. While the fight could potentially still be two regiments on one, the heavier throw weight and skill of the Twelfth might very well prove decisive, especially with detachments from the Fourth MAC and First Canopian Lancers being forced to cover their DropShips and the NMA.

As with all things, however, McNamara's plan was predicated on the Capellan commanders dancing to his tune.

"Do we have an update on results from the minefield?" he asked his aide.

Major William Keddon gave a sad shake of his head. "We have reports of five BattleMechs down, several more with leg damage. Unfortunately, they found most of the vibrabombs before they could do much damage."

McNamara nodded, having expected as much. A true minefield, though far more effective, would've immediately tipped off the Capellans that the defenders were unafraid of collateral damage in that part of the city. The vibrabombs had been a good compromise: battle armor and hovercraft were not heavy enough to trigger them, but the multi-ton footfalls of BattleMechs had triggered them and inflicted severe leg damage on the attacking forces. This proved even more effective for their goals, as every fallen 'Mech would need protection while it was down, especially with Hastati battle armor in the field. That meant the Capellans needed to leave behind a second unit to watch their downed comrades or risk having them threatened by Hastati light forces.

Unfortunately, the Capellan commander had expected this sort of a gambit and had exercised caution in committing her heaviest units. While the mines had damaged the initial scouting elements, they hadn't stopped as many of the heavier units as McNamara had hoped.

Still, that might leave a new opportunity.

"Major," he said, "new orders for our striker units. Their heavier recon units have taken losses, let's try to take advantage of that. Also, all forces should concentrate fire on the approach lane. I want to cause maximum damage while they are still bunched up."

"Do you want me to order artillery or air support on the area?"

McNamara shook his head. "Not yet. I don't want to show our hand too early."

Keddon smiled lightly and gave the orders. As McNamara watched on the main screen, a Hastati *Nightsky* leapt from the cover of a low building and ambushed a Fourth MAC *Men Shen* by landing at its rear. The heavier Capellan 'Mech shuddered as the *Nightsky*'s pulse lasers bit deep into its lighter rear armor, damaging the engine, according to the surge of heat that flashed on infrared. The *Men Shen* desperately tried to turn in the narrow street's tight confines, but by the time it brought its heavier armament to bear, the *Nightsky* had already jumped away. The same scene played in microcosm on the various screens, but the Twelfth had as many losses as victories. On one screen, he watched a Capellan *Pillager* and *Ti Ts'ang* brutally savage a Hastati *Thunderbolt*. The 'Mech went down hard, likely suffering from gyro damage, and he saw the flurry of activity as several command center technicians dispatched a recovery team to the area.

Everywhere he looked, screen after screen showed the desperate defense of Northwind's capital. BattleMechs fought at point-blank range as the Capellan forces attempted to press through the outer defensive line, all while well-entrenched Republic forces desperately tried to whittle down the enemy's numbers before they were overwhelmed.

On one screen, a Capellan *Wraith* jumped behind a Republic Regulator hovertank and savaged the tank's rear armor with its large laser, and a vicious kick sent the crippled tank careening into the side of a nearby building. On another screen, a black-and-gold *UrbanMech* trapped a Capellan *Eyleuka* in a blind alley and fired before it could jump away. The *Eyleuka*'s stealth armor offered no help at point-blank range as the *UrbanMech*'s heavy autocannon eviscerated the 55-ton 'Mech.

On a third screen, a squad of Fa Shih battle armor swarmed all over a Republic *Night Stalker* in the close confines of a cross street. The *Night Stalker* crushed a single trooper in its clawed right hand while slashing its left-arm lance to keep the rest of the squad away. The killed trooper's squadmates responded viciously by cutting open the *Night Stalker*'s cockpit with their lasers, heedless of the damage they took.

McNamara glanced upward as his aide came alongside him. "Sir, we are reaching CLG," Keddon announced quietly.

McNamara gave a small nod to confirm he had heard. Combat loss grouping was the point when the cumulative damage across a unit reached a level, where further damage could potentially cascade and cause the loss of the whole unit. Right now, they could ill afford such a chain of critical losses.

"Start pulling them back to their designated fallback positions, Major," he replied, making sure his voice could be heard throughout the room. "We've done everything we set out to do here."

Despite his proud words, he knew it wasn't going to be enough. He had hoped that the unexpected strength of the Republic resistance would convince the Capellans to pull back from the city, at least temporarily, giving them valuable time to redeploy and prepare for the next attack. Unfortunately, the Capellan commander proved to be just as determined as he had feared. By forcing the Twelfth to abandon the outer areas and pull farther into the city, the Fourth MAC ensured that McNamara's troops would have to fight to regain every meter of ground later.

McNamara had little choice. If he did not retreat now, he would lose the forces necessary for the battles to come. Saving as many people as he could in the early phases of the conflict would help with later objectives, making it no choice at all.

"Get me the NMA," McNamara ordered, turning back to the main screen.

"Halloran." The voice came through the command channel clearly, despite the distance and continued heavy fire the NMA campus was enduring.

"Status report, Colonel."

"Things continue well here, sir. Our forces are picking at the Canopian forces from a distance, and we have several enemy 'Mechs confirmed down. We're suffering from reduced accuracy due to lack of spotters, however. I believe the Canopians finally caught on, so what few spotters remain have been ordered to go to ground."

McNamara smiled tightly, pleased that at least something was going better than planned. Construction teams had been working on the 'Mech-sized redoubts since the news of the invasion had reached the planet, and they had pressed the training 'Mechs into service to aid the defense as best they could. A mix of instructors no longer on active duty and some of the brighter pupils had been given the opportunity to defend the campus, keeping a second front open against the invading forces.

Unfortunately, a distraction was all he could use them for. Most of the training 'Mechs were partially functional, most having been loaded with real ordnance for the first time in decades. If they moved out into the field, they would suffer quickly, especially against the lighter, more advanced Canopian force.

"Continue the engagement with energy weapons, and do what you can to hold the line. I've ordered our defensive forces in the city to pull back and redeploy."

There was a long pause on the line before Colonel Halloran responded. "General, I've been working on some contingency planning with my fellow instructors. The students have been moved into some of our less-mobile units, and the instructors have switched out for our light strikers. On your order, I can field a company-sized force to distract from your breakout."

Keddon looked over at him, but McNamara was already shaking his head. "Request denied, Colonel. Your 'Mechs won't make it ten meters against the Canopians, and it would only get you all killed. You have a defensible position, and we have forces in place that can relieve you if you're in danger of being overrun. Your orders are to hold in place."

A squeal of static came over the line, as if someone was leaning on the comm button. "Sorry, sir—I'm having a little trouble—"

"Don't try that squelching bullshit with me, Colonel!" McNamara's voice rang through the command center, catching the attention of anyone who hadn't already been eavesdropping. "I am giving you a direct order to hold that academy. You will not risk your lives on some damned selfless quest for glory. Confirm and acknowledge!"

Halloran's voice was husky as he responded, "Orders received and acknowledged, sir."

"Good," McNamara replied, his voice returning to normal. "Now, keep me in the loop if anything changes. With the Capellans pressing forward, they may decide to attack you to try splitting our focus."

Halloran confirmed his understanding of his orders, and the channel went silent as McNamara sighed heavily. Seeing that several of his staff were still watching, he fixed them with a steely glare that sent them scurrying back to their duties, holding it until Keddon stepped up beside him.

"It was a courageous offer to make," the major said quietly, and McNamara considered his aide for a moment before giving him a small nod.

"It was. Unfortunately, he knows it'd be a suicide mission. I have no doubt he'd have given as good as he had got, but centuries-old 'Mechs are not going to be our salvation here." He shook his head mournfully. "If only Lady Maeve's plan had worked."

Keddon nodded silently. For all of their preparations, the additional 'Mechs stowed on the DropShips had not even gotten into play. By striking at Fort Barrett with two full regiments, the Capellans had forced Second Battalion to defend from within the fort, negating any mobility advantage that the Twelfth's light forces could have imparted. With that being the case, Maeve had decided to hold her little surprise until it would actually be effective. Unfortunately, that meant there wouldn't be any support rushing to the rescue on New Lanark anytime soon, either.

Straightening, he looked up, every centimeter the confident commander. Damned if he was going to show his disappointment at the missed opportunity to strike the Capellans. "Captain, let me look at the deployments for our inner line..."

Having watched the situation from the back of the room, a shadowy figure stepped out and moved unhurriedly to the second level of the command area. He gave a small nod to the guard posted at the doorway and casually headed out into the main concourse, taking great care to not garner any unwanted attention. Moving steadily through the concourse, he adjusted his gait until he reached one of the nearby wall-walks between the parapets, far enough away from the command area for the bleed of military-strength jammers to not interfere with his personal equipment, and he pressed a memorized number into his communicator.

The line clicked with the confirmation of a positive link. "The general is pulling back the troops, preparing to leave the city," he transmitted. "The Capellans will be moving within the hour."

A careful silence stretched on the other end of the line, and then a voice responded, clear and certain. "We are prepared. What are your orders?"

Looking over the parapet, he laid the perscomm carefully on the stone. His gaze reached outward, taking in the beautiful sight of the pristine fields outside of the city and the gentle current of the Grand Thames sending up small white-capped breaks in the crystal-clear water.

His gaze slipped toward Tara, where ugly clouds of smoke rose in the distance, the occasional burst of visible energy making it look like a thundercloud growing to consume the entire city. His expression tightened, and he thought of what would happen when the city fell.

He'd been in the command center for the entirety of the battle so far, and had seen how dire the situation looked for the Twelfth Hastati. While highly capable fighters, the Republic troops were at a significant disadvantage, as being forced to protect too many objectives was crippling their ability to operate offensively. If ever there was a time to capitalize on the chaos, it was now. There would be no better time to take action than with the Twelfth in full flight, when he could capitalize on their disorganization.

Still, he had kept his secret for so long it seemed wrong to bring things into the open like this. He thought back to all the years he had spent to keep his mission from discovery, of all the sacrifices he had made...

But now the time had come. The avalanche had begun; the rocks no longer had the chance to vote.

He took a deep, steadying breath, picked the perscomm back up, and spoke a single command:

"Activate the Grey Watch Protocol."

CHAPTER 10

"Don't you know I would like to send them more forces? We've evacuated everyone from the academy who was willing to go. All we can do for the others is hope they can sell themselves as dearly as possible."

—Brigadier General McNamara to his staff,
23 November 3150

NORTHWIND MILITARY ACADEMY
NORTHWIND
REPUBLIC OF THE SPHERE
23 NOVEMBER 3150

In the shadow of the Northwind Military Academy, things were even grimmer than was visible in the command center. Declan's lance had been deployed into the woods behind the NMA, prepared to hold open the back door if the defenders were under threat of being overrun. Due to his role as support for the NMA, he was conferenced in on their command channel.

He also knew what General McNamara hadn't said. That despite their best efforts, it probably wasn't going to matter either way.

From his position inside the forest, Declan could see the Canopian forces re-forming, preparing for a major push. From what Fairchild's sensors could gather, it was mostly lighter units without the long-range weapons to capitalize on the siege of the compound. The general hadn't wanted the academy's defenders to sacrifice themselves by leaving their battlements to strike at the Canopian forces, but Declan had no doubt they would soon find the battle they sought.

"*Tian-Zong* sky-lining itself! Take it!" Oedhe's voice came over the lance channel, and Declan's eyes shot up to the ridgeline. The heavy BattleMech was taking careful aim from the top of a nearby hill but had sacrificed the safety of the surrounding forest for a clear shot into the NMA compound.

Declan intended to show them their mistake.

Whipping up his *Marauder II*'s arm, he discharged his ER PPC while Oedhe did the same with his heavy PPC; both shots struck the Canopian's right torso. The enemy 'Mech reeled forward as Declan fired another PPC, which hit its left leg.

The shock of losing several tons of armor at once was too much for the *Tian-Zong*'s pilot, and the 'Mech collapsed bonelessly to the ground. The MechWarrior quickly attempted to rise, but a laser fired from the NMA grounds capitalized on the earlier damage, ripping the left leg off of the 75-ton BattleMech and sending it tumbling back to the earth.

Using the sniper method, Declan and Oedhe moved through the underbrush to new positions. While they weren't opposed to taking advantage of an opportunity, their orders were to protect the NMA force if they had to retreat, not to start a new front with the Canopians.

Declan focused on his scanner again, trying not to think about the current situation. Despite the training he'd done with Lady Maeve and her lance, she left him behind with the rest of the Hastati when she was called to Fort Barrett. *Did she ever intend for me to be part of her team, or was this all a ploy to string me along on her mole hunt?*

He forced his thoughts back to the present as a new threat icon popped up on his screen. "Hold position. I think someone may have missed that *Tian-Zong*. New contact coming our way."

As he spoke, a PPC shot shattered the bole of a nearby tree, and he swore. His sensors registered his assailant as a *Vindicator* before it disappeared back into the trees. He held perfectly still, resisting the urge to return fire, not knowing whether he had actually been seen or whether it was an attempt to flush them from cover.

"Do they know we're here, or just got lucky?" Oedhe whispered.

They waited for several moments, but no additional fire came. It seemed the *Vindicator* pilot just need a way of venting their spleen at the loss of a lancemate.

"Hold position for now. We'll see where things go from here."

Fairchild, who was positioned closer to the academy's western wall, came over his headset. "One, I am getting a couple of odd magscan readings on the far end of the tree line."

"Hostiles?"

"I don't know," the sergeant responded, a rare note of uncertainty in her voice. "It was just a couple of blips, heavy tonnage, on magscan."

Declan paused for a moment. At that tonnage it could be a Capellan support lance, but it seemed unlikely that Capellan troops would be coming in this direction with the battle for Tara still in progress. "Keep an eye out to see if it comes back, Sergeant. Something doesn't seem right about this."

Before he could dwell further on the mystery, Oedhe sent an emergency broadcast. "Boss, I think we have a problem here..."

Declan switched over to Oedhe's data feed and instantly saw the issue. The Canopians had realized the futility of attacking BattleMechs partially hidden behind defensive emplacements, and had instead begun concentrating on the rear wall of the compound. As he watched, a portion of the outer wall started to buckle under repeated fire, the outer layer crumbling in places where the armor had already been sheared off. The defending Republic BattleMechs, realizing the threat, increased their fire to hold the attackers off, but it had little effect. Inspired by the small victory, the Canopian forces were pushing forward in the forest, their weapons fire increasing as they targeted the crumbling outer wall.

"If that wall comes down, things are gonna get real hot in there real fast." Oedhe said, his voice tense.

And he was right. The Canopians had been holding fire discipline so far, but if they could make a breach in the wall—or worse, multiple breaches—they might take the risk to flood the compound itself. Once they were inside, the battlements would be as much of an impediment to the defenders as to the attackers, and the Canopians' greater maneuverability would prove telling. While the enemy still had to be wary of a trap, the fact that heavier forces had not come to push them back told them that the resistance from inside the NMA was all the defenders had. It was still a risk, but if the Canopians took the NMA out of play, they would be able to devote more forces to supporting the Capellan push on Tara.

"Keep your eyes peeled. I have a feeling we're about to have company." Switching to the command channel, he got through to Major Keddon immediately. "Commander, Backdoor One. We have multiple breaches in the rear wall of the compound and Canopian forces rallying to strike from the woods. Orders?"

The major's voice was solemn. "Backdoor One, hold position until the NMA forces make a breakout. If the Lancers strike, support any escaping NMA units, but abandon the compound if the enemy breaches. Provide cover for withdrawing units, but you must depart in good order and preserve your forces."

Declan fought the urge to respond sharply, but Major Keddon was correct. His company didn't have the firepower to repel a full Canopian thrust, and the NMA was a symbol, not a primary goal for the enemy attackers.

"Lieutenant..." Fairchild transmitted, an odd tone in her voice. "We're not going to just do nothing, are we?"

Declan was surprised by the statement, coming from the normally staid sergeant, then he cursed himself for forgetting that her husband taught tactics courses at the NMA. While she hadn't mentioned it before this mission, he was likely one of those still inside, defending the campus with the other volunteers, and it must have torn her apart to be ordered to do nothing while her husband remained at risk.

Before Declan could reply, his throat tightened as the first ranks of Canopian 'Mechs emerged from the woods, firing at the damaged wall from the opposite side, keeping up a steady barrage to keep the NMA forces from attempting a breakout. He watched as successive lances of Canopian 'Mechs pressed forward through the clearing, lasers and tracer rounds tearing into the reinforced walls and chipping away at the protection of the forces inside.

On the walls, several defending 'Mechs faced the new threat, but it was too little, too late. A *Whitworth* turned an instant too slowly and was skewered on two large laser beams that slashed armor from its arm and rear torso. Surrounded by a battalion's worth of 'Mechs, the defenders fought valiantly, but even Declan saw them taking damage.

Seeing their valiant stand against the larger Canopian force, he straightened in his command couch and lowered his targeting reticule on a nearby *Marshal*. "All units, stand ready..." He opened a channel to the command center again, but stayed his hand as he heard an emergency call from Fairchild.

"Contacts coming from the forest! Multiple contacts!"

"Report!" he replied harshly. "Who are they?"

"I...I don't know!"

Something in Fairchild's otherwise unflappable voice caused him to look up, just in time to see a *Marauder* step out of the tree line. It had been stripped down to a bare coat of gray primer over most of its birdlike body, but what was most startling was the exquisitely rendered tartan that ran down one side of the torso, wrapping around the hip like a kilt. Declan tried to identify the familiar-looking pattern but was too startled by the unexpected arrival to let it register.

To his surprise, the 75-ton *Marauder* was an old 3R model, complete with the autocannon and original Magna Hellstar PPCs, its hunched profile burned into his memory from decades of his grandfather's stories. With almost contemptuous ease, the 'Mech pointed an armored vambrace at the 55-ton *Marshal*, sending a bolt of man-made lighting searing into its chest. The lighter 'Mech reared back and then shuddered again as the *Marauder* followed up with an autocannon fusillade that stitched a line of death across its hip and into its torso.

The Canopians' momentary shock at the appearance of the heavy 'Mech abated, the other Canopians turned to face the new threat. A second *Marshal* stepped up beside its lancemate and aimed its large laser as a second gray-primer 'Mech, a *Phoenix Hawk*, stepped into the fray and skewered the *Marshal* with a trio of laser strikes. As Declan watched, additional gray 'Mechs stepped from the trees, ancient models he remembered from the stories of old. A *Warhammer*, followed by a *Rifleman*. They came out in a staggered formation, creating a sort of battle line that hadn't seen regular use in two centuries, their overlapping arcs of fire turning the clearing into a kill zone.

"Does anyone recognize that paint scheme?" Declan asked, his attention rapt despite himself.

He watched the *Warhammer* fire one of its PPCs, then the other, staggering the shots with professional care. The first shot hit a nearby *Men Shen* in the leg, and the other took out the knee actuator, causing it to limp back as it withdrew.

Fairchild risked a brief transmission. "Do you see that? The *Warhammer* is staggering its fire... I think it only has standard heat sinks."

Instantly the firing patterns made sense: Declan was thinking of these new ' Mechs as old because they were probably using Succession War-era technology. Still, that raised even more questions than it answered. *Upgrade kits for these 'Mechs have been available for decades. Why hadn't they been brought up to current standards? Could someone have found a* lostech *cache of equipment on Northwind itself?*

"What do we do, One?" Fairchild asked, just as confused as everyone else. The sergeant had regained her composure with the arrival of the surprise rescuers, although the excitement in her voice told Declan how ready she was to act.

"Stay concealed," he said. "but capitalize on the confusion if you get the opportunity. Right now they seem to be doing pretty well on their own."

They didn't have to wait long. The Canopians, seeing their vanguard destroyed, repositioned to rush the lance of newcomers, hoping to overwhelm them with sheer numbers. A pair of new 7M *Shadow Hawk*s squared off against the ancient *Rifleman*, hoping to use their maneuverability for a quick kill.

Unfortunately for them, the *Rifleman* had anticipated the maneuver. Despite taking a pair of light Gauss-rifle rounds in the torso and a medium laser to the barrel of its left-arm autocannon, it fired a large laser and an autocannon, which ripped into the centerline of the nearest *Shadow Hawk* as it closed. The newer 'Mech shrugged off the first salvo, but the second, concentrating on a damaged leg, sent it tumbling to the ground.

The *Shadow Hawk*, now seeing an opportunity to strike at the *Rifleman*'s notoriously thin rear armor, took to the sky on its jump jets and leaped over the larger 'Mech, firing its medium laser and SRMs at its target's back. The *Rifleman* shuddered for a moment, but the *Shadow Hawk* never got to celebrate its victory, as the *Warhammer* turned its full complement of short-range weapons on it. The barrage of medium lasers, machine guns, and short-range missiles ripped into the *Shadow Hawk* and forced it to one knee as it stumbled upon landing. Without bothering to turn, the *Rifleman* rotated its arms with the casual menace of cocking a pistol, and streams of depleted-uranium slugs punched through the *Shadow Hawk*'s chest. The pilot ejected, fleeing from the combined firepower of the heavy 'Mechs.

The remaining *Shadow Hawk* attempted to get to its feet, but the *Rifleman*, now at close range, stomped down with a single foot, crushing the arm-mounted light Gauss rifle. Between the damage from the *Rifleman* and the pent-up energy in the Gauss rifle's capacitors, the arm blasted apart; the painful neurofeedback from the explosion ensured the pilot wouldn't get their 'Mech up anytime soon.

Skirting around the combat, a *Vindicator* 3Lr rushed the mysterious 'Mechs and fired its snub-nosed PPC into the *Rifleman*'s chest. The arcing beam sought out the already-damaged torso and stripped away the last of its armor, leaving it dangerously exposed. The *Vindicator* raised its PPC to fire again, but in a show of expert precision, the *Marauder* put its own PPC through the *Vindicator*'s faceplate and filled the cockpit with a sickening blue light. The uncontrolled 'Mech went down, and Declan could only imagine the panic the Canopians were enduring.

"Lieutenant, the academy!"

Hearing Fairchild's voice, Declan turned his focus back to the NMA compound and found that the defenders had not been idle. Whether they had known what was occurring in the clearing or not, they had moved quickly: BattleMechs covered a pair of IndustrialMechs that were securing new armor plates and moving concrete barriers to repair and reinforce the breached walls, making them stronger than before. They might be breached again, but for now the NMA had been given a breather.

The newcomer force must have realized the same thing, as they were beginning a careful retrograde back into the forest. As the *Rifleman* stepped back, Declan caught a glimpse of a path that had been purposefully cut through the trees, probably sewn with sensor-dampening blinds that had allowed the 'Mechs to sneak up on the Canopians. Whoever these people were, they had been planning this strike for some time.

Regardless, the tactical situation had changed significantly. The Canopians had only made such headway because they weren't dealing with mobile forces. Whoever these mysterious new combatants were—the tartaned BattleMechs belonged to no Highlander unit he had seen—they were clearly friends of the people in the academy, and that meant poor things for the invaders. Declan resolved to learn all he could about these newcomers once he returned to the Castle.

He watched the *Marauder* take a step backward into the trees, leaving the lighter *Warhammer* to cover its departure with a mixture of weaponry able to deal with threats at all ranges, despite the Canopians seemed none too eager to follow. Moving BattleMechs blindly through the woods against a heavier opponent that clearly knew the terrain was a recipe for defeat.

Declan had to make a decision. Whoever the older 'Mechs were, they had decided that now wasn't the time for a definitive fight, and he had to agree.

"All right, team. The Canopians are likely going to redeploy after these new developments, so let's get out of here while the getting is good." He relayed the information back to base, including the revelation of the new 'Mechs.

"You're not the first we've heard this from," Major Keddon replied. "Lady Maeve just messaged us from Fort Barrett saying a company of gray 'Mechs just tore up the attacking force. Wasn't enough to drive them back for good, but the attack has been halted for now." There was a pause, as if the major heard something outside the channel. "New orders, Lieutenant. Charlie Company is en route to relieve you. Return to the Castle as soon as they are on station."

For the briefest of moments, Declan wanted to argue, but there was little point. Charlie Company was a lighter formation that would be able to provide better cover for the NMA. His own battle lance would be of greater use against the heavier Capellan forces.

He acknowledged the order and passed it along to the rest of the lance, then they moved to new defensive positions to await Charlie Company. As he eased his 'Mech behind a tree scored by earlier fire, his eyes locked on the spot where he'd last seen the *Marauder* before it disappeared into the darkened woods.

Taking the brief moment of respite, he opened a channel to Fairchild. "Did you get a shot of that *Marauder*?"

The speed in which the picture appeared on his secondary screen told him that she recognized it too.

The Casey tartan—*his tartan*—gracing the chest of the mysterious 'Mech.

CHAPTER 11

"Three months, and we're no closer to knowing why the Northwind HPG still works when so many of its contemporaries remain down. What makes it different?"

—Senior Researcher Bianca Haller to her team,
Project Sunlight-Northwind

COMSTAR HPG COMPOUND
TARA, NORTHWIND
REPUBLIC OF THE SPHERE
23 NOVEMBER 3150

Bianca Haller stifled a sigh as she looked out over the quiet compound. Standing on the steps to a side entrance into the compound, she had taken a moment to appreciate the stillness of the evening, still wearing her work jumpsuit and wrapped up in a heavy coat. A late-night snowfall had covered everything in a crisp blanket of unbroken white perfection, and she found great comfort in the small slice of normalcy she'd managed to find for herself.

At least, for a few brief moments.

"What're you doing out here, Bianca?" a voice hissed from behind.

Turning slowly, she saw Nicole Kates, her roommate and a fellow technician, bundled up in her traditional bedwear of thermals and a heavy plaid robe. Nicole looked around furtively, as though a young student afraid of being caught after curfew.

Bianca smiled at Nicole to allay her concerns. "I just came out for a bit of fresh air, and I forgot my keycard. You're not going to get in trouble for letting me back in."

Unfortunately, Nicole was not mollified in the least by her friend's glib attitude. "You heard what the precentor said! We're supposed to stay inside the compound! Do you really want to risk catching a stray bullet?"

Bianca sighed theatrically. "We're not prisoners, Nicki, we're employees! They can set down recommendations and guidelines, but they can't just keep us here against our will!"

Well, they can, but they'd be a lot more subtle about it.

From the exasperated look on Nicole's face, she was thinking the same thing. "And why's it so important that you need to sneak out in the middle of the night? Going back into town to see your MechWarrior again?"

Bianca shrugged coyly, to make it seem like no big deal. "What would you have me do, sit in the command center and pray?"

It was exactly the wrong thing to say, and Nicole glared in betrayal. Her family, unlike Bianca's, had been with ComStar since the Third Succession War, before it had become the secularized institution it was today. Bianca knew all too well how the company was considered by outsiders in the wake of the Word of Blake Jihad; even joking of the time when ComStar was a quasi-religious order would get them both in big trouble.

Bianca put her hands up in apology. "I'm sorry. That was wrong. I'm just feeling so trapped in here. I can't stand it."

Nicole nodded, momentarily appeased. She put an arm around Bianca's smaller frame and gave her a wan smile. "I know, B. It's not easy for me either, being away from my family, but luckily it's only for a little while, and we can go home as soon as we crack the secrets of this HPG."

Bianca smiled wanly and gave a small nod. "Thanks, Nicki. It's good to know that..."

Her voice trailed off as she caught sight of a box truck driving down the snowy road as it pulled into the nearby BanMart's parking lot.

Nicole looked at the truck as well, confused. "What's wrong?"

"They restocked VitaOrange yesterday..." Bianca replied, gesturing to the truck. "Not to mention, due to the curfew, they shouldn't be letting trucks into the..." She hesitated as a pair of armed security officers moved toward the gate nearest the truck.

Pulling open the door with her free hand, Bianca pushed her roommate inside. "Nicki, we need to go..."

For a moment, Nicole hesitated at her friend's sudden change in demeanor. "B, you're scaring me..."

"Go!" Bianca yelled.

Before she could say anything else, there came a screech of tearing metal, and the back of the truck was ripped open from the inside, the walls and ceiling of the truck bursting outward. Bianca watched in horror as the inhuman face of a green-and-gold Ying Long battlesuit ripped its way out of the cargo compartment like some horrific alien creature and mowed down the two guards with a burst from the man-portable plasma rifle it carried. The flames reflected off the snow as three more armor troopers emerged from the wrecked truck. The air around them rippled and shimmered, and the quartet of creatures seemed to disappear before Bianca's eyes.

Despite not being military, she knew mimetic camouflage, and that meant they were in deadly trouble.

Nicole froze, still staring at where the armored trooper used to be, and Bianca pushed her into the hallway as she stumbled after her, reaching over to pull the alarm box on the wall. A siren wailed, and she placed her hands on either side of Nicole's face, forcing her friend to look at her. "Listen to me. Those things must be here for the compound. I need you to get back to your room and stay quiet. I don't think they want to hurt us, but I don't want you in the crossfire. Can you do that?"

Despite the abject terror in Nicole's eyes, she managed a nod, and Bianca gave her shoulder a squeeze as she directed her down the hall. Nicole made it only a few steps before breaking out into a run, nearly careening into the security officers that bolted down the hall, weapons at the ready. Bianca saw the head of security, Richard Dalton, stop for a brief moment to let Nicole through, then hurried down to where Bianca was watching through the window. As she expected, the sound of the battle armor had brought the patrolling Hastati *Firestarter* around the corner of a nearby building, the lights from the compound reflecting off the golden highlights on the 35-ton 'Mech.

The Ying Longs had made it into the courtyard, visible only by the imprints they made in the snow, and they were positioned to prevent the *Firestarter* from firing indiscriminately at them, as a stray shot might damage the HPG.

The *Firestarter* lit off a flamer instead. The gout of superheated plasma caught the rippling apparition of a camouflaged battlesuit, disrupting its mimetic camouflage as it melted and burned. The other Ying Longs, upon seeing the gruesome death of their comrade, took to the air on plumes of jump-jet exhaust to grapple onto the 'Mech, and their battle claws ripped off shards of armor.

The *Firestarter* flailed its arms, slamming one of the troopers to the ground with a hollow *thump*, but the others clung to the 'Mech's back, arm, and chest. Distracted, the MechWarrior never noticed the battlesuit that sneaked around from behind until it lit off its plasma cannon, bathing the *Firestarter* in burning plasma. With a single, well-coordinated movement, the remaining battle armor leapt off the 'Mech. The *Firestarter* raised its right arm, eager to gain a small measure of revenge, but the remaining battle armor recovered too quickly and fired off their plasma rifles, wreathing the 'Mech in flames. Bianca couldn't help but watch helplessly as the *Firestarter* became a towering inferno.

The sudden heat increase quickly overwhelmed the light 'Mech's heat sinks, causing the *Firestarter* to lock in place then to slump forward as the immense heat from the burning plasma shut down its fusion engine. As she watched, the mimetic armor of the battle armor send ripples across the snowy landscape as they circled their prey. A pair of Ying Longs leapt onto the burning *Firestarter*, heedless of the heat, and tore at the cockpit like vicious animals.

Dalton turned toward her, his expression taut. "Get back to your station. They're already inside our defensive perimeter. Try to get a message to the Hastati, let them know the compound has fallen."

Bianca looked at him incredulously for a moment, but he merely shook his head sadly in response to her unasked question.

"There's no way the Hastati will force them out in time. There's too great a chance of collateral damage." Dalton shook his head grimly. "The only thing we can do is keep our heads down and wait for the tactical situation to change."

She wanted to say something, anything to refute the point, but she knew he was right. If the Capellan forces were already within the perimeter, they would make a fight of it, and the last thing either side wanted was a night firefight in front of the compound, where an errant shot might damage the precious HPG linkages vital for interstellar communications. No, if the Hastati wanted to take back the station, they were going to have to do something other than a frontal assault.

"What are you going to do?" she asked, her glance slipping to the automatic rifle in Dalton's hands.

He gave her a grim smile. "What I was trained to do. Now, go!"

Any chance she might have had to argue with him was lost as he smashed out the window with the butt of his rifle and fired a burst from what little cover the door provided. "*GO!*"

The die being cast, she ran down the hall, staying as low as possible as she heard the security chief firing behind her, covering her escape. There was a deafening crash from behind her, but she forced her concentration on putting one foot in front of the other, running desperately for the transmissions center.

She burst through the doors, conscious of the terrified faces who began shouting questions at her. Ignoring them, she raised her voice over the din. "Activate emergency protocols! Everyone secure your stations!"

Reacting to the note of command in her voice, the ComStar technicians dashed to their consoles to lock away the most sensitive data. Reaching her own console, Bianca entered the memorized sequence of keystrokes she had been given for just such an eventuality, a grim smile of pleasure crossing her face as the secured files locked themselves in a series of hidden folders that it would take a team of specialists to find, assuming anyone even knew what to look for.

Other faces stared up at her expectantly, and she gave an approving nod. "All right, everyone, back to your quarters and follow your training. Remember, we're just low-level techs. Just do what they ask you to do, and do not resist!"

She caught a few nervous smiles, but the sound of running, metal-shod feet down the hallway caused an immediate stampede for the door. With a final appraising look around the room, Bianca slipped out, hoping she had done enough to keep the murderous Capellan forces from taking advantage of their new prize.

San-ben-bing Eric Sears pushed his way through the door into the narrow corridor, his weapon at the ready. In the hall, a security officer was gasping for breath while trying to stanch the flow of blood from his shoulder. When the man saw Sears, he instinctively reached out for his weapon, but Sears was too quick, silencing him with a burst of automatic fire.

Sears gave a nod to the two troopers who followed him, and seeing no further threats, they cleared the rest of the hallway before moving on to clear the next. His unit had been dispatched from the Maxim APC parked outside the compound gates, escorted by a squad of Fa Shih battle armor that rapidly deployed mines around the compound. As he watched, light forces from the Fourth MAC secured the nearby intersections, engaging in brief firefights with the remaining Hastati forces pulling back from the compound. Deeper into the city, small fires sent up threads of smoke, and energy weapons reflected off windows as the Hastati tried to hold on but were forced back.

Sears wished he were out there on the front lines, but he was proud to be involved in this part of the mission. The Chancellor himself had demanded the capture of the HPG compound, and Sears was the one destined to accomplish it.

Out of the corner of his eye, he saw a burst of movement down the hall, and he raised his rifle before giving a tight smile. The running figure was a young woman fleeing down the hallway. Despite her posing no threat and only trying to get away, he aimed at her, sighting down the barrel.

Sears stiffened, gasping as he felt a blade slip through the flexible joint in his body armor, sliding deeply between his ribs. An icy cold sensation spread throughout his body, and he swayed on his feet. He attempted to turn, but the knife dug deeper into his side, and his legs collapsed, unable to support his armored body any longer. He heard his rifle clatter to the floor, surrounded by ruby splatters as he tasted blood in his mouth.

A blurry outline swam before his eyes, but his vision couldn't focus.

He slid down the wall, his eyes darting around to identify his attacker, but the darkness encroaching on his vision rent his sightline into pinpricks. He tried to reach for his radio, but his bloodless fingers would not respond.

In his final moments, he wondered what he had seen...

Plaid?

CHAPTER 12

"My lady, we are reading additional BattleMech forces
approaching the compound from the south! They are firing
on the Capellan forces!"

—Captain Kyle Traeger,
Twelfth Hastati Sentinels

THE CASTLE
NORTHWIND
REPUBLIC OF THE SPHERE,
24 NOVEMBER 3150

On the main screen, standing larger than life, the gray *Marauder*
stood proudly, locked into immortality by Declan's gun-cam
footage. Without the rush of battle fueling him, Declan could
take a closer look at the mysterious 'Mech, noting the same
signs he had noticed in the field. While the *Maurader* may have
been an antique by modern standards, it had still proven to
be in fine fighting form. And aside from the expertly painted,
hauntingly familiar tartan, it remained completely free of
visible insignia, stark to the point of deliberate anonymity.

"I was hoping you might be able to provide an explanation,"
Maeve Stirling began, gesturing toward the screen. Like
Declan, the Knight had quickly identified the tartan, and he
was conscious of her intense scrutiny. She had just flown over
from Kearney to reevaluate their battle plans in the wake of the
NMA strike and the loss of Tara, and had personally requested
that he accompany her to the general's strategy meeting as her
aide, despite his rank. Around the table, the other company

and battalion commanders sat at the large circular table, awaiting the arrival of General McNamara.

Declan gave her a small shrug. "I'm sorry, my lady. It's definitely my family's tartan, but we've never painted it on our 'Mechs like that."

The general's aide nodded from his seat at the main interface console. "That's not the only curious thing, however..." With a flip of a switch, Major Keddon switched to a view of the *Rifleman,* and played the footage at half speed.

Declan watched the *Rifleman* take a glancing blow from a large laser. Keddon paused the screen and enlarged the damaged area on the screen. Painted under the gray primer, though partially flaked away from the heat, was a claymore on a red-plaid shield: the traditional emblem of the Northwind Highlanders.

Declan was not surprised. The instant he'd seen the tartan, he suspected the Highlanders had once again come back to protect their own, and he had a sneaking suspicion about knew the source.

Colonel O'Hara shook his head. "That's impossible. I know every Highlanders parade scheme by sight, and that is not one of ours."

"We can look up the other tartans from the battleROM footage," Maeve interjected, glancing over at Declan. "The Casey tartan was not the only recognizable one."

"That won't be necessary," came a familiar voice from the back of the room. General McNamara moved with purpose down the aisle, two men in tow. The first was, unsurprisingly, Declan's grandfather, and the second man was only beginning to go gray, his distinguished mustache oddly familiar. The general had changed into a fresh uniform, but the two men with him wore identical black vests with the Northwind Highlanders crest and grey camouflage pants that he recognized as standard Republic issue.

Maeve raised an eyebrow at the new arrivals. "I know Major Casey, of course," she said to the mustached man, "but I don't believe we have been introduced, sir."

"I'm afraid I am a bit before your time, Lady Maeve. Colonel Michael Griffin, at your service."

Recognition struck Declan in a flash. Griffin was older than remembered, but he had been Countess Campbell's head of intelligence during the Steel Wolf attacks.

"Ah, yes, the countess's spymaster," Maeve responded. "I thought you retired shortly after the Steel Wolves attacked Terra."

"'Retired' is a bit of a strong word," Griffin replied lightly. "I stepped down from my position as head of intelligence, but I took up a new role after the strikes on Northwind."

"And what role would that be, sir?" Colonel O'Hara asked, his voice painfully respectful.

Griffin gestured toward the 'Mechs up on the screen.

"I am the commander of the Northwind Highlanders' Grey Watch regiment."

"Forgive me, Colonel," said Silas O'Malley, one of the company commanders, "but I have never heard of the Grey Watch before."

"An impression we've gone to great lengths to cultivate, Captain," Griffin said respectfully. "In fact, it's a relatively new regiment, officially formed after the first Steel Wolf attack on Northwind."

Maeve's dubious expression matched Declan's thoughts on the matter. "Is that so? Was the Exarch aware of this unit's formation?"

"Far be it from me to guess what the Exarch might or might not know, ma'am," Griffin replied. "As to our origins, that would require a bit of explanation, but for now, suffice it to say we are here and ready to do our part to protect our home."

For his own part, Declan was astounded that Maeve managed to keep her temper so far. Turning to the general, pointedly avoiding Griffin. "And when were you going to inform me of another armed force on the planet I've been entrusted to protect, General?" She smiled thinly at McNamara. "I'm assuming you knew, at the very least?"

While Griffin remained respectful, he was also not cowed by the woman's ire in the least. "You would've been informed when the time was right, my lady...which is why we are here now."

Declan glanced over at his grandfather at Griffin's us of *we*, but Seamus was focused on the Grey Watch 'Mechs still on the screen. He quickly turned his attention back to the byplay between the two commanders.

"You didn't think including your unit in my deployments would've helped with planning strategy?"

General McNamara stepped in between the two commanders, his voice carefully neutral. "Colonel, my lady, there will be more than enough time for recriminations later. While I understand tensions are particularly high at the moment, perhaps we can get back to the matter at hand?"

Maeve looked like she wanted to take issue with that, but gave a small nod of acceptance. "Please, Colonel...continue."

Griffin bowed his head slightly. "I do apologize, but the secrecy was necessary. A major part of our effectiveness was that no one knew we existed, and there have been security concerns to be addressed before we could come out into the open. In fact, if not for the dire situation that we found ourselves in, I likely wouldn't have revealed the unit as quickly as we did."

"Well, I appreciate that you were here," the general replied, gesturing to the screen. "It certainly helped at the NMA."

"And at Fort Barrett," Maeve replied grudgingly.

The colonel bowed his head in acknowledgement. "It was our duty. However, a lot of our 'Mechs are older, using Succession War technology, and we haven't had the chance to upgrade most of them."

Declan immediately saw what Griffin was trying to say. While the Canopians were still slowly reaching regular CCAF standards and Laurel's Legion was rebuilding, both regiments would still field far more advanced equipment than the Grey Watch. Compared to cutting edge forces like Warrior House Imarra and the Fourth MAC? The technology gulf would be a chasm.

Yet apparently not insurmountable.

"While our equipment may not be cutting edge, however, you will find that everyone on our roster is an experienced warrior, some of whom have literally been piloting their 'Mech for decades." Griffin gestured proudly to the screen. "As you've seen, we still have a lot of fight left in us."

The Knight gave a small, careful nod and looked up at the elder man. "From your participation today, am I to believe that you'll be placing your unit under our command?"

Once again, the tension in the room was palpable, but clearly General McNamara was ready for this exact question. "As a point of fact, in the absence of Countess Campbell and the legate, I have taken it on myself to purchase the services of the Grey Watch on behalf of the Republic. While they technically serve Northwind, they are more than willing to work in a joint-command structure with you, as if the RAF had hired them on contract."

Declan nodded, impressed with the elegant solution. While Lady Maeve's demeanor showed her displeasure at leaving this new regiment in the hands of someone who had deceived her, she wasn't going to look a gift horse in the mouth. Declan glanced over at her, wondering if she had also noted how McNamara hadn't said exactly *when* he had hired the unit...or known about their existence.

Everyone watched the Republic Knight square off against the elder Grey Watch commander. After several interminable moments, she gave a small nod and reached out her hand, which Griffin took warmly. "Welcome to the fight, Colonel. It is always a pleasure to fight beside the Northwind Highlanders."

Around the room, fists pounded silently on tables and consoles, a solemn but respectful recognition of her response. After a few moments, the room stilled in quiet relief, and the general gave a small nod of thanks.

"Well, with that out of the way...perhaps we can move on to tactical planning?"

They all sat back at the table, and Keddon brought up the first display.

Declan had purposefully avoided looking at his grandfather for most of the meeting. He already had enough to do without wondering about his grandfather's role in the whole affair. After the meeting ended, Declan moved over to Maeve, who stood between him and Colonel Griffin.

"Colonel," Maeve said, "have you met Lieutenant Casey?"

"Indeed." Griffin proffered his hand with a grin, providing a deceptively strong grip. "Congratulations on your work out there today, son. From your grandfather's stories, I've always expected great things from you."

Declan nodded at the casual mention of Seamus, and he applauded the spymaster for making him glance in his grandfather's direction. "I didn't know the two of you were still acquainted, sir."

"Seamus and I happen to go way back," the colonel replied noncommittally. "Most recently he's been occasionally assisting me with some organizational items."

"Is that so?" Declan said carefully. "He's always been more of a frontline man, especially when he was in his 'Mech... a *Marauder*, as I seem to remember."

Seamus nodded. "My first 'Mech, from the bad old days."

Declan nodded, but he didn't get the chance to say anything more before a voice came from behind them.

"I am still waiting for that explanation, Colonel," Silas O'Malley said. To his credit, he remained stock still, formally perfect in every way, except for the strained tension in his voice.

Griffin glanced at him, his voice carefully neutral. "An explanation, Captain?"

"Yes, sir. You mentioned earlier that the Grey Watch's origins required a bit of explanation. I would very much like to hear it."

Declan was impressed with the veneer of calm Griffin maintained. "It sounds like you have a different question to ask, Lieutenant. Why don't you put it out there where we can face it like warriors?"

"Where were you?" Silas asked simply, his eyes bearing the unspoken accusation. "You said the Grey Watch was formed after the first Steel Wolf attack on Northwind, yet I've heard nothing about your unit until today. When the Steel Wolves attacked our planet a second time, far too many good warriors died defending us, and continued to do so when Countess Campbell took the rest of the Highlanders to Terra. So, once again, Colonel, I will respectfully ask you: While our people were fighting and dying for our homeworld, where were you?"

For a long moment the question hung in the air, and Griffin remained silent, ensuring everyone had a chance to hear it before responding.

"I'm afraid I cannot give you a satisfactory answer, Captain, at least to the first part of your question. Luckily, the second is far easier. The reason why we aren't on Terra is because Countess Campbell wanted us here, to protect Northwind. You will never know how she agonized about her decision to support the Republic by returning to Terra. She is as loyal to Northwind as any of us, perhaps more so with the weight of responsibility she carries for her troops, but she did not want to risk letting the homeworld be attacked while she was away. As such, she did the best she could, and we are the result. I wish that we were in place to assist during the earlier attacks as well, but we're here now." He took a step forward, his eyes burning like hot coals. "As for me, personally? I was on that line with those who fought and died, so I understand your frustration."

Declan swore under his breath as he made another connection, but had to put that aside to concentrate on the colonel's words.

Griffin's passionate response had at least dulled the edges of Silas's anger, but his voice was still sullen. "Why do I get the feeling that we're not getting the whole story, Colonel?"

"Because you aren't, *Captain*," Griffin replied, stressing Silas's rank and allowing some of his own frustration to show through. "I've told you what you need to know, which is exactly what I'd tell any of my own troops."

Silas looked like he wanted to say more in response, but Declan placed a careful hand on his shoulder. He had let this play out this long because he had the same questions as every other member with the Highlander blood in the unit, but he also wasn't going to let this devolve into a brawl. "Captain, may I speak with you outside, privately?"

For a moment, it looked like Silas was going to turn on him, but something in Declan's tautly reasonable tone must have cut through the haze.

Silas's mouth opened to reply, but then he merely gave a nod before turning back to the others. "Thank you, Colonel. If you'll pardon me?"

Griffin nodded, and they gave Silas a moment to leave the area.

Declan was the first one to break the silence. "You handled that well, Colonel."

Griffin looked suddenly tired, despite himself. "I only wish I had better answers to give him. One of the reasons I joined intelligence in the first place was because I hated going out with no idea what was going on." He chuckled. "Unfortunately, all that's gotten me is to where I'm the one who has to tell the troops only what is need-to-know."

"I can certainly understand that feeling, sir. Being out of the loop can be difficult under the best of circumstances."

Despite not looking at Maeve, Declan could feel the icy focus she directed at him.

The colonel straightened, raising in his chin thoughtfully as he locked eyes with Declan. "It sounds like you have your own questions, Lieutenant."

"Not as many as you might think, sir," Declan replied with strict formality. His eyes flickered to the Knight for a moment. "At least, not necessarily for you. I'm just looking for some confirmation on some things I've already suspected."

Griffin gestured with his hand to continue. "I'd be happy to help, if I can."

Declan smiled thinly, and turned to Maeve. "You sure you want to hear all of this again? After all, I'm sure you already know the story."

If the room had been cold before, it became positively icy when Maeve replied. "What exactly are you saying, Lieutenant?"

He didn't flinch away from her stare. "I am saying, ma'am, that despite the admirable performance before, I believe you've known about the Grey Watch from the beginning."

Griffin turned carefully to the Republic Knight, his eyes narrowing. "That's quite the accusation, Lieutenant."

"Not an accusation," Declan said, "just an observation. I noticed how careful you were to intimate that the Grey Watch was formed following the first Steel Wolf attack, but I found that a little strange. Countess Campbell requisitioned all the equipment she could get her hands on following Gray Monday, and I doubt she would've left all this equipment here if she'd known about it. My guess is that all of the Grey Watch's equipment was squared away much earlier, probably before the Republic's inspectors ever came to Northwind." He glanced over at Maeve. "As you said, that was before our time, so it makes me wonder who would've had the access and the ability to make sure things went smoothly. Perhaps a newly minted Paladin of the Republic?"

Declan nodded, not needing to explain the rest. It was well known that many private 'Mech owners on Northwind had hidden equipment away before the Republic inspectors came through, conveniently losing paperwork so their equipment could not be seized by the buyback program. While the practice was not nearly as widespread as some imagined, it was still fairly prevalent, and on a planet that relied on a 'Mech-based economy, many families were willing to cover for others. The Republic inspectors, finding fewer BattleMechs than expected, had come in force to check the city, so all the equipment would have been moved out into the highlands. Although the inspectors had tried to check the highlands as well, it was difficult for them to find anything to confiscate when the whole populace of Northwind had a vested interest in keeping these 'Mechs hidden and safe.

It took a moment, but colonel gave a wry nod of understanding. "It was before my time, so I never really thought about it." He looked over at the Knight. "Your mother?"

Maeve smiled, not bothering to deny it. "Once a Highlander, always a Highlander. My mother and I both believed that a strong Northwind is in the best interest of the Republic."

Griffin nodded in understanding. "If you knew of our existence, why didn't you try to find us?"

Maeve gave Declan a wry glance. "Care to venture a guess?"

"For the same reason we are all tiptoeing around the situation: one of the threats the Grey Watch was created to defend against was the Republic," Declan replied. "She knew there were additional resources on Northwind, but she also had the same question that Silas did regarding your motivations. If the 'Mechs still existed, why had they not participated in defending against the Steel Wolf strikes?"

"I assume you know the answer to that as well," Maeve said, a teasing note in her voice that Declan chose to ignore.

"My guess is they never got the chance. Colonel, you said you took command of the Grey Watch after the passing of their previous commander. Should I assume that was Colonel Borden of the NMA?"

Griffin nodded, giving a grim smile. "The commandant originally let the Countess know of the Grey Watch's existence. During the first attack on Northwind, several 'found' 'Mechs made their way into the battle, although most of them were too far from the capital to do any good. Most of our units are broken down into lance-sized groups, run by a cell system. That way, if any portion of the cell was compromised, the regiment as a whole would remain viable."

"A wise decision, considering what happened later," Declan said. He took some small joy in seeing the shot hit home with a thinning of the Knight's lips. "That's why the Grey Watch didn't get into the fight for the second attack, wasn't it? The commandant died before he could rally the unit."

"Exactly," Griffin replied. "The Grey Watch was already on the march when the second attack began, and we were moving into position to take the Steel Wolves out once and for all. Unfortunately, on the night Colonel Borden was killed, no one was in place to transmit new orders to the regiment. In the absence of orders, each lance fell into defensive positions, protecting their assigned areas. The Steel Wolves were not here to stay that time, however, and by the time the Grey Watch received new orders, the threat had passed."

The colonel momentarily looked his age, the dark circles around his eyes more pronounced. "I wasn't lying about how the countess agonized over the choice to follow after the Wolves. She wanted to protect the Republic and honor the sacrifices of those who had died on Northwind, but she wasn't willing to leave the planet undefended. That night, one of the Grey Watch officers came forward and explained the situation. It wound up being exactly what was needed at the time: the countess could leave a devoted force at her back to defend Northwind, and she could still fulfill her own pact with the Republic. Honestly, I don't think I'd seen her happier since..." His voice trailed off, and he quickly changed the subject. "While she wasn't sure how well they would fight, she was confident they could hold off any threat long enough for her to return to the planet."

Declan was going to comment about the potential leak of information and the death of NMA Commandant Borden, but something in her expression made him hesitate. *Is there still something else she's not telling me?* They locked eyes for a moment, and he resolved to follow up with her when they were alone.

"And when did you take over the unit?" Maeve asked.

"When the battle on Terra was over. I initially returned to Northwind to act as a liaison with the Grey Watch and just sort of fell into the position. The countess began rotating regular forces to watch the planet, but with the Fortress in place, it seemed best to keep us as an ace up her sleeve."

Declan gave another nod, confident he'd gotten all he could out of the colonel. "Well, I am happy you're here, sir. As Lady Maeve said, it is always an honor to fight alongside the Highlanders."

"And vice versa, Lieutenant," Griffin replied, offering his hand. "Now let's make sure the Capellans know they've been in a fight."

CHAPTER 13

"Besides the battle itself, there is nothing so terrible as waiting."

—Major Seamus Casey

THE CASTLE
NORTHWIND
REPUBLIC OF THE SPHERE
24 NOVEMBER 3150

Stepping back out into the brisk winter air, Declan was not surprised to find his grandfather speaking softly with Silas O'Malley at the foot of the now-familiar *Marauder*. While he was too far away to hear what was being said, he did see Seamus put his hands on the larger man's arms and Silas bowing his head respectfully, almost as if in prayer. Knowing full well the effect that his grandfather had on younger warriors, Declan let the two men have their moment, waiting until Seamus had sent Silas off with a comradely slap on the back before approaching. Measuring his steps to let Silas get out of earshot first, he stepped up beside his grandfather and watched Silas walk away. "Is he going to be all right?"

Seamus nodded, not bothering to look over at Declan. "He'll be fine. It's just the usual mix of uncertainty over what's going to happen, and still being angry at not getting a chance to do more the last time Northwind was attacked. I reminded him that he's here now though, and the threat is even greater than when the bloody Wolves were at our door." He took a deep breath, holding the bitter cold air in his lungs for a moment. "He's got his head on straight now, and he'll give it his all."

"Are we still talking about Silas?" Declan asked, glancing at Seamus accusingly.

To his complete lack of surprise, Seamus met his eyes levelly. "If it's an apology you're wanting, lad, you have quite a wait ahead of you. The colonel explained it best. The fewer who knew about us, the better."

"And you couldn't trust me?" Declan retorted, betraying a measure of his anger. "Your own blood?"

For a moment, Seamus remained silent. When he spoke again, his voice held the familiar softness it had when young Declan had skinned his knee, or when he had fallen out of one of the immense trees in their backyard. "I dinnae tell you *because* you're my own blood...and you swore an oath of service to the Republic. I dinnae want to force you to make a choice between your oath and your family."

Declan gave a small nod, glancing up at the *Marauder*, conscious of the tightness in his chest. His grandfather was right, of course. As a member of the Republic Armed Forces, it would have been his duty to report the existence of additional military forces that could combat the Capellan threat, but it would've been at the cost of betraying his family, and the Northwind Highlanders.

"It's funny..." Declan kept his voice level, his eyes locked on the BattleMech before him. "I must have seen this 'Mech a hundred times, but when I saw the old girl out at the academy, I had no idea it was you. I thought you had her upgraded?"

Seamus nodded proudly. "I did. Damn, I couldn't wait to get the new ER PPCs into her when they first came in. But when we expanded the unit, we found ourselves with a mixed bag of tech. A lot of the newer 'Mechs aren't as robust as these old warhorses, and a lot of them aren't compatible with the newer tech. I still had the old Hellstars on hand, so I gave the new stuff to folks who needed it, and I put the old girl back into classic configuration." Seamus gave a thin smile. "It's also the same reason I haven't traded up for something bigger. I know how to fight with her, and how to win. No one knows the old girl better than I do."

Remembering how his grandfather had taken out the charging *Vindicator*, Declan couldn't argue the point. "I know that. I just don't understand why you think you need to be on the front lines for this battle. You just told me your 'Mech is running old tech, and I'm going to bet the others are in roughly the same condition. You can still help, you just don't need to be at the tip of the spear anymore. That's for those of us whose tech can keep up with the Capellans' equipment."

Seamus smiled sadly. "It's not about the equipment, lad, it's the people. I've always taught you that. You saw the battle at the academy. It's not about all the fancy targeting computers in the world, it's about experienced MechWarriors who know their equipment and know how to fight. Some of you youngsters think we're relics of a bygone age, but I remember the battles and the people who used this tech all too well. A *Marauder* like mine was on Mallory's World, the defense of New Avalon, probably pounding up the steps behind the Star League forces ready to kick down the doors to Stefan Amaris's throne room. Hell, even the Bounty Hunter used one for a while."

"Pops..." Declan began, but Seamus cut him off, his voice no longer as friendly and laid back as usual.

"I know what you're going to say, Dec. And I'm going to be honest, I would say the exact same thing if I heard this from my own grandfather. It goes beyond all the logical rationalizations in the world. What it comes down to, lad, is that I am not going to sit on the sidelines while another damned invader tries to take this planet. I will not dishonor my family, my home, or the legacy of the Northwind Highlanders by sitting back while others fight for me.

"And if you think that I'm going to let you take the lead without me at your back, Declan Casey, you're a damned fool." His eyes were piercing, and his words hit like a rotary autocannon on full automatic. "And while I may have raised a stubborn mule, a mouthy child, and a damn fair warrior... I dinnae raise no fool."

Declan, for the first time in recent memory, was at a loss for words. He merely nodded, and his grandfather put a paternal hand on his shoulder, before turning back to his 'Mech.

It took every bit of strength Declan had to turn around and walk back toward his own lance on the far side of the tarmac, and he was not surprised when another member of the Grey Watch stepped up to him. His concerns momentarily abated, he threw an arm around the newcomer warmly. "Uncle Tommy!"

"Decky-Boy!" Tommy Finnegan hollered, and wrapped his muscular arms around him in a comradely hug. He was also in warriors togs, but these were the tan of the Highlanders. "Yer granddad dinnae tell us you'd be joining us on the grand adventure today!"

"I don't think he knew," Declan said.

Tommy gave a slight frown under his bushy mustache as he tried to analyze his nephew's face. "You're not angry at us, are you, lad?"

"Not angry..." Declan began. "In your shoes, I'd probably do the same thing. I'm just..." He looked squarely at the shorter man. "You fought your battles, Uncle. The only reason I'm here, why any of us are here, is what you accomplished. You held Northwind for us in trust, and it just..."

"It cuts against the grain to see us having to take up the mantle again," his uncle replied, getting a small nod out of him. "You'd rather we carry ammunition to the front in his jeep?"

Declan looked at him curiously, and Tommy laughed. "You do know that was what he did the second time the Steel Wolves attacked, don't you?"

"I thought he would've been in his 'Mech..."

Tommy laughed, a hearty guffaw. "Trust me, so did he! As it happens, however, he was here for your nephew's birthday, and by the time we heard about the fighting we were too far away to get back.

"But your grandpappy doesn't know how to do much more than love his family, tell stories, and fight, and the damn fool isn't going to be happy unless he does them in that order. When your brother was out on the front lines, and Seamus wasn't close enough to get to his 'Mech, he grabbed me and we were running ammo to the damn ground pounders." He laughed. "You should have seen it: the two of us, with a trunk full of ammunition, slaloming through the mountains to try to get to the infantry. I don't think I've heard him swear so much in his entire life. But when your brother went down..." Tommy's words trailed off, and he just shook his head. Glancing back up, he saw Seamus watching, and gave him a knowing nod. "Well, I better get back to my checklist. The boss is quite the taskmaster." He looked squarely at Declan with a wry smile. "Shoot straight and keep your head down, kid."

"You too, Uncle," Declan replied, and moved back toward his lance, feeling better for the exchange. He hadn't known that about his grandfather, and he wondered what else he didn't know about the man. He'd always been a doting grandparent, and no one had been prouder than Seamus when Declan graduated from the NMA. He had always related to him as a grandparent, and not as much as a fellow MechWarrior.

Turning, Declan found Fairchild, Oedhe, and Taggart, each standing respectfully out of earshot. They waited for him among a cluster of other MechWarriors, watching the preparations with the Grey Watch 'Mechs, but Taggart's furtive glances in his grandfather's direction belied their seemingly casual demeanor. He'd heard from her instructors that she'd been Highlander-mad since entering the academy, and this was her first chance to fight with them.

Fairchild stepped up to him, and he gave the tall sergeant a nod of thanks for the private moment with his grandfather. Once again, the tall, powerfully built woman was perfectly in control of her surroundings; her relief at hearing that her husband had survived the battle at the NMA did wonders to bring her back to her normal self. From the reports Declan had heard during his return to the Castle, the Canopian forces had pulled back from the academy and maintained their cordon around the campus but remained on the prowl for additional surprise strikes from the forest.

"We just heard about the Grey Watch," Fairchild stated drolly. "That must've been quite the surprise."

"For all of us," Declan said, putting the question to rest without having to voice it. While not everyone would believe he hadn't known anything about the Grey Watch, especially with his grandfather's clear involvement, they would either believe him or they wouldn't. He glanced over at Taggart, who was bombarding Oedhe with observations about the Grey Watch BattleMechs that loomed above them. Oedhe, having met many of the assembled warriors during his own training at the academy, merely smiled down at her. "How are they doing?"

"Oedhe took the news pretty well. Give it a couple of weeks, and he'll be telling everyone that he knew the whole time. Ellie...well, you can see. I don't think she's ever been so happy."

Declan smiled despite himself as he watched the young MechWarrior push a lock of red hair over one ear while she continued talking Oedhe's ear off, and he turned back to

Fairchild. Unlike the Taggart, Fairchild had her hair shorn tight to the scalp, setting off her ebony skin and piercing brown eyes. He caught her looking at him with a thin smile, and she answered his next question before he could ask it. "Don't worry, sir. They'll be ready when the time comes."

Declan was about to thank her when he overheard a raised voice from nearby, one of Silas's MechWarriors: "Great, just want we need. Geriatrics in broken-down 'Mechs."

His ire started to rise, but he clamped it down with iron control. "Is there a problem, MechWarrior?" To his credit, the sergeant didn't shrink away from Declan's challenge, although he did glance at his rank insignia. Catching the glance, Declan shook his head. "Ignore the rank for a moment. You're entitled to your opinion, so let's hear it."

Several people nearby turned to listen, and he knew that still more were pretending not to. Ignoring them all, he faced the sergeant square on. It took him a moment, but he finally recognized the MechWarrior: Daniel Kerry.

Kerry raised his chin slightly. "No offense to your grandfather, sir, but all of these warriors...they've been off the battlefield for decades, running equipment that was ancient during the Succession Wars. I'm glad they want to fight, but what do they really think they're going to accomplish here?" He shook his head. "They're out of their league, and we have enough to worry about without having to babysit them."

Declan made a show of giving a considerate nod. "I can see what you're saying, Sergeant..."

"Yer a damned fool, Daniel Kerry!"

Taggart forced Declan a step back as she pushed past him and locked in on the larger man. "Fine words, especially from someone whose diapers these warriors probably literally changed at one time or another." She looked angry enough to spit on the tarmac, and if anyone was bemused by the sight of the slight young woman taking on a larger man, they wisely kept their opinions to themselves. "You might look around and see warriors who've been out of the game for a while, but I'll tell you what I see." She pointed over at the man speaking to Seamus. "You know Declan's granddad, and many of you trained with him. But the man across from him is Tommy Finnegan, who fought with Jaffray on Wildcat, going toe-to-toe with Clanners using that *Rifleman* over there, and he came back to tell the tale." She continued pointing at the other Grey

Watch MechWarriors within view. "Evelyn Kaemil led a lance that was ambushed on a routine patrol. She took down two assault 'Mechs by herself and got her recon team to safety with no losses. Thomas Olsen is nearly a hundred years old, and his *Commando* is even older, but he can still make it dance. Pally O'Brien, he gets a personalized message from Wolf's Dragoons every year on his birthday, asking him to join them after a joint op three decades ago. Jaime Wolf may be long gone, but he still gets the invite every year."

She took a deep breath, completely unaware that she had the attention of everyone around her. "These people aren't just your friends or family. These are some of the most elite mercenaries the Inner Sphere has ever seen. They fought off the Capellans, the FedSuns, the Clans, and everyone else who sought to subdue them. Many of them trained you, but don't you dare forget what they did to earn that right. These are the Highlanders who saw the Clans firsthand, who fought their way through hell and back and never failed in their duty. What you forget is it's not their duty to protect you. It is *yours* to uphold the legacy they have worked so hard to maintain for you. Call them grognards, call them rooted in the past. That's your prerogative. But you also can't argue that they were the best at what they did, and they've earned their stripes. Have you?"

She waited for an answer, but Kerry saw the tide of public opinion shifting against him, causing him to stay silent.

"So if you don't want to fight with them at your back, that's on you." Her eyes belied her words, piercing Kerry like twin daggers. "However, I'd damn sooner have *them* covering my ass than *you*."

The crowd laughed, and from her self-conscious expression she realized what she had said and how many people had been listening. She straightened her shoulders, giving the larger MechWarrior a final glare, and then turned sharply on her heel as she strode toward her own 'Mech.

Declan stopped her with a glance as she reached him, and he could feel her vibrating with anger and embarrassment for her outburst. She looked up at him squarely, expecting a rebuke, but he surprised her with a tight smile and a respectful nod. She smiled proudly, and then continued on her way, taking Fairchild and Oedhe in her wake like an honor guard, both men bemused by the entire scene.

Declan watched them head to the staging area, then turned back to the gathered Grey Watch warriors hard at work on their own preparations, seeing them as if for the first time. The young woman, Highlander-mad as she was, had seen what he hadn't: these warriors had been the top of their field for longer than Declan had been alive. Yes, they might be running equipment older than they were, but they had also outlived scores of their contemporaries, fighting against threats just as bad, if not worse, than what they faced now.

For a moment, he caught his grandfather's eye. He gave the elder man a respectful nod, and Seamus smiled, flashing him a quick fist of acknowledgment, a silent message of support.

Declan gave a wan smile and a raised fist of his own, then followed the rest of his lance, feeling better despite himself.

They might die today, but they won't die alone.

CHAPTER 14

"We can now officially state that the HPG on Northwind is no longer responding to messages from Terra, although ComStar still registers the maintenance signal confirming that the station is operational. While it does not appear to be the same issue as the one that affected the entire HPG network on Gray Monday, what this means for the status of the planet is unknown."

—Ann Helzer, *Voice of the Galaxy*
(independent broadcast, Terra affiliate)

COMSTAR HPG COMPOUND
TARA, NORTHWIND
REPUBLIC OF THE SPHERE
26 NOVEMBER 3150

Having parked her *Pillager* outside of the main HPG center, Lindsey Baxter opted to trade her BattleMech cockpit for the comparative warmth of the ComStar compound. She hustled down the rungs of the egress ladder as quickly as she could manage without slipping. Like most MechWarriors, she wore little in the blast furnace that was her cockpit, but things were very different when exposed to the relentless chill of a Northwind winter.

A young *sao-wei* met her at the foot of her 'Mech, and she gratefully accepted the heavy Fourth MAC jacket he offered as she quickstepped toward the entrance to the ComStar facility. Taking the shallow steps two at a time, she let her gaze roam upward, to the immense receiving dish that dwarfed even her 100-ton BattleMech. "The compound is secure?"

"Yes, *Sang-shao*," the young officer replied. "Per your orders, we've had our infantry clear the compound, and no threats were found. The ComStar employees put up no resistance, and they are responding to our orders. We also have made contact with the *gao-shiao-zhang* on Kearney, and he asked to have you contact him on your arrival."

He opened the door for her, and Lindsey gave him a nod of thanks, stifling a sigh of relief as she moved out of the wind.

"Thank you." She continued farther into the compound without bothering to let the officer show her the way. All ComStar buildings had a familiar layout, which meant she already knew how to reach her destination.

At the command center, Lindsey gave a small nod to the *sao-wei*, who instructed one of the nervous ComStar acolytes to pull up a direct channel to Grand Master Hui at Fort Barrett. Within moments, the *gao-shiao-zhang* appeared larger than life on the primary screen dominating the far wall.

Lindsey gave the image a respectful bow. "Congratulations on your victory at Fort Barrett, *Gao-shiao-zhang*."

The Grand Master bowed his head, quickly deflecting her praise. "My efforts are minor compared to your own, *Sang-shao*. Despite the interference of new elements..." He was referring to the mysterious gray 'Mechs that intelligence efforts had identified as the 'Grey Watch,' a previously unknown Northwind Highlanders unit. "You have already secured our primary objective. The Chancellor will be quite pleased."

She bowed her head respectfully, but not fast enough to hide her small flush of pride. The night raid had been a risk, but Baxter considered herself a talented poker player. By making the major push in the city center at night, she had forced General McNamara to make a choice: attempt a fight in the heart of the city in the darkness, or cede the HPG in the hopes of reclaiming it later. As expected, the chance to keep collateral damage to a minimum had been foremost on the general's mind, and that had allowed Lindsey to seize her prize.

"How go your preparations to take the Castle?" Hui asked.

Built from local stone, the immense fortification sat atop a massive hill high enough to provide overwatch for the entire region. From within its thick walls, rows of parapets, each reinforced to support BattleMechs, provided a powerful redoubt against the most determined attackers. The remaining Hastati forces were using the ancient, stately edifice as a staging area, and Lindsey had no doubt it was their last major bastion on the planet. Originally she had planned to strike there before taking the HPG, but the opportunity to secure the lightly defended ComStar compound had been too tempting to ignore.

"With the compound secure, I have my battle armor loading up for transfer to our staging area west of the city. My main battle elements have already mustered there in preparation for the strike on the Castle itself, and they are ready to move on my command. Colonel Tompkins-Centrella is shifting some of her forces to take over the defense of the HPG center, and I anticipate being able to strike within the next twenty-four hours."

"Excellent," the *gao-shiao-zhang* replied in support of the wisdom in her plan. By placing her troops between the two major targets, Tara and the Castle, she forced any Highlander reinforcements to run a gauntlet of her own making in order to reach the HPG compound. With the NMA still encircled by the Canopians and no reinforcements coming from Fort Barrett, Task Force Clarity's eventual victory was assured.

"I support your choices, *Sang-shao*," Hui continued, but his voice held a note of concern. "However, due to our success at Fort Barrett, I am planning to garrison Laurel's Legion at the fort while I bring House Imarra to New Lanark."

She smiled to cover her sudden unease. It was only natural for the *gao-shiao-zhang* to want to take part in the destruction of the famed Twelfth Hastati, but she remained fully confident she could take the Castle without his implied assistance. *Not to mention,* she thought, *if I hold the attack until the Imarra forces arrive, the gao-shiao-zhang himself will be the senior commander on the battlefield, not me.*

The Grand Master caught the flicker of concern on her face. "You are currently the commander on the ground, however. If you feel able to take the Castle before I arrive, I support your decision." He looked at her seriously. "I only ask that you do not move in haste. Remember, the only thing that truly matters is our eventual victory for the glory of the Confederation."

"Of course, sir," she replied automatically, despite not truly agreeing. While she both understood the tactical considerations of waiting for reinforcements and respected the honor he was trying to show her, he was wrong about it being the only thing that mattered. A greater personal imperative could not be denied: her victory here would clear the stain of defeat they had suffered on New Canton. While the capture of Tara had gone a long way toward rectifying past failures, she was knew that crushing the Republic forces at the Castle would forever overshadow the memories of her former commander's death."

Taking the opportunity, she gave another deep bow, holding it out of respect. "Thank you for your counsel, *Gaoshiao-zhang*."

He smiled benevolently. "May the Chancellor's wisdom be with you, *Sang-shao*."

The signal cut out, and Baxter turned to the others in the mobile command center. "Get the *sao-shao* on the line. I have new orders for him."

Lindsey's *Pillager* rushed forward with loping strides to find the battle for the Castle had already been joined.

Conscious of House Imarra's impending arrival, she had ordered Second Battalion to besiege the Republic compound early, preceding the main attack with artillery and long-range sniper fire as she brought First Battalion from Tara. As requested, Colonel Tompkins-Centrella had sent two of her Lancers battalions to take over security for Tara and the HPG compound while her remaining battalion maintained overwatch of the blockade around the NMA. The lighter, more maneuverable Canopian 'Mechs would be especially effective in an urban combat environment, while the siege of the Castle would require the Fourth's heavier elements.

First Battalion had hit some initial resistance as they left the city, engaging Republic pickets that had been left to slow them down in just such a situation, but she turned the tables on the enemy by taking several pages from their own playbook. By hugging tight to the buildings on the outskirts of the city, her forces made the Republic troops hesitate to return fire, and she ordered the use of only energy weapons for this phase of the attack to husband their munitions for when the battle was truly joined. Despite the restrictions she imposed on her people, their sheer numbers allowed them to break through the pickets, leaving them for the Canopians to mop up while she pressed forward at the best speed her battalion could muster.

Despite the distance, the light show between the fort and the attacking Second Battalion 'Mechs was visible to all as she approached, which provided a hypnotic vision to focus her mind on the battle to come.

Having achieved all of her objectives so far save one, she looked forward to neutralizing the remaining defending forces on-planet to prevent a guerrilla campaign, providing communications support for the Confederation's eventual assault on Terra, and finally closing the book on the conquest of Northwind.

Her battle plan was straightforward, to avoid the dangers of over-complication. Second Battalion, split between a long-distance firing line and a diversionary strike at the western wall, had so far kept the Republic forces focused on themselves. Once First Battalion finally arrived, Lindsey's troops would strike the Castle from three different directions, providing a wealth of threats and using their mobility to break the Republic lines. With the Castle invested, she would spread the defenders as thinly as possible to force an opening in their defense.

She was confident that when they did force a breach, her battle armor and scout lances would be ready to take advantage. *Sang-shao* Qiao had proven especially helpful in that regard: while she had claimed her outdated knowledge of the Highlanders was of no help, her historic knowledge of their fortifications, like the Castle, had proven invaluable. Lindsey had provided maps of hidden egress points to each lance commander, and several companies were positioned specifically to counter any breakout from the Castle's network of tunnels.

Should the House Imarra forces arrive in time, they would hammer the final nail in the Twelfth's coffin, providing the extra throw weight required to guarantee the destruction of the Republic fortress.

Throttling her *Pillager* back to a walk, she led her forces into extreme range of the Castle at the head of her heavy battle line. At her side, the rest of the Fourth MAC followed suit, eager as she was to end this conflict once and for all.

This close, what had been an artistic light show from a distance took on the gritty reality of true warfare. At her feet, a broken *Yao Lien* from Second Battalion burned, and she stepped around it, keeping the warning of the downed 'Mech foremost in her mind.

As she listened, her commanders brought their forces into the shifting strike lines they had so dutifully practiced, with heavier units to the front behind a column of her fastest armor. An old Steiner formation practice that they had adapted, the heavily armored assault 'Mechs would provide tempting targets as a mobile skirmish line, pressing the attack as the lighter units used them for cover to get close enough to swarm the enemy with raw numbers. The majority of Second Battalion continued to provide covering fire, eager to have their own revenge on the defenders that had brought down their comrades.

Lindsey gave one final approving glance at her formation before opening the command channel and sounding the call to battle: "First Battalion...*forward to victory!*"

At her command, the armored column bolted forward, following meticulously practiced serpentine paths that looked erratic but made them difficult to hit while supporting their lancemates. It was largely effective, but a lucky shot from an autocannon struck a Fox armored car broadside, tearing a large rent into the maneuvering skirt and sending it into a flat spin that ended with a fiery detonation against the bole of a large oak.

Fortunately, the second phase of the attack was already in the offering. Her heavy battle line was already in motion, with heavy and assault 'Mechs laying down a withering curtain of fire as they pressed forward in an unstoppable wave. As she watched, an *Awesome*, resplendent in the green-and-ivory livery of the Fourth MAC, fired three of its PPCs at the Castle defenders, daring them to face its firepower. While most of the shots missed and spent themselves harmlessly against the Castle's thick, reinforced walls, e shot struck true. A *Malice* reeled off the line, one of its four LB-X autocannons sheared off by the lucky hit.

"Maintain fire!" she ordered. "Sharpshooters, take advantage where you can!"

The *Awesome* pushed forward to take advantage of her command, and a *Stalker II* stepped into its place, the 85-ton 'Mech's extended long-range missiles leaping out from its shoulder-mounted launchers on wings of flame.

With limited immediate threats to their position, her BattleMech forces barraged the entrenched Republic forces. Extended-range energy weapons, missile launchers, and

Gauss rifles fired off sporadically, showing the remarkable fire discipline any commander expected of her people. While the range was extreme, many of the defending 'Mechs remained in place, making them easy targets.

Her headset buzzed with an incoming message from the nearby mobile command center that was coordinating the attack, despite the communications jamming. "*Sang-shao*, we have a priority message from *Sang-shao* Qiao."

She listened carefully to the prerecorded message, which Qiao had transmitted earlier in the day and it had only reached Lindsey now via the MCC's comms relay due to the omnipresent jamming curtain the Castle laid down when they landed. According to the message, General McNamara had made his own desperate gamble on Kearney, attempting to retake Fort Barrett with the remnants of the Twelfth's Third Battalion and the mysterious Grey Watch forces. She saw it as a transparent attempt to divide her attention, but even the combined Republic forces couldn't be enough to take on the reconstituted Legion. In any other circumstances, she might have been concerned for Qiao, trapped between the gray 'Mechs and the bottled-up Hastati, but the Legion had solidified their defensive position before the attack, and their interior defense forced the Republic troops to come to them. It also helped that Qiao's message had arrived so late: there was no use in worrying about a battle that had probably already ended, especially since Lindsey had a fight to concentrate on here.

She sent a quick query to Qiao and promptly put the situation out of her mind. With the battle joined, the status of the Legion was a concern for the *gao-shiao-zhang*: Lindsey had enough on her plate at the moment.

Concerned that the Republic forces may have had other surprises in store, she attempted a quick check on her Canopian allies but was not surprised to receive nothing but the angry squeal of jammed communications. The Republic forces were blocking all frequencies except those they were using, and the Castle-mounted jammers were significantly more powerful than anything other method. While it didn't stop Lindsey's troops from using line-of-sight transmissions or relays, it did keep her from hearing from the outside world.

Forcing herself back to the battle at hand, she watched her forces reach the rally point and proceed to scatter. Without requiring further orders, her hovercraft and light armor made a mad dash for the Castle walls, taking shots of opportunity where they could, as they attempted to slip beneath the wall of fire from the battlements. The abrupt change in aspect should have momentarily thrown off the defenders' targeting, but few of the seasoned Hastati warriors fell for the ruse. They extracted a terrible price on her forces, destroying tank after tank before they could get into range. While the speed of her armor had always been its greatest advantage, range restrictions against a fortified target proved a significant equalizer for both sides.

Along the Castle's exterior, a single Pegasus tank slipped into a crevasse, which provided cover from the defenders' attacks as the hovertank fired its weapons as quickly as they could cycle. A Grey Watch *Panther* emerged from behind one of the battlement's merlons to shoot its PPC at the Pegasus, but Lindsey fired a Gauss round that nearly ripped off the light 'Mech's arm, forcing it to pull back.

With the defenders momentarily focused on her armor, her main battle line found the range, and her lighter 'Mech forces spread out, flooding the enemy with targets. Near the front of the line, an *Anubis* closed to point-blank range with a defending *Commando* on one of the Castle's lower cutaways, and savaged it mercilessly with lasers and missiles before moving on to the next target. On the lower levels of the Castle's battlements, things devolved into a close-range brawl, a fight her forces excelled at, as her jumping 'Mechs took to the air in an attempt to breach the Castle's interior. With a quick glance at her secondary monitor, she gave a small chuckle as the mission timer counted down to the next phase of her plan.

From what she could observe of the battle, her forces were wearing down the defending 'Mechs within the Castle. Although the enemy had a strong defensive position, her numbers and greater freedom of movement allowed her to pull back between attacks and deploy fresh forces to capitalize on the previous wave without risking critical damage. The relentless attacks were slowly whittling down the Hastati and Grey Watch forces, and she knew it was only a matter of time before they could no longer sustain their own defense. Eventually she would strip the remaining Republic forces from the battlements and bring in her aerospace squadrons to pounding the Castle into rubble.

Spotting a Grey Watch *Rifleman* on the battlements attempting to track the *Anubis*, she smiled grimly and aimed both of her *Pillager*'s Gauss rifles.

It'll all be over soon.

CHAPTER 15

*"Keep trying to cut through the jamming. I want to
coordinate as quickly as possible. This needs to end now."*

—Gao-shiao-zhang Jiang Hui

**THE CASTLE
NORTHWIND
REPUBLIC OF THE SPHERE
26 NOVEMBER 3150**

Declan swore as he wrenched his *Marauder II* to the side,
narrowly avoiding the twin large lasers that carved away part
of the rock outcropping he was using as cover. He returned fire
with a single PPC but didn't see whether the stream of charged
particles had hit the Capellan *Penetrator* that shot at him.

Following the battle plan designed by General McNamara
and Colonel Griffin, the majority of the Hastati 'Mechs were
outside the Castle, engaging the approaching Capellan forces,
while the Grey Watch and the Twelfth's long-range support
lances provided covering fire from the Castle itself. The
battle had turned vicious quickly, as the Capellan forces were
attempting to overwhelm the defenders through sheer force
of numbers, but the defenders had held their own so far.

Despite Declan's private misgivings about the effectiveness
of their equipment, the Grey Watch had given an excellent
accounting of themselves so far, taking out threat after threat
as waves of Capellan forces approached. The quiet, self-
assured warriors were not as boisterous as their younger
counterparts, but the occasional rebel yell escaped onto the
command channel, earning several chuckles.

Despite the Capellans' range advantage over the Grey Watch 'Mechs, the Castle's defensive emplacements made the ancient 'Mechs devilishly hard to hit. Furthermore, once the Capellans came within range of the Grey Watch's inferior weapons, the training of the elder Highlanders more than evened the score. While the Fourth MAC was made up of some of the best MechWarriors in McCarron's Armored Cavalry, the Northwind Highlanders were in a class of their own. Their gunnery skills, honed over decades, negated the attacker's speed advantage. Declan watched in awe as a Grey Watch *Warhammer* battled its younger Capellan twin at long range, hitting it with shot after shot from its standard PPCs as fire from the newer 'Mech struck the battlements again and again. Eventually the elder 'Mech capitalized on earlier damage it had done, blasting off the right leg and sending the Capellan 'Mech crashing to the ground.

Unfortunately, the Grey Watch couldn't keep up that sort of return rate forever. Over the radio Declan heard lance after lance pulling back due to heavy damage. The Republic forces slowly but surely were being ground down by the relentless Capellan advance.

The radio crackled to life in his headset. "C&C to all Centurion lances, reorient to the south tunnel at best speed for a recon-in-force. We have reports of APCs and 'Mechs on approach."

Declan confirmed the transmission, and ordered his lance back into the side tunnel they had been guarding as he mulled the situation over.

Armored personnel carriers? Why would they use APCs...

Realization struck Declan like a capacitor discharge: the attack on the walls was intended to pressure the Republic forces to flee through the escape tunnels.

They know where the tunnels are.

"C&C, this is Watch Two, we have contact," the familiar voice of Cadha Jaffray said on the command channel before Declan could relay his thoughts. Lieutenant Colonel Jaffray, granddaughter of Loren Jaffray, was Seamus's former commander, another of the esteemed warriors who had unsurprisingly signed on with the Grey Watch. "We confirm heavy Capellan forces on direct approach to the south tunnel. My lance is holding the line."

Declan's voice caught in his throat. Outside the Castle's protective barriers, the Grey Watch 'Mechs would be at an even greater disadvantage when faced with the more maneuverable Capellan BattleMechs.

Colonel Griffin broke onto the line. "Reinforcements are en route, Watch Two. Pull back to the tunnels and make your stand there."

"No, Michael," Griffin's second-in-command replied, ignoring radio discipline. "This is the major push. If we hold them here it will give our warriors the chance to get out one of the other tunnels. They can't have enough forces to cover them all."

The frustration in the colonel's voice was plain as he desperately tried to argue with the elder Highlander. "Fine, then hold the tunnel for us, and we'll come in to cover you—"

"It's too late, sir," Cadha replied, her voice sorrowful but determined. "We are already engaged."

Coming down the final ramp to the tunnel entrance, Declan took in the entire scene. Jaffray's company had pushed out from the Castle, forming a battle line against the encroaching Liao forces. A Capellan *Vandal* shot forward, its rotary autocannon chattering, cutting a swath of damage across the familiar silhouette of his grandfather's *Marauder*. One of his lancemates, a *Black Knight*, fired back with his large laser, but was quickly engaged by an approaching *Emperor*, its gleaming armor reflecting light from the snow as it stomped toward the Grey Watch line.

A pair of old *UrbanMech*s held the line at the end of the tunnel, their heavy autocannons rending the attackers as they closed, acting as powerful mobile turrets as the attackers attempted to breach the compound. A *Lu Wei Bing* from the *Emperor*'s lance kept up a steady stream of fire at the *UrbanMech*s, slowly grinding away at them from long range before attempting to go toe-to-toe with its heavy autocannon. Arcs of energy ripped across the battlefield from the *Lu Wei Bing*'s paired light PPCs, interspersed with missiles from its Doombud multi-missile launcher. Every ruptured armor plate the *UrbanMech*s suffered underscored the futility of a ranged battle against the much larger 'Mech.

A single glance at the positioning of the Capellan forces made everything crystal clear. The Capellans had been set up along the tunnel ridgeline, ready to ambush anyone who escaped through the tunnel, but they'd been spotted too early. Without the element of surprise, the commander of the attacking forces had gone with a new alternative: if they couldn't get the defenders as they escaped, they would use the tunnels to open a new front.

With her fellow Grey Watch warriors at her side, Lieutenant Colonel Jaffray's *Highlander* turned toward the approaching Capellans and accelerated her immense BattleMech into a run, firing her weapons as she went. "For Northwind!"

As Declan watched, something solidified deep within him. He straightened in his command couch and pushed his own 'Mech faster down the tunnel. Since his reconnaissance mission had been rendered moot, he knew he had a new imperative, one that he had been born with. "Lance—"

"*For Northwind!*"

Declan's head shot up at the battle cry just in time to see Taggart's *Osprey* burst past him at full speed. Seeing his lancemate take the lead, he pushed his own 'Mech to follow, but a number of threat icons suddenly flared onto his screen.

Careening around one of the *UrbanMech*s, a Capellan Maxim transport swerved around the tunnel wall and quickly disgorged its cargo of Fa Shih battle armor.

Any hesitation he'd felt evaporated in that moment. "Lance, follow Four! Fight through the battle armor!"

The rest of his lance attempted to catch up with Taggart, firing at the spry infantry as they went, but the *Osprey* was too fast for them. The lighter 'Mech's birdlike legs ate up meter after meter, blackened snow churning up behind them. She dove forward and blew past the Grey Watch line as they engaged with the waves of encroaching Liao forces. She kept up a constant barrage of fire, each of her weapon interlocks going off in sequence to keep from overheating.

"*For Northwind!*" A ferrous slug shot out from her Gauss rifle and struck an enemy *Dervish* in the torso, shattering armor plates over its chest and sending it reeling.

"*For Northwind!*" Extended-range medium lasers slashed out with brilliant emerald beams and sliced off the hand of a Liao *Wasp*. Missiles from her own multi-missile launcher severed the rest of the arm and carved deep into the torso.

"*FOR NORTHWIND!*" Return fire blazed around her, projecting a halo around the nimble 'Mech, but nothing seemed to touch her. It was as if her sheer, righteous purpose protected her and revitalized the defenders for a few brief moments—

Until it all came crashing down.

A stray Gauss-rifle round, intended for a Republic JES missile carrier that had moved to support the Grey Watch 'Mechs, took Taggart high in the hip and rocked her 'Mech dangerously to one side.

Her aura of invincibility gone, Taggart was immediately bracketed by a flight of missiles, several of which impacted against her 'Mech's head and sent her reeling. A second Gauss round plowed deep into the torso-mounted missile storage and set off a chain of sympathetic explosions, dropping the gutted 'Mech to its knees.

With a bone-deep howl of agony, Oedhe throttled his *Lament* into a run and fired at all comers as he desperately pushed through the wave of Capellan 'Mechs to get to the downed *Osprey*.

Realizing that tactical considerations had taken a momentary backseat to the necessity of keeping the rest of his lance alive, Declan tried to cover Oedhe as best as he could. He fired his PPCs and lasers into the scrum, punching through the chest of the damaged *Dervish*, and an ammo explosion devastated the Capellan 'Mech.

A new threat icon came up on his HUD, and he watched in horror as a 90-ton Capellan *Emperor* approached the 55-ton *Osprey* as Taggart desperately strained to stand despite the crippling damage her 'Mech had taken.

The *Emperor* gazed down at the *Osprey* for a moment, and then raised its arms. Declan pushed his *Marauder II* to full throttle, scraping paint off one arm as he brushed against the tunnel wall at a run, desperate to get into range.

He knew wouldn't make it, but he still had to try.

The *Emperor* lit off two shotgun blasts from its arm-mounted LB-X autocannons, rending holes in the *Osprey*'s torso, arms, and head. The smaller 'Mech bucked from the fire at point-blank range, and Declan's heart caught in his throat.

He only breathed again when he heard a reedy voice in his headset. *"For Northwind..."*

He couldn't tell whether the Capellan MechWarrior had heard her, or if they simply refused to show mercy. Regardless, the *Emperor* lit off its plasma cannon in response, bathing the downed 'Mech in fire. Taggart's defiant cry mutated into a horrific scream, and then everything went mercifully silent.

For Declan, everything went white.

A Fa Shih trooper took to the air, leaping for his torso, but Declan slammed it into the wall with his PPC's gauntlet, crushing the battlesuit's chest. He rushed forward, calling the rest of his lance to him as he charged, his voice raw with unbridled emotion. In that instant, his only conscious thought was to avenge the loss of a lancemate who had risked it all to defend the world she loved.

In response to the charging Republic forces, the *Emperor* stepped up, aiming over the charred *Osprey* at Declan's charging 'Mech. Declan fired both PPCs into the Capellan's chest, barely noticing lasers flash past on his right as Fairchild forced the nearby *Lu Wei Bing* to backpedal. He fired again and struck the *Emperor*'s torso, heedless of the rising heat in his cockpit.

Fighting for air in the stifling cockpit, he aimed for the *Emperor*'s shoulder and shot two beams of raw energy into the arm, ripping it off at the shoulder. The heat in his cockpit spiked into the red band. An autocannon burst from the *Emperor*'s remaining arm took him high in the chest with a crash like thunder, and he tasted blood.

Alarms screamed in the confines of the cockpit. He pounded the shutdown override and fired again from point-blank range as he struggled for breath. The *Emperor* reoriented its deadly plasma cannon, seeking to heat him up enough to force his 'Mech to shut down.

"C'mon, c'mon, cool down..." he coaxed his *Marauder II*.

Whether from the heat or just the stresses of the last few weeks, his thoughts kaleidoscoped, catching fragments of all that had happened. Seeing Bianca so frightened...pulling his knife on Maeve...seeing the colonel's *Black Watch* crashing to the ground during the exercise...

Ellie...

Heedless of Fairchild's voice in his headset, he shoved his throttle to the stops and *charged.*

The sound of two 'Mechs hitting each other was like striking a massive gong, and damage alarms screamed as they both collided. The damage-display wireframe erupted into a solid mass of yellows and reds, and when he glanced down, he saw coolant leaking out from his 'Mech's torso like a mortal wound.

The damage to the *Emperor* shocked him even more, however, its own armor crumpled by the impact. Lacking an arm to help roll with the fall, the 'Mech had landed heavily, and he could only imagine the impact shock the other pilot had endured. Through his cockpit, he could see the other MechWarrior was clearly disoriented but desperately tried to do anything to save themself.

With careful precision, Declan raised his 'Mech's right arm, the ER PPC aimed straight for the *Emperor*'s cockpit. He breathed slowly, watching his heat drop back into the yellow band. He saw the wide-eyed look of the other MechWarrior through the armored cockpit glass as they desperately strained against their safety straps to reach forward and shut down the 'Mech. Declan could hear Fairchild and Oedhe in his headset, both telling him different things, but all he heard was Ellie's final, terrified scream...

He fired.

His left-arm PPC, aimed at the *Emperor*'s remaining arm, spat the fury of man-made lightning, and the spike of pure cerulean energy slagged the autocannon. He lashed out with one leg, kicking the damaged arm off, then continued on, leaving the downed 'Mech behind him as its pilot finally managed to shut down their fusion engine to surrender.

His cooling vest fought down his temperature as his breathing steadied; his eyes roamed the battlefield as he attempted to control his thoughts once again. The *Lu Wei Bing* was only a smoldering hulk now, and the *Vandal* fled back to the re-forming Capellan lines. The final 'Mech of the lance, the *Penetrator* he had engaged earlier, had crumpled behind a rocky outcropping; its tortured leg lay at a grotesque angle.

While the conflict still raged, the loss of the *Emperor* halted the Fourth MAC's forward motion, and they were now trading fire with the combined Republic forces. Ellie's brave actions had given the Grey Watch enough time to bring reinforcements to the fore, and Cadha Jaffray's *Highlander* formed the core of a new heavy battle line that had clear fields of fire through the valley. As Declan watched, a round from Jaffray's Gauss rifle and a pair of PPC strikes from Seamus cut down a *Raven II* that had ranged too close to their line. The wave of fire overwhelmed the lighter MAC forces, and they slowly began pulling back.

The line was *holding*.

Switching to the command channel, he tried to get a sense of the larger battle but caught a message from Colonel Griffin instead.

"General, you need to sound the retreat." The signal showed the voice as coming from a massive *Awesome* on the center of the battlements. "The Grey Watch will act as the rear guard at the Castle and hold the back door. You need to re-form your regiment and get to the secondary rally point now."

Declan could almost hear the General McNamara shaking his head. "This is the best position left, Colonel. We will hold here."

"Be reasonable, General!" Griffin's voice was harsh. "If you're going to succeed in a guerrilla war, you need lighter, more advanced units, not heavy relics that'll only slow you down. This is the battle we were born to fight...and every Capellan we take down here will mean one more defender of Northwind who can fight another day." There was a long pause before the colonel's solemn voice continued. "It is the duty of the Grey Watch to protect Northwind. It is your duty to make sure our sacrifice is not in vain."

Declan knew General McNamara wanted to argue the point, but even he could see that Griffin was right. Even with the help the Grey Watch provided, the disparity in numbers was just too large to surmount. If the next step was to deny the planet as a whole to the Capellans, he would need the more-advanced units of the Twelfth Hastati. If there was any chance for the Republic to retake the planet, they would have to use the same tactics used so successfully against the Clans and hold out as long as possible. Declan again thought back to Loren Jaffray, the former Capellan Death Commando who returned to the Highlanders fold, who had been forced to wait for reinforcements deep in the Periphery on the world of Wayside V.

He felt a painful ache in his chest as he remembered that the unit that had survived Wayside V was Stirling's Fusiliers. Andrea Stirling's unit.

For a long moment he thought the general was going to refuse, but Griffin's logic was inescapable. Through a heavy heart, McNamara ordered the Hastati forces to begin a retrograde action toward the underground tunnels that would allow them to escape into the forest. While Declan had no doubt the Capellans would follow, it would take them time to consolidate their gains, and he doubted they were in any condition for meaningful pursuit.

Slowly, one by one, the various Hastati 'Mechs pulled back, until the remainder of his lance was all that was left. Declan watched each of them pull back, the hard knot in his chest refusing to let go as he switched back to his lance channel to radio his teammates. "You all heard the orders. Head to the tunnels. I'll hold open the back door until you're safe."

Something in his voice must have tipped off Fairchild, because she immediately responded. "Sir—"

"You first, Sergeant." Declan's tone brooked no argument.

There was a long pause before she responded. "Think I'll just hold back a little longer, if you don't mind. John, you want the lead?"

"You're both morons," Oedhe said. "I'm not going anywhere either."

Declan narrowed his eyes as he saw what they were trying to do. "This is a direct order, people. I want you through that tunnel yesterday."

"Court-martial us later," Fairchild replied, stepping her *Ostsol* next to her commander. "For now, we fight. Do you want to call the targets, or shall we?"

Despite his anger at their choosing to disobey his orders, he was secretly pleased that here, at the end, he was not alone.

"All right, you heard the colonel. Every 'Mech we take down here is one less that our brothers and sisters have to fight down the road. Target that *Pillager*... I have a feeling it's one of their commanders." He looked around, seeing his two lancemates beside him as he moved his 'Mech toward the end of the Highlander line. "For Northwind."

A lone voice whispered over the channel: "For Ellie."

He switched his channel over to Lieutenant Colonel Jaffray and said, "Colonel, my lance stands ready to assist you."

"Thank you, Lieutenant." Her voice hardened as she switched to the main command channel, allowing all of Northwind's forces to hear her. "*Highlanders...*"

Declan took a deep breath, his hand gripping his throttle, his eyes locked on the approaching ranks of enemy BattleMechs that marched inexorably toward them.

"*Forward!*"

CHAPTER 16

"General, we've lost communication with our forces at the jump point..."

> —Lieutenant Kyla Torrance,
> Twelfth Hastati Sentinels

THE CASTLE
NORTHWIND
REPUBLIC OF THE SPHERE
26 NOVEMBER 3150

Lindsey gave a grim smile of pleasure as she watched the Grey Watch forces surge toward her re-formed battle line. While it appeared the sneak attack on the southern tunnel had been less effective than anticipated, it seemed she would still get the decisive battle she'd sought from the very beginning.

The Grey Watch 'Mechs were forming a battle line, keeping the Castle to their back; they had apparently made the decision to fight the decisive battle here. To be fair, it was the best of several poor options: the obsolete BattleMechs they piloted would be run down and destroyed piecemeal by her faster, more advanced equipment. At least here they could maximize their advantages for the short time they had left. Even with the technical skill they had shown, Lindsey had no doubt the Castle would be hers by nightfall.

As she stepped her *Pillager* to the front line, the rest of her lance formed up on her: Rao's *Ti Ts'ang* at her right, Endrin's *Victor* to her left, and Palos's *Penetrator* covering the rear.

"Beta Company, pull back through Alpha to get clear. You've borne the brunt of it so far, now it's our turn. Alpha

Company, cover Beta and press forward. Charlie Company, once we are engaged, turn on axis and hit the right flank. As soon as we have an opening, we'll turn the enemy your way and crush them against you." She smiled grimly at the thought. "We're the hammer, you're the anvil."

A chorus of affirmative responses followed, and she throttled her 'Mech forward, taking only two steps before firing a Gauss-rifle round that leapt out toward the Grey Watch lines a struck a *Black Knight* in the chest. Alpha Company, in response to her orders, pushed forward across the snowy landscape, the hovertanks breaking into pairs as befit their loadouts. Two Regulators lashed out with their Gauss rifles, while a pair of Pegasuses savaged a Hastati *Spider* that had the temerity of closing range.

The *Spider* fired at a Pegasus with its medium laser but merely scored a glancing blow off the glacis protecting the front of the hovertank. It attempted to shift position, but two barrages of SRMs wreathed the light 'Mech in flames, sending it crashing to the ground.

Lindsey had focused so intently on the duel with the *Spider* that she hadn't noticed the blinking light on her comm board that showed a signal trying to punch through the jamming.

"Spear, this is Talon, please respond."

Lindsey smiled at the sound of the Grand Master's voice. If he was close enough to defeat the jamming, it meant the forces she needed to finally crush the Republic were at hand!

"Talon, this is Spear. Welcome to the battle. We are engaged with Grey Watch forces, I am sending you grid coordinates now. If you—"

To her surprise, Hui cut her off. "Spear, re-form your unit and return to the HPG compound immediately."

Lindsey shook her head. Had she heard him right? They couldn't just give up, not now, not when they were so close! "Talon, please repeat."

"Multiple DropShips are on final approach. We believe they are Republic reinforcements. We must consolidate our forces ASAP or risk being cut off from the city."

A sickening feeling settled in her stomach. Was the timing of this rally planned? Was this all part of some elaborate trap?

She struggled to focus on the situation. "Do we have positive ID on the DropShips?"

"No, but our DropShips in orbit have spotted them deploying fighters. I have diverted our own fighters to intercept, but that means they will be unavailable to cover our withdrawal."

Lindsey hissed under her breath, but the House Imarra leader was correct. If those were Republic fighters, they had to be dealt with immediately or deadly strafing attacks would devastate her forces in the open fields around the Castle.

She switched back to her regimental channel, momentarily leaving the *gao-shiao-zhang* on the secondary line. "Cavalry, we need to break into that Castle yesterday! All forces forward close distance, and force them against the rocks!"

It was a desperate gamble, but they had to get under the defensive fire coming from the Castle. If she could get into the Castle itself, there was an excellent chance the *gao-shiao-zhang* would allow her to press the attack, especially as it looked like they might soon need a defensive position of their own.

Before she could give further orders, however, an ear-piercing squeal played over her speakers.

For a moment she thought she'd taken a cockpit hit before the battle had even been joined, but around her she saw momentary hesitation on both sides of the conflict, letting her know that the signal she'd just received had gone out on an open channel to both sides. Her comm system tried to filter the sound through the jamming, but Lindsey's stomach dropped; her breath caught in her chest as she identified the sound without the need of the computer's filtration.

Bagpipes.

She shifted her head in an attempt to stifle the sound, but immediately straightened as a familiar voice came over the neurohelmet's headset:

"This is Countess Tara Campbell of the Northwind Highlanders."

The voice was crystal clear, and would've been identifiable even if the countess hadn't stated her name. "You have invaded Republic space and forcibly invaded the planet of Northwind. By the authority of the Exarch of the Republic of the Sphere, I demand that you immediately cease hostilities and prepare to leave the planet as quickly as possible." There was a slight pause, and her icy voice came back harsh and unforgiving. "If you do not immediately comply, my forces are prepared to engage."

Lindsey wanted to laugh at such an ultimatum, but instead she quickly sorted through the many variables. From the class and number of incoming DropShips, she could be looking at close to five battalions—enough to make a true fight of the planet, especially if the defenders could hold the Castle.

The tactical situation was far more dire than she could've imagined. Instead of a last, desperate charge into overwhelming odds, Campbell's incoming Highlanders forces could be the hammer to shatter her against the anvil of the Republic forces already on-planet. Lindsey's units were spread out in the open, and if she let the new forces link up with the old, she would risk being defeated in detail.

The Grand Master had the same thought. "*Sang-shao*," he radioed, "we need to regroup on the city now. Incoming aerospace forces have already stripped our satellite cover, and the DropShips are en route to the Castle. We must pull back."

No!

"Respectfully, sir, we can still take the Castle before they land."

"Not in time," Hui replied. "Those DropShips are moving between us and the city."

She instantly saw the dilemma: if the DropShips landed behind them, she would be forced to fight through the same gauntlet she'd tried to use on the Twelfth Hastati earlier. Not only would the Highlanders be fresh, but they would be the ones with Hastati at their rear.

Her choice was terrible but obvious. "All forces, pull back into the city! Rally on the HPG compound!"

She knew it was the right call, but abandoning the strike on the final major bastion on the planet made her cringe. Her priorities were clear, however: she had to hold the HPG at all costs, and if that meant postponing her revenge on the Republic, she would do it. All she needed to do was to maintain an orderly withdrawal ahead of the enemy reinforcements.

"*Incoming!*"

A shadow passed over her, and for the briefest of moments she thought that it was a solar eclipse.

No, not fighters...

DropShips.

The aerodyne DropShip, a Republic *Avenger*, flew right above her at full burn. As she watched its trajectory, several small figures rained down from the DropShip and fired jump jets to slow their descent.

Battle armor.

"Pull back to the city! Now!"

She couldn't afford to get cut off from Tara, especially if the Republic was dropping their elite battle armor into the fray. Too many of her Fa Shih troopers had been killed during the initial conquest of the city and the HPG compound, and the rest had been split into squads to capitalize on the eventual breach of the Castle walls. With assistance from the locals, the Republic battle armor could be a horrifying foe, one that she'd have to keep from the HPG compound at all cost.

Her sensors showed the first tan-colored BattleMechs finally coming around the far side of the Castle in formation, advancing with deadly purpose. The DropShips must have combat-dropped the first of the arriving Highlanders 'Mechs on the far side of the Castle, into the lighter concentration of Second Battalion to have the greatest effect. Her mobile armor broke into smaller units to harry the newcomers, but the Highlanders needed no encouragement to force the Fourth MAC backward, with weapons fire crashing down on the withdrawing armor like a typhoon.

As her nimble light armor attempted to support her heavier forces, the 'Mechs under her command pulled back in an orderly fashion, peppering the newcomers with fire. A *Lao Hu* held its position for a moment, seeking to capitalize on the damage that its extended-range large laser and long-range missile rack had visited on an approaching *Orion*. The *Lao Hu* pilot allowed the Highlander 'Mech to close range, and then fired off a shotgun blast from its immense LB-X autocannon. The cloud of cluster rounds peppered the *Orion*'s armor, but one of the submunitions blasted into the Gauss-rifle capacitor in the arm. With a silvery flash of arcing electricity, the Gauss rifle split open down the middle, shattering the 'Mech's primary weapon, and rending armor from the inside out. Lindsey willed the Highlander 'Mech to fall, but the MechWarrior bravely fought the burst of feedback that ripped through their neurohelmet connections.

Unfortunately, the Gauss rifle wasn't the *Orion*'s only weapon.

A cloud of smoke shot up from the battlements, and a pair of immense Arrow IV missiles bore in on the *Lao Hu*. The pilot, seeing the danger they were in, backpedaled quickly but couldn't avoid the *Orion*'s TAG laser, which guided the two missiles to their target. Both warheads struck the *Lao Hu* within an instant of each other, wreathing the 'Mech in fire, and the Orion's LRMs only fed the maelstrom.

Endrin slowed, ready to go to the *Lao Hu*'s aid, but when the smoke cleared, there was no need. The upper half of the 'Mech was gone.

To her horror, a PPC bit deeply into the hip of Endrin's *Victor*, causing him to stumble. The actinic blue beam nearly severed the leg outright, but he somehow managed to keep trudging forward, refusing to disobey her last order. The leg damage hampered his speed, however, and she instinctively turned her *Pillager* to assist him.

"No, ma'am!" Endrin's voice roared in her earpiece. "You must return to the city."

"Not without you," she responded with a calm she didn't feel, and she desperately looked around for assistance. Rao was backpedaling in step with her, but his limited long-range profile would be of no help to Endrin. In the corner of her eye, she saw Palos's *Penetrator* under heavy fire, trading shots with a Grey Watch *Rifleman* that was mercilessly savaging him with its autocannons and lasers.

From downfield, an advancing *Marauder* laid into Endrin's *Victor* with all its might. Despite the age of the Highlander's weaponry, the two cerulean beams struck the 'Mech, followed by a burst from the dorsal autocannon. Both PPC shots wrecked the arm, but Lindsey watched in raw terror as the autocannon rounds slashed into the lower torso. For the briefest of moments, she thought the shot had only grazed him, but then the *Victor* fell to its right, its left leg still locked upright. She howled in rage as the 'Mech landed heavily on its side, unable to reach out with its remaining arm to dissipate the force of the fall. She felt the vibration as the *Victor* struck the ground, and she leaned forward to get a better view.

"Kyle? *Kyle*?"

Every element of her being screamed at her to go back for him, but she couldn't. With the Grand Master still out of range, it was her duty to maintain the defense of the HPG compound. If the Republic battle armor somehow managed to reach the city, the results could be devastating, especially if the damned jamming kept her from communicating the threat to the garrison in time.

She looked back at the *Victor*, motionless and half buried into the snow, as the encroaching Hastati forces neared. A black-and-gold *Marauder II* held the center of the line, its weapons aimed at the downed assault 'Mech, but it made no move to fire.

As she stared with revulsion, the memory of something the Grand Master said at his dinner party rang through her ears.

The only thing that matters is victory.

Fighting the tears that threatened to run down her face, she slid between the two buildings, and as quickly as she had come, she was gone.

CHAPTER 17

"We may have lost a battle, but the war is far from over. When it comes to the Celestial Wisdom, you must realize there are always plans within plans, even if we do not see them."

—*Gao-shiao-zhang* Jiang Hui
to *Sang-shao* Julie Qiao

TARA
NORTHWIND
REPUBLIC OF THE SPHERE
26 NOVEMBER 3150

From her perch high above Tara, *Sang-shao* Lindsey Baxter closed her eyes tightly, reveling in fresh air that was free from the stink of coolant, fire, and death. The rising winds picked up her hair and blew it freely. The breeze felt clean and sharp against her skin, sending a goose bumps up her arms as she stared out over the city.

She had found this location by accident, a rarely used maintenance platform designed for inspecting the curved surface of the immense dish antenna that sat on top of the HPG compound. Ringing the base of the dish, it towered above the facility, giving her a commanding view of the area the city and allowing for a dim view of the distant Castle. Small movements in the distance were occasionally discernible: 'Mechs on patrol, their immense size hidden by the encroaching twilight.

In the wake of the battle for the Castle, things had quickly devolved into a rough stalemate. The Fourth MAC had pulled back to the spaceport for repairs, while fresh House

Imarra warriors held a new defensive line outside the city. The Canopian Lancers continued providing support within the city itself, but she knew the *gao-shiao-zhang* intended to return them to the NMA as soon as the Fourth returned to combat readiness. The Canopians had managed to eke out a small victory in the terrible battle by shattering an attempted breakout at the NMA, but no one was comfortable with how adeptly the Grey Watch forces could move through the terrain.

We came so close!

With the aid of House Imarra's warriors she had managed to withdraw the remainder of her forces from the Castle in good order, but at a terrible cost. Now, with the Republic reinforcements having linked up at the Castle itself, there was little chance of her taking the Star League-era fortress without suffering heavy losses. *Hell, if not for their reluctance to risk collateral damage to the city, they'd probably be fighting us right now.*

To make things worse, she'd also heard that Republic reinforcements had dropped onto Kearney. Laurel's Legion had withdrawn in an orderly manner, but it had cost them Fort Barrett. While the base would probably be of no benefit to either side for the moment, it was just another loss to make her regret not seizing the Castle sooner. If she had, House Imarra could've remained to support Laurel's Legion, and they both would've had the advantage of secured fortifications when enemy reinforcements arrived.

She found herself wishing for the opportunity to consult with Qiao but quickly abandoned the thought. The Legion's commander was still in transit, and considering the toll the battle had taken on all of their forces, Lindsey didn't want to risk distracting her over something minor.

"There you are."

She whirled on the voice that came from behind, and instinctively raised her hands in a defensive posture. To his credit, the *gao-shiao-zhang* did not flinch, merely smiling tolerantly at her reaction. To cover her embarrassment for not noticing his approach, she quickly shifted the motion into an attempt to straighten her jacket, then she bowed her head respectfully as he stepped fully out of the building. No doubt the Grand Master took the hand-to-hand combat aspects of Warrior House discipline as seriously as everything else, and while she liked to think she could take him on, she also had no doubt that he would be a spirited opponent.

She fought the instinct to snap to attention as he stepped up beside her on the catwalk. Like her, the Grand Master had traded his rank insignias for a plain duty uniform to hold back the chill, and she did not want a salute to betray his rank. While she doubted any snipers were in range, there was always the chance someone was watching them at that very moment.

Both of them looked out over the approaching twilight for a moment before Hui decided to speak. "You are a difficult woman to find, *Sang-shao*."

She glanced down at her communicator, verifying that it was active. "Forgive me, *Gao-shiao-zhang*. I specifically left my communicator on..."

He waved off her explanation with a small smile. "Oh, I could have messaged you, but I preferred the challenge of finding you myself. The tracker said you were still in the compound, but none of your staff knew quite where. I had just happened to be speaking with *Sang-shao* Qiao, and she had a good idea of where to find you."

"Is that so, sir?" She gave him a curious look, wondering exactly what he might be implying. She had grown friendly with Qiao and found a great deal in common with her, but had he alluded to something more?

"Indeed," he replied, which did nothing to alleviate her concerns. "She said if you weren't behind a stack of paper or old-fashioned maps in your office as you planned a retaliatory strike, then you would be surveying the battlefield from the highest vantage you could find, until you were absolutely certain you had wrested whatever secrets it might contain. Since all of our aerospace forces are grounded to backstop any Republic aerospace maneuvers, I made an educated guess that you would come up here." He laughed lightly. "I suppose I should be grateful that you did not make me climb all the way to the top of the dish."

She smiled politely at his response, and the *gao-shiao-zhang* turned back to the view, sharing the companionable silence before he continued. "*Sang-shao*, I have been considering our current predicament, and I wanted to consult with you about our options."

"Of course, sir."

The House Imarra commander's expression tightened. "We must face facts, *Sang-shao*. The Republic has reinforced Northwind in greater strength than we had anticipated. Aside from the remains of the Twelfth Hastati and the Grey Watch, we now have Tara Campbell's Highlanders battalion, a Stone's Defenders battalion, and two battalions of the Sixth Fides Defenders. That gives the Republic commander a troop strength nearly on par with our own, and those reinforcements are fresh. Thanks to your efforts they have been bloodied, but we no longer have the numerical superiority we were counting on. While I feel confident we can provide an excellent accounting of ourselves, our ability to permanently hold this planet has suffered a major setback." He looked over at her, his expression filled with pride. "Yet you still achieved a great victory today, even if it is not everything we had hoped for. Our goal was to take the HPG compound, and you succeeded admirably."

She looked up, surprised, but had thought much the same herself. While he was the overall commander, and would gain the accolades for the success of this mission, he had also failed to hold Fort Barrett, and had been late to the party after his initial victory on Kearney.

"However," he said, "I think it may be time to inform the CCAF of our situation."

Her eyes widened, and she couldn't help but feel revulsion at the thought. A regiment of McCarron's Armored Cavalry calling for support? It felt like a betrayal.

Still, she knew her commander was right. The enemies massing against them had grown too numerous. For Task Force Clarity to have any chance for a lasting victory, they had to find a way to seize the initiative again. Still, something in the way Hui had so calmly stated his intentions roused her suspicions, and her lips narrowed as she focused on him. "The Highlanders were always expected to come here, weren't they?"

"It might be more accurate to say that it was not unexpected. However, no one anticipated them bringing three additional battalions as well, nor to have responded so soon."

Thinking back to her briefing on Sian, Lindsey remembered all the contingency planning around what the task force must do if Campbell's Highlanders did return to Northwind. Their plans had centered on leaving a large-enough force to keep the Highlanders mired on Northwind while disengaging the rest to join the eventual strike on Terra.

Unfortunately, with Task Force Clarity now outnumbered, Lindsey needed all of the assets at her disposal to ensure that none of the Republic forces could follow them off-planet and threaten the plans for invading Terra.

Her mind raced with the possibilities. "Under other circumstances, this might be ideal. Any resources Stone sent here will not be able to defend Terra when we strike."

Hui nodded in agreement, and for a brief moment she considered his words. Might the Chancellor be willing to inform one of the Clans about the Republic's potential weakness? Either the Wolves or the Jade Falcons would gladly jump at the chance to be the first Clan to step foot on Terra and conquer the weakened Republic. Hell, Daoshen might message them both and see what remained for the taking after the two Clans had battered themselves bloody.

She shook her head before the thought was fully formed, knowing the Chancellor would never risk it. While the Confederation had rarely gone head-to-head with Clan warriors, they knew well enough to be wary of such a threat. No, the best course would be to keep the HPG from informing Stone about Northwind's fate until DropShips bearing the golden *dao* of House Liao were eclipsing the sun as the made their final approach.

"I can certainly see the advantages, sir," she replied. "Do you want me to have a message prepared for you? The HPG staff maintains their neutrality in our conflict and will send what we require."

To her surprise, hesitated a moment before speaking. "I appreciate the offer, *Sang-shao*, but I believe it might be best if *Sang-shao* Qiao sent out the message."

Confusion set in at first, and then that gave way to the first stirrings of true anger in her chest. "Is that the true reason Laurel's Legion was added to the task force? As a scapegoat should things go wrong?"

To his credit, Hui did not deny her theory. "It was deemed to be...incompatible with the prestige of the Warrior House Orders if a request for reinforcements came from House Imarra."

"Of course," Lindsey replied, careful not to let any hint of her rising anger creep into her voice. "It would work out for all involved if it came from a unit that had been disgraced before... especially a unit the Chancellor has deemed expendable."

For the first time, she saw flinty hardness in the Grand Master's eyes. Had she finally gone too far? "Respectfully, *Sang-shao*, we are *all* expendable, especially in this particular instance. We are at the closest point to taking Terra since the end of the first Star League, and it is our sworn duty to ensure that we do everything in our power to bring that goal to fruition. I have no doubt of Qiao's loyalty to both the nation and our shared purpose. It is imperative that we hold this planet, and I shall use whatever means necessary to do so." His voice softened, and he looked at her carefully. "If you have an alternative, I would be happy to hear it."

She hesitated, wondering what those dark-brown eyes were hiding. Could he suspect what she wanted to propose? Had he set her up for this conversation? She raised her chin, equal parts defiance and false confidence buoying her up. "What if I were to make the request?"

He watched her carefully. "The request for reinforcements?"

"Yes. You said it was inappropriate for House Imarra to put out the call, but our loyalty to the Chancellor is well-known, and many independent units would jump at the chance to go into battle alongside the Fourth MAC. They are more likely to respond to a distress call from a McCarron's Armored Cavalry regiment than a less renowned regiment." *Not to mention, if one was suspicious about ulterior motives, I provide all of the same opportunities and none of the drawbacks.*

He made a good show of considering the proposal. "It would also leave Laurel's Legion out of the spotlight should things go wrong. You would be taking a great deal of responsibility on yourself, however. Do you think *Sang-shao* McCarron would approve of this course of action?"

She straightened. "Cyrus trusts me to use my best judgment in all situations, and he has never regretted that decision."

The *gao-shiao-zhang* gave a thoughtful nod and glanced at her appraisingly. "Then I suppose I can only ask whether you are doing this for the good of the mission or to protect someone you consider a friend."

This time she did smile. "As the Celestial Wisdom has said many times, the loyalty of McCarron's Armored Cavalry is without question. We have always done what is best for our nation and the Capellan people and have never shied away from the hard calls. If this is what needs to be asked of me to ensure our victory on Northwind and to protect a valuable ally, I will do it without hesitation."

For a brief moment, she thought he would press the issue, but he merely nodded and gestured to stairwell that led back inside. Nodding at him respectfully, she preceded him down the stairs and walked silently with him to the command center. Stepping down into the communications pit, she turned to the closest ComStar technician, a young blond woman in a brilliant white jumpsuit.

"Technician, I need to send out an HPG message."

The young, mousy woman nodded, happy to do a task she understood, and moved to the other side of the room. Baxter glanced over at the Grand Master silently, and she considered how to word this message.

Still, Hui's question rang in her head. Was she really doing this for the good of the Confederation, or to spare a friend?

Must the answer truly be one or the other?

CHAPTER 18

"There are two types of Highlander burials. One is bad. One is worse."

—Major Seamus Casey

THE CASTLE
NORTHWIND
REPUBLIC OF THE SPHERE
27 NOVEMBER 3150

Even with more people in the room than during the previous meeting, Declan felt the space seemed somehow emptier. With the Highlanders and the Republic reinforcements maintaining the perimeter, much of the Hastati forces had been pulled back for repairs, allowing the command staff to attend the briefing. While as a lance commander he would have been invited, he had once again been tapped by the Republic Knight to accompany her.

Declan's gaze slid over to Maeve in the seat beside him at the table, and attempted to read anything in her taut expression. She had only recently returned from Kearney, having managed to break the Laurel's Legion blockade, but it had cost them dearly. Her company had been in the thick of the fighting, and she had lost several MechWarriors, including her second-in-command.

We've all lost far too much.

His eyes wandered to the empty chair to his left, and his expression hardened.

Silas O'Malley hadn't made it. Rumor had it that he died avenging a Grey Watch warrior who saved his lance from an ambush, but he was on the long list of those who had still missing in action, so no one knew for sure.

Before he could go too far down that mental path, the heavy metal doors on the far side of the room slid open. Everyone snapped to their feet as Countess Tara Campbell entered, General McNamara in her wake. The commander of the Highlanders wore a simple tan jumpsuit with the Highlanders crest on either shoulder, but Declan would've recognized her anywhere. The weight of her obligations etched deeply into her face, but she retained the same powerful intensity that had inspired the Highlanders to take up the banner whenever she called.

Stepping down to the central table, she caught sight of Colonel Griffin, her former head of intelligence, and moved toward him. For a long moment, the two just stood at arm's length, and she smiled warmly. "It's been a long time, Michael."

"Countess..." Griffin's voice caught, and he bowed his head.

Tara reached out and pulled him into a tight embrace. She said something Declan couldn't hear, and Griffin stepped back, his composure returned, aside from a shininess near his eyes betraying how deeply her presence had moved him.

"I'm sorry that we couldn't keep the secret for longer, ma'am," he said.

"The secret never mattered," the countess responded softly, her voice holding the same star quality Declan remembered from holovid broadcasts. "Northwind is what matters, and you helped to defend her once again. Thank you."

Griffin bowed his head once more, and he turned to introduce the Republic Knight. "Countess, may I present Lady Maeve Sterling."

The countess smiled at Maeve, and for the first time Declan caught a firsthand glimpse of what had captured the hearts and minds of the Highlanders. "Lady Maeve and I are well acquainted, Michael. I can't tell you how much I appreciate you coming to our aid, Maeve. I am in you debt."

"Any debt belongs to those who are no longer here," the Knight replied, glancing at Declan. "I only wish we could've done more for you, Countess."

"No, my lady," Campbell replied, her voice stern. "You did everything you could, and I know better than most how many of your people gave everything." She raised her voice so everyone could hear them. "When the Highlanders first agreed to become a part of the Republic, Devlin Stone made us a promise that he would be there, should we need him." Her eyes swept the whole room, taking everyone under her steely gaze. "Even though it would weaken his own defensive position on Terra, the Exarch not only provided me with the means to get here in time, but he also sent supporting forces from Stone's Brigade and the Sixth Fides. Whatever may have happened in the past, he made good on that promise today—a covenant that has been sealed with your blood and sacrifice.

"Unfortunately, this is well and truly everything the Exarch could spare. That puts an extraordinary responsibility on us, ladies and gentlemen." She looked around the table at everyone present. "Before, we merely had to drive these invaders from our planet, but now we need to shatter the entire Capellan presence on Northwind."

"Ma'am?" For the first time in Declan's experience, General McNamara sounded incredulous.

Countess Campbell turned to him squarely. "General, I have maintained contact with Paladin Lakewood on the way in, and the DMI believes the Capellans have grossly overextended themselves to free up the forces necessary for this campaign."

"Which would explain why they sent a task force comprised of primarily former mercenaries and their Canopian allies," Maeve answered.

"Exactly," Campbell replied with a nod. "Intelligence believes they planned to leave Laurel's Legion and the Canopians in place to hold the planet, while House Imarra and the Fourth MAC press onward to Terra to rendezvous with additional Capellan forces." Her grim expression turned into a predator's smile. "Unfortunately for them, we've blunted their assault, and their planning must have been predicated on all of their regiments being combat ready at the end of the mission."

The general nodded in understanding. "If they hold the planet but can't use their forces to move on Terra, they'll have to bring in others, which will take time."

"Time that, by all accounts, they may not have. Between our strikes on other fronts and their own standing defensive requirements, the Capellans are stretched thin—potentially too thin to bring in anyone else without compromising their grander plans. The signing of the Unity Pact has allowed them to significantly reduce their defensive requirements on some fronts, but that has only been enough to get them where they are. While the Capellan military is in the best shape it's been in centuries, it has also engaged in some of the heaviest fighting since the Fourth Succession War. Furthermore, the Capellans not only have to conquer Terra, they need to *hold* it. And make no mistake, General, the Clans *are* coming."

"Countess, the Chancellor must've suspected you would return home when Northwind was threatened," Griffin interjected. "The Confederation worked with the Highlanders for a long time. They know you would never give up Northwind without a fight."

McNamara nodded again, but glanced over at the countess. "But what's to keep the Capellans from bypassing Northwind and striking Terra directly? We can pin their troops here, but that pins us down as well."

"A fair point, General, but my plan is to shatter the Capellans so that *none* of their forces make it off-planet intact. Once we do so, we will be able to strike back at the Capellans."

Declan's eyes widened, and he looked at Tara Campbell with newfound respect.

The general agreed with her assessment. "And Northwind would be a staging point for opening a new front with the Capellans."

"Exactly. Even the threat of a new front should keep the Confederation at bay and ensure that the Exarch can concentrate on more immediate foes."

Declan nodded in understanding, finally realizing exactly how vital the defense of this planet was the Republic as a whole. He had been focusing on the attack as a threat to his ancestral home, but it could potentially become the defining conflict of the Republic's survival. The Exarch had gone out on a limb to uphold his promise to the Highlanders, and he had bet everything on an extraordinary toss of the dice.

"What do you need us to do, Countess?" McNamara asked, quietly deferring to her authority.

"As we speak, Stone's Defenders are taking over the Castle's defenses. They are Stone's specialists in this particular area, and you'll find few better. The Sixth Fides will be searching for ways to break into the city, and you and I are going to drive the Canopians back to their DropShips. The Highlanders are in the process of configuring for city combat, and we will take point in Tara."

"And the Grey Watch?" Griffin asked.

The Countess gave him a small smile. "Your regiment won't be kept out of the battle, Colonel. Many of your 'Mechs sustained heavier damage than their newer counterparts, but they're getting priority repairs. We'll need them to work with the units that don't know Northwind as well as we do. Once we've fully secured the Castle's defenses, we are going to break the Canopians away from the NMA and take my namesake back from them."

"What about Fort Barrett?"

"We'll leave it be for now. They might leave Laurel's Legion there to hold it, but I doubt it. If I were their commander, I would be redeploying to make sure they can keep us out of the city for as long as possible. They have two major advantages: they know we want to avoid collateral damage to our homes, and they already control the HPG. That means we'll need to be a great deal more circumspect about our attack plans than normal."

She looked around and then stood. "However, I think that is enough for now. You have all been through hell and back, and I think we can take a couple hours to rest and regroup. My forces are fairly fresh, so they will hold the line while we reorganize, but I don't think we have anything to fear from the Capellans for tonight at least. See to your people. Get some food in you, grab some shuteye, and we will reconvene here tomorrow morning at oh-eight-hundred." She smiled at them all, giving an encouraging nod. "Rest well. We have a war to win."

Everyone moved to leave, and Declan was about to turn to Maeve when he saw Fairchild appear in the doorway, her expression serious. Seeing the sergeant's grim mien, Declan quickly said his goodbyes and followed her out.

A long row of caskets had been lined up down the middle of the main 'Mech bay, the only space large enough to hold them as repairs continued. It seemed as though the quiescent BattleMechs nearby were standing watch over their lost warriors, an image only exacerbated by the dark storm clouds that gathered beyond the Castle's walls.

Fairchild led Declan down the row, allowing them to take in each coffin as they walked, until they reached John Oedhe, who stared mournfully at a single polished casket identical to the others. Without needing to read the inscription on the small golden plate, Declan and Fairchild stepped up on either side of their lancemate, although Oedhe didn't seem to notice them. He was still in his MechWarrior togs, having not left the 'Mech bay since the search-and-rescue teams had begun bringing in the remains they could recover.

Around them, others gathered—warriors, technicians, and support staff from the various units, all intermingled in their shared grief. Grey Watch warriors mixed with Twelfth Hastati as they mourned their dead, and the air filled with the pain of their collective loss.

Across the bay Declan saw Lady Maeve Stirling sharing soft words with one of her troops, whose shoulders trembled visibly even from a distance. The two shared a quick glance, but when Fairchild straightened, Declan turned to realize they'd been joined by several others, including Countess Campbell, Colonel Griffin, and his grandfather.

He instinctively straightened to attention, but the countess shook her head. "At ease, Lieutenant." She gestured to the coffin before them. "What was their name?"

"Ellie Taggart, ma'am," Declan responded. "She took point on supporting the Grey Watch."

From the thoughtful nod Tara gave, Declan had no doubt that all three of the senior Highlanders had seen the battleROM footage. When he returned to the Castle following the battle, he had been prepared to suffer the consequences of his lance's unauthorized support of the Grey Watch, but General McNamara had retroactively approved his support of the Grey Watch in the wake of their victory. While Declan had no doubt he was due for a significant reaming from Captain O'Hara, he remained at peace with his decision.

"A brave young woman," Colonel Griffin said, looking down at the casket.

"Just a damn kid," Oedhe said, surprising them all when he spoke. His voice was gravelly, as if he hadn't said anything in days. He looked up at the colonel, his eyes sunken and hollow. "She was just so damn *proud* to be fighting alongside the Northwind Highlanders, to be in the thick of it with her heroes." He shook his head, as if trying to expel the memory. "She knew each and every one of you, all you'd done in the past, all you'd risked... she waited her whole life to be in that moment.

She thought it was all some grand adventure. All because she wanted nothing more in life than to be a Highlander."

Seamus looked sharply at him, but his expression softened as he saw the raw agony written across Oedhe's heart.

"I'd say she was both," Seamus began, his voice soft, but rising so those nearby could hear him without disrupting the solemnity of the moment. All around them, the others looked up from their grief to listen to his words. "A young woman, who put her love of her homeland and her nation before thoughts of herself, who bravely led a charge against the Capellan hordes that dared to invade our world. One of far too many..." He paused for a moment; his gaze slid over the various coffins, his voice taut with emotion. "Yet each and every one of them gave their last full measure of devotion to protect our planet, and they will have my respect until long after I have joined them." Seamus reached into his pocket, pulled out a small patch that Declan recognized as the Grey Watch insignia, and stepped forward to place it reverently atop of the casket.

Stepping back, Seamus looked up at Oedhe, his gaze unwavering. "Ellie Taggart sacrificed her life on the banks of the Grand Thames, giving of herself to protect those she swore would come to no harm, and she did so with Northwind's name upon her lips. That made her a Highlander, now and forever."

Oedhe swallowed heavily, clearly unable to speak, but he nodded in response, his eyes glistened in the 'Mech bay's dim light. All around the bay, Declan heard muttered agreement and saw the sharp nods from the assorted warriors and technicians.

Seamus looked around at the crowd and gestured to the row of fallen warriors. "With their help, we've won the first battle, but we still have many more before us before we drive these Capellan invaders from our soil. I may not know what tomorrow will bring, but I do know two things." He threw two fingers up into the air. "This is our world, and no damned Capellan is ever going to take it from us!"

This time the agreement was full-throated, and Declan felt a warm swell of pride in his chest.

Seamus pointed at Taggart's casket, his voice building to a full throated roar, "And I know that if every one of us fights with even *half* the spirit this lass possessed, we'll for damn sure send those Capellans to the hell where they belong!"

By all rights, the thunder of agreement that followed should have brought the walls of the 'Mech bay crashing down around them.

CHAPTER 19

"People always seem to forget that sometimes, when you scream into the void...it answers."

—Countess Tara Campbell
interview with ColCast News, 3150

GOVERNOR'S MANSION
INGRESS
DIERON MILITARY DISTRICT
DRACONIS COMBINE
28 NOVEMBER 3150

From where he stood in front of the large, floor-to-ceiling doors that led out onto the balcony of the governor's private study, *Sho-sho* Hisao Ikeda, commander of the Hikage, proudly watched his troops diligently repair the damage to the governor's compound. When the Hikage had first arrived on-planet, intelligence from the local Internal Security Force claimed that the planetary governor was secretly supporting the rebels that had been staging guerrilla raids on Ingress. As such, he had felt it a priority to pay the governor a personal visit.

Unfortunately, such visits tended to have a high collateral cost.

A yellow light above the door flashed, indicating he had a visitor, followed by a green light a moment later, confirming that his security had verified the visitor's identity. For all of his flaws, the governor had a flair for efficiency that Ikeda, as a House Kurita officer, respected.

He registered all of this in his peripheral vision, and for several long moments he focused on the scene outside.

Satisfied with the continued progress, he returned to his desk, took a brief moment to center himself, and pressed one of the small gold buttons inlaid in the desktop.

The door to the hallway opened with only the whisper of air, and a young *gunjin*, stepped in and snapped to attention. As always, Ikeda took a brief moment to ensure that every aspect of the *gunjin*'s kit was impeccable, and then gave a small nod. "Yes?"

The young man spoke formally, his eyes still locked forward on the far wall. "*Gunjin* Takeo Hitaki reporting. Please pardon my interruption, *Sho-sho*. We received a priority message from an inbound JumpShip, and I was ordered to bring it to you straightaway."

Ikeda nodded. "From the Warlord?"

He saw a flicker of discomfort across the *gunjin*'s face, but it was gone in an instant. "The message is from *Sang-shao* Lindsey Baxter of the Fourth McCarron's Armored Cavalry, a request for assistance from any allied forces within range."

"Oh?" Ikeda raised an eyebrow in curiosity and waved the young soldier forward. "And what do our dear Capellan allies have to say for themselves?"

Taking the question as an order to continue, the young man forced himself to look directly at his commander. "The Fourth is a part of a Capellan task force that has struck Northwind, and they are requesting reinforcements."

Ikeda took a moment to consider the information, thinking back to his daily ISF briefings. If he remembered correctly, there had been reports of the Fourth MAC being en route to Republic space in the company of Warrior House Imarra, Laurel's Legion, and the First Canopian Lancers. He'd thought it interesting at the time, but it had nothing to do with his current mission.

"They've encountered something that four regiments cannot handle?" he finally asked, bemused. "Have one of the Clans attacked?

The younger officer remained stock-still. "The message reports that reinforcements from the Northwind Highlanders and the Republic of the Sphere have arrived on-planet, and they are seeking assistance in completing their mission."

Once again, Ikeda reached over to press another button on his desk, and the door opened again. His aide, *Chu-sa* Ivan Hallow, entered without hesitation, coming alongside the young *gunjin*. Hallow, older than Hitaki by nearly a decade, had been with Ikeda for over six years. He was one of the few officers in Ikeda's inner circle, and knew his commander better than most.

"Has this information been confirmed?" Ikeda asked.

"Yes, sir," Hallow replied. "Intelligence traced the message as originating from Northwind, and it confirms the data from our recent ISF reports."

Ikeda leaned back in the chair and returned his gaze to the balcony, where light streamed in across the carpeted floor. "As I seem to remember, Northwind has one of the few working HPG stations in the region."

"Yes, sir," Hallow replied. "Although no one knows why it still works." His aide's expression was unreadable. "Regardless of the reason, capturing a working HPG would be a benefit to the Combine. Not only would it facilitate military communications in the region, but having our own scientists study it might help us learn how to repair our own HPGs."

"Indeed." Ikeda nodded thoughtfully. "What other regiments in this region are combat ready?"

To his credit, Hallow had the answer ready, having anticipated the question. "The Fourth Dieron Regulars are preparing to move to their secondary staging area before returning to rotation. All other regiments are currently engaged. If you would like me to rearrange our deployments, we can safely break free a different regiment within eight days."

"That will not be necessary," Ikeda replied, turning back to the young soldier that had remained perfectly still. "*Gunjin*, have your commander draft new orders for the Fourth Dieron over my signature, and have him inform Command that we are immediately moving to support our allies under the auspices of the Unity Pact."

After the *gunjin* confirmed the orders, Ikeda dismissed him with a nod and watched him leave with a palpable aura of relief. He shared a small smile with Hallow at the *gunjin*'s discomfort, now that the two men were alone. "I assume two regiments will be enough to deal with the situation?"

"If the data the Capellans sent is accurate," Hallow said, "two should be more than enough. The Twelfth Hastati has taken significant damage, and with our assistance the Capellans should be more than capable of taking on the Republic reinforcements. Depending on our objectives, we should be successful in anything short of full planetary conquest, as we can call on reinforcements more quickly than the other contenders for the planet."

Ikeda nodded, in full agreement with his aide's analysis. While there was a thin chance that the Capellans might have additional troops on the way, it was doubtful: if the forces had been available earlier, they would have been sent with the first wave.

As for the Republic, he had seen the same intelligence reports that their allies had. If the Republic had managed to send this large of a force to Northwind, they must have drawn them from Terra, thus weakening Terra's defense. If Ikeda could take out the Republic forces on Northwind and either capture the HPG or deny the Republic its use, the Draconis Combine would be within a stone's throw of taking the birthworld of humanity itself.

When such an opportunity presented itself, it was his duty as an officer of the Draconis Combine to take advantage of it. The Coordinator and the *gunji-no-kanrei* had placed him in command of the Hikage for a reason, and this was a certain way to solidify their faith in him.

Turning back to Hallow, he stood carefully. "Make sure my message to the Warlord goes out first. I am sure he may be able to find us additional troops for such a worthy objective. However, all of our forces should be prepared to leave immediately."

Hallow glanced over at the balcony. "And our work here?"

Ikeda moved toward the balcony, Hallow following with practiced precision. He carefully opened the twin glass doors, and both of them stepped out into the cool night air.

Outside, two light 'Mechs, a *Rokurokubi* and an older *Owens*, bathed the courtyard in the blinding brilliance of their searchlights, turning night into day. Lined up in the center of the courtyard, the former planetary governor and his staff kneeled in a single line; the terror etched on their faces was clear even from this distance.

For a long moment, Ikeda made a careful showing of looking at each face below, as if committing them to memory. He looked out into the night beyond the courtyard itself and nodded once, passing judgment.

Without further prompting, the *Owens* lit off its machine guns and cut down the kneeling figures in a hailstorm chatter that drowned out most of the screams. Ikeda watched unblinking as the grisly duty was completed, and he did not turn away until the final body dropped to the blood-soaked grass.

"See to the preparations, *Chu-sa*," Ikeda said quietly, his gaze never leaving the courtyard. "We have a call to answer."

ABOUT THE AUTHOR

Michael J. Ciaravella has been a passionate devotee of the *BattleTech* universe for over twenty years, most recently having the honor of writing the "Secrets of the Sphere" articles for the new *BattleTech* Magazine, *Shrapnel*. A regular sight on the convention circuit, Michael has earned multiple championship titles, including several *BattleTech* Open and Solaris Melee Championships as well as the coveted Pryde Bloodname. In what little free time he has not devoted to writing and gaming pursuits, Michael is also an award-winning theatrical producer, director, and actor in New York, where he lives with his beloved Amy and their three cats: Tuxberious Nova Cat, Pancetta Kurita, and Princess Waffles Francesca Peregrine.

BATTLETECH GLOSSARY

AUTOCANNON

This is a rapid-fire, auto-loading weapon. Light autocannons range from 30 to 90 millimeter (mm), and heavy autocannons may be from 80 to 120mm or more. They fire high-speed streams of high-explosive, armor-piercing shells.

BATTLEMECH

BattleMechs are the most powerful war machines ever built. First developed by Terran scientists and engineers, these huge vehicles are faster, more mobile, better-armored and more heavily armed than any twentieth-century tank. Ten to twelve meters tall and equipped with particle projection cannons, lasers, rapid-fire autocannon and missiles, they pack enough firepower to flatten anything but another BattleMech. A small fusion reactor provides virtually unlimited power, and BattleMechs can be adapted to fight in environments ranging from sun-baked deserts to subzero arctic icefields.

DROPSHIPS

Because interstellar JumpShips must avoid entering the heart of a solar system, they must "dock" in space at a considerable distance from a system's inhabited worlds. DropShips were developed for interplanetary travel. As the name implies, a DropShip is attached to hardpoints on the JumpShip's drive core, later to be dropped from the parent vessel after in-system entry. Though incapable of FTL travel, DropShips are highly maneuverable, well-armed and sufficiently aerodynamic to take off from and land on a planetary surface. The journey from the jump point to the inhabited worlds of a system usually requires a normal-space journey of several days or weeks, depending on the type of star.

FLAMER

The flamethrower is a small but time-honored anti-infantry weapon in vehicular arsenals. Whether fusion-based or fuel-based, flamers spew fire in a tight beam of bright orange that "splashes" against a target, igniting almost anything it touches.

GAUSS RIFLE

This weapon uses magnetic coils to accelerate a solid nickel-ferrous slug about the size of a football at an enemy target, inflicting massive damage through sheer kinetic impact at long range and with little heat. However, the accelerator coils and the slug's supersonic speed mean that while the Gauss rifle is smokeless and lacks the flash of an autocannon, it has a much more potent report that can shatter glass.

JUMPSHIPS

Interstellar travel is accomplished via JumpShips, first developed in the twenty-second century. These somewhat ungainly vessels consist of a long, thin drive core and a sail resembling an enormous parasol, which can extend up to a kilometer in width. The ship is named for its ability to "jump" instantaneously across vast distances of space. After making its jump, the ship cannot travel until it has recharged by gathering up more solar energy.

The JumpShip's enormous sail is constructed from a special metal that absorbs vast quantities of electromagnetic energy from the nearest star. When it has soaked up enough energy, the sail transfers it to the drive core, which converts it into a space-twisting field. An instant later, the ship arrives at the next jump point, a distance of up to thirty light-years. This field is known as hyperspace, and its discovery opened to mankind the gateway to the stars.

JumpShips never land on planets. Interplanetary travel is carried out by DropShips, vessels that are attached to the JumpShip until arrival at the jump point.

LASER

An acronym for "Light Amplification through Stimulated Emission of Radiation." When used as a weapon, the laser damages the target by concentrating extreme heat onto a small area. BattleMech lasers are designated as small, medium or large. Lasers are also available as shoulder-fired weapons operating from a portable backpack power unit. Certain range-finders and targeting equipment also employ low-level lasers.

LRM

This is an abbreviation for "Long-Range Missile," an indirect-fire missile with a high-explosive warhead.

MACHINE GUN

A small autocannon intended for anti-personnel assaults. Typically non-armor-penetrating, machine guns are often best used against infantry, as they can spray a large area with relatively inexpensive fire.

PARTICLE PROJECTION CANNON (PPC)

One of the most powerful and long-range energy weapons on the battlefield, a PPC fires a stream of charged particles that outwardly functions as a bright blue laser, but also throws off enough static discharge to resemble a bolt of manmade lightning. The kinetic and heat impact of a PPC is enough to cause the vaporization of armor and structure alike, and most PPCs have the power to kill a pilot in his machine through an armor-penetrating headshot.

SRM

This is the abbreviation for "Short-Range Missile," a direct-trajectory missile with high-explosive or armor-piercing explosive warheads. They have a range of less than one kilometer and are only reliably accurate at ranges of less than 300 meters. They are more powerful, however, than LRMs.

SUCCESSOR LORDS

After the fall of the first Star League, the remaining members of the High Council each asserted his or her right to become First Lord. Their star empires became known as the Successor States and the rulers as Successor Lords. The Clan Invasion temporarily interrupted centuries of warfare known as the Succession Wars, which first began in 2786.

BATTLETECH ERAS

The *BattleTech* universe is a living, vibrant entity that grows each year as more sourcebooks and fiction are published. A dynamic universe, its setting and characters evolve over time within a highly detailed continuity framework, bringing everything to life in a way a static game universe cannot match.

To help quickly and easily convey the timeline of the universe—and to allow a player to easily "plug in" a given novel or sourcebook—we've divided *BattleTech* into six major eras.

STAR LEAGUE
(Present–2780)

Ian Cameron, ruler of the Terran Hegemony, concludes decades of tireless effort with the creation of the Star League, a political and military alliance between all Great Houses and the Hegemony. Star League armed forces immediately launch the Reunification War, forcing the Periphery realms to join. For the next two centuries, humanity experiences a golden age across the thousand light-years of human-occupied space known as the Inner Sphere. It also sees the creation of the most powerful military in human history.

(This era also covers the centuries before the founding of the Star League in 2571, most notably the Age of War.)

SUCCESSION WARS
(2781–3049)

Every last member of First Lord Richard Cameron's family is killed during a coup launched by Stefan Amaris. Following the thirteen-year war to unseat him, the rulers of each of the five Great Houses disband the Star League. General Aleksandr Kerensky departs with eighty percent of the Star League Defense Force beyond known space and the Inner Sphere collapses into centuries of warfare known as the Succession Wars that will eventually result in a massive loss of technology across most worlds.

CLAN INVASION
(3050–3061)

A mysterious invading force strikes the coreward region of the Inner Sphere. The invaders, called the Clans, are descendants of Kerensky's SLDF troops, forged into a society dedicated to becoming the greatest fighting force in history. With vastly superior technology and warriors, the Clans conquer world after world. Eventually this outside threat will forge a new Star League, something hundreds of years of warfare failed to accomplish. In addition, the Clans will act as a catalyst for a technological renaissance.

CIVIL WAR
(3062–3067)

The Clan threat is eventually lessened with the complete destruction of a Clan. With that massive external threat apparently neutralized, internal conflicts explode around the Inner Sphere. House Liao conquers its former Commonality, the St. Ives Compact; a rebellion of military units belonging to House Kurita sparks a war with their powerful border enemy, Clan Ghost Bear; the fabulously powerful Federated Commonwealth of House Steiner and House Davion collapses into five long years of bitter civil war.

JIHAD
(3067–3080)

Following the Federated Commonwealth Civil War, the leaders of the Great Houses meet and disband the new Star League, declaring it a sham. The pseudo-religious Word of Blake—a splinter group of ComStar, the protectors and controllers of interstellar communication—launch the Jihad: an interstellar war that pits every faction against each other and even against themselves, as weapons of mass destruction are used for the first time in centuries while new and frightening technologies are also unleashed.

DARK AGE
(3081-3150)

Under the guidance of Devlin Stone, the Republic of the Sphere is born at the heart of the Inner Sphere following the Jihad. One of the more extensive periods of peace begins to break out as the 32nd century dawns. The factions, to one degree or another, embrace disarmament, and the massive armies of the Succession Wars begin to fade. However, in 3132 eighty percent of interstellar communications collapses, throwing the universe into chaos. Wars erupt almost immediately, and the factions begin rebuilding their armies.

LOOKING FOR MORE HARD HITTING BATTLETECH FICTION?

WE'LL GET YOU RIGHT BACK INTO THE BATTLE!

Catalyst Game Labs brings you the very best in *BattleTech* fiction, available at most ebook retailers, including Amazon, Apple Books, Kobo, Barnes & Noble, and more!

NOVELS

1. *Decision at Thunder Rift* by William H. Keith Jr.
2. *Mercenary's Star* by William H. Keith Jr.
3. *The Price of Glory* by William H. Keith, Jr.
4. *Warrior: En Garde* by Michael A. Stackpole
5. *Warrior: Riposte* by Michael A. Stackpole
6. *Warrior: Coupé* by Michael A. Stackpole
7. *Wolves on the Border* by Robert N. Charrette
8. *Heir to the Dragon* by Robert N. Charrette
9. *Lethal Heritage* (The Blood of Kerensky, Volume 1) by Michael A. Stackpole
10. *Blood Legacy* (The Blood of Kerensky, Volume 2) by Michael A. Stackpole
11. *Lost Destiny* (The Blood of Kerensky, Volume 3) by Michael A. Stackpole
12. *Way of the Clans* (Legend of the Jade Phoenix, Volume 1) by Robert Thurston
13. *Bloodname* (Legend of the Jade Phoenix, Volume 2) by Robert Thurston
14. *Falcon Guard* (Legend of the Jade Phoenix, Volume 3) by Robert Thurston
15. *Wolf Pack* by Robert N. Charrette
16. *Main Event* by James D. Long
17. *Natural Selection* by Michael A. Stackpole
18. *Assumption of Risk* by Michael A. Stackpole
19. *Blood of Heroes* by Andrew Keith
20. *Close Quarters* by Victor Milán
21. *Far Country* by Peter L. Rice
22. *D.R.T.* by James D. Long
23. *Tactics of Duty* by William H. Keith
24. *Bred for War* by Michael A. Stackpole
25. *I Am Jade Falcon* by Robert Thurston
26. *Highlander Gambit* by Blaine Lee Pardoe
27. *Hearts of Chaos* by Victor Milán
28. *Operation Excalibur* by William H. Keith
29. *Malicious Intent* by Michael A. Stackpole
30. *Black Dragon* by Victor Milán
31. *Impetus of War* by Blaine Lee Pardoe
32. *Double-Blind* by Loren L. Coleman

NOVELLAS/SHORT STORIES

1. *Lion's Roar* by Steven Mohan, Jr.
2. *Sniper* by Jason Schmetzer
3. *Eclipse* by Jason Schmetzer
4. *Hector* by Jason Schmetzer
5. *The Frost Advances (Operation Ice Storm, Part 1)* by Jason Schmetzer
6. *The Winds of Spring (Operation Ice Storm, Part 2)* by Jason Schmetzer
7. *Instrument of Destruction (Ghost Bear's Lament, Part 1)* by Steven Mohan, Jr.
8. *The Fading Call of Glory (Ghost Bear's Lament, Part 2)* by Steven Mohan, Jr.
9. *Vengeance* by Jason Schmetzer
10. *A Splinter of Hope* by Philip A. Lee
11. *The Anvil* by Blaine Lee Pardoe
12. *A Splinter of Hope/The Anvil* (omnibus)
13. *Not the Way the Smart Money Bets (Kell Hounds Ascendant #1)* by Michael A. Stackpole
14. *A Tiny Spot of Rebellion (Kell Hounds Ascendant #2)* by Michael A. Stackpole
15. *A Clever Bit of Fiction (Kell Hounds Ascendant #3)* by Michael A. Stackpole
16. *Break-Away (Proliferation Cycle #1)* by Ilsa J. Bick
17. *Prometheus Unbound (Proliferation Cycle #2)* by Herbert A. Beas II
18. *Nothing Ventured (Proliferation Cycle #3)* by Christoffer Trossen
19. *Fall Down Seven Times, Get Up Eight (Proliferation Cycle #4)* by Randall N. Bills
20. *A Dish Served Cold (Proliferation Cycle #5)* by Chris Hartford and Jason M. Hardy
21. *The Spider Dances (Proliferation Cycle #6)* by Jason Schmetzer
22. *Shell Games* by Jason Schmetzer
23. *Divided We Fall* by Blaine Lee Pardoe
24. *The Hunt for Jardine (Forgotten Worlds, Part One)* by Herbert A. Beas II

ANTHOLOGIES

1. *The Corps (BattleCorps Anthology, Volume 1)* edited by Loren. L. Coleman
2. *First Strike (BattleCorps Anthology, Volume 2)* edited by Loren L. Coleman
3. *Weapons Free (BattleCorps Anthology, Volume 3)* edited by Jason Schmetzer
4. *Onslaught: Tales from the Clan Invasion* edited by Jason Schmetzer
5. *Edge of the Storm* by Jason Schmetzer
6. *Fire for Effect (BattleCorps Anthology, Volume 4)* edited by Jason Schmetzer
7. *Chaos Born (Chaos Irregulars, Book 1)* by Kevin Killiany
8. *Chaos Formed (Chaos Irregulars, Book 2)* by Kevin Killiany
9. *Counterattack (BattleCorps Anthology, Volume 5)* edited by Jason Schmetzer
10. *Front Lines (BattleCorps Anthology Volume 6)* edited by Jason Schmetzer and Philip A. Lee
11. *Legacy* edited by John Helfers and Philip A. Lee
12. *Kill Zone (BattleCorps Anthology Volume 7)* edited by Philip A. Lee
13. *Gray Markets (A BattleCorps Anthology),* edited by Jason Schmetzer and Philip A. Lee
14. *Slack Tide (A BattleCorps Anthology),* edited by Jason Schmetzer and Philip A. Lee